I0586170

Layers of Deception

Neive Denis

Book 11 in the Sonoma Whittington, Private Investigator, series

Copyright

First published in 2023
Copyright © Neive Denis 2023
All rights reserved.

No part of this book may be reproduced or transmitted in any form or by any means, electronic or mechanical, including photocopying, recording or by any information storage and retrieval system, without prior permission in writing. The Australian *Copyright Act* 1968 (the Act) allows a maximum of one chapter or 10 percent of this book, whichever is the greater, to be photocopied by any educational institution for its educational purposes provided that the educational institution (or body that administers it) has given a remuneration notice to the Copyright Agency (Australia) under the Act.

Cataloguing-in-publication data
Creator: Denis, Neive, author

Cataloguing-in-Publication details are available from the National Library of Australia
www.trove.nla.gov.au

ISBN: 978-0-6454907-6-3 (paperback)
ISBN: 978-0-6454907-7-0 (digital)

Main cover image: Chele_Bero Images (Michele Beresford, Townsville, Australia)
Cover design: T A Marshall, Mackay, Australia

Disclaimer

This novel is a work of fiction. All characters and events are the product of the imagination of the author. While some of the characters might remind you of people you know, they are fictitious and any resemblance to anyone living or dead is purely coincidental. Although some locations also may seem real and familiar, most places referred to in this work constitute a collage of places the author has known and are fictitious. Any resemblance to an existing location is coincidental.

Chapter 1

"Good God, Janine, is this left over from your incident in the park, or is it something new?" I asked as I scrutinised my battered and bruised new client, Janine Thomlinson, now sporting bits of plaster and bandages in various places.

"Yeah, it's not a great appearance, is it? But it looks a lot better than it did a couple of days ago. I've brought the information you asked for, or at least as much as I could find," she said, trying for a wry smile despite a still swollen cheek.

"It's good you are out of hospital, but are you sure you should be here today and not still resting?"

"I'm fine, and I don't want to delay this any longer."

"If you are sure, can we rewind to when you first came to see me? It will allow me to make sure my file is up-to-date and accurate. According to my notes from that previous occasion, you came to see me because you suspected your husband was seeing another woman. Is that correct?"

"Yes, I suspected he was having an affair. Nothing's changed. I mean, nothing's happened to change my mind about that."

"Okay; you felt your husband had become withdrawn and secretive. He was going out at night more than usual without saying where he was going or who he was meeting. Was this a recent development, or had it been ongoing for some time before you came to see me?"

"In the last few days, I've had plenty of time to think about things. I realised it's been building over a few months. Before that, a few of his mates would get together at another mate's house to watch a major footie match on a big TV. And whenever a visiting team was playing here in Millhaven, or it was an important game like a local grand final, he would go to watch the match with some of those mates. Don't get me wrong. I was never given details of where he was going, who would be there, or when he'd return. But I used to be able to work out roughly where he was going."

"And this has changed to some degree over the last few months?"

She nodded without lifting her eyes from her hands in her lap.

"So, you weren't given many details in previous times. How has that changed? What happens now?"

"These days, he goes out a lot more often at night, and seems to be out somewhere a lot over the weekends. As I said, I only used to have an idea of where he might be going and who he would be with from hints I picked up. After we were married a while and I got to know him better, there were clues I could pick-up. Now there is nothing. I'm not getting any hints, clues, or even warnings that he's leaving. The first I know about it is when he gets dressed and is on his way out the door. Sometimes he comes home from work and then goes out again before dinner, but he doesn't tell me beforehand he won't be eating dinner with me or eating it later on his own."

I did a quick scan of the paperwork she brought with her. Quite a few questions on my form relating to her husband, Blake Carter, remained unanswered. She saw me flicking through it and rushed to apologise.

"I'm sorry. I couldn't find the answer to some of the questions. So I've had to leave them blank. Will that stop you taking the case?"

"No, of course not... As I told you earlier, gathering this information helps me recognise your husband, and better understand his habits. Those things help with planning surveillance work to establish where he goes, who he goes with, and what he does there."

We revisited the information from her previous visit, which

was the total of my thin case file so far.

Then, I focused on the accident that put her in hospital for a few days She remained adamant it wasn't an accident, despite what the police believed. She was convinced the bloke on the motorbike rammed her deliberately while she was cycling through the park. I questioned how she could be so sure.

"After hazing me for some distance through the park, he chose the best place to execute his plan. His only problem was, the plan didn't come off quite as he expected. The little bridge across the stormwater drain in that more-deserted area of the park has waist-high stone-pitched walls along both sides. I was on the bridge when I heard him closing in on me. I sped up, pedalling as fast as I could to get across the bridge and get out of his way. Bad move…! I was going flat out and about halfway across when he chose to ram my rear wheel. Except for a quirk of fate, the incident should have sent me over the wall and down about three metres into the concrete-lined stormwater drain below. Instead of flying over the wall as intended, I struck the wall and bounced back onto the bridge decking's grass verge."

As the original case Jasmine wanted me to investigate focused on her husband and his recent behaviour, I needed to know where he was when the incident occurred.

"It happened on Friday night, after he had left that morning to fly to Tasmania for a week of trout fishing with a couple of his mates who still live there. He wasn't home when it happened. So he wouldn't have missed me. I could have been lying injured on the bridge for goodness knows how long, if the joggers hadn't found me when they did."

"Does he often go off to Tasmania? Do you sometimes accompany him?"

"Uhmm, yeah, he does go back there a bit. He is originally from Tasmania and only moved away after university. I was going to say he didn't return there often, but now I've thought about it, he has made a few trips since we've been married. And, no, I've never been invited to accompany him – not that

I would want to anyway. His trips always are for camping, hiking, or fishing with his mates. No place for females on those excursions, not according to their thinking anyway."

While, to a sceptic like me, it all appeared too convenient for him to be so far away when Janine's incident happened, it did provide me with a starting point for my investigation. After Janine left, I checked if her husband did fly to Tasmania on Friday morning, and whether he had a return flight booked.

By lunchtime, I knew his story did not hold up as Janine recounted it. And her husband hadn't given himself the alibi I thought he might have been aiming to set-up. He had not flown to Tasmania that Friday morning, nor did he have a return flight booked for any time in the next fortnight. I think things were already not looking good for Mr Blake Carter. I reminded myself that I must keep an open mind. It was too early yet to form opinions about any player in this new case.

For the next hour or so, I did a lot of thinking and planning. Before going any further, I needed an investigation plan. I set up a spreadsheet and started listing specific points to pursue, when and where to research, and who might be able to assist with information. A comprehensive list resulted. As I noted its resultant outcome, it was satisfying to tick-off as completed the item listed as 'check Carter's flights'.

What to tackle next? The matter of the motorbike being in the park. It shouldn't have been there. Still, it must have been a motorbike. Janine would hardly be mistaken about what rammed her. Perhaps a visit to the park might be in order to familiarise myself with the site of the incident.

Ooh, yes… I sensed an interesting investigation ahead. And I saw a client shedding quite a few tears before the case was closed. Despite everything she told me, I sensed she was still fond of the man she married. And, despite initiating this investigation into her husband's activities, she remains in denial. It's likely her feelings will change in the near future.

A few phone calls scuttled my intention to head to the park soon after Janine left my office, and an appointment after lunch further delayed escaping my office. The delay allowed me to devote some thought to my crime scene survey. I decided the best way would be on my recently-purchased e-scooter. So, having decided visiting the crime scene might uncover something useful, I dashed home from my city office at four o'clock to collect the necessary equipment before going to the park.

After using its hydraulic wheelchair lift to load my e-scooter into the cargo compartment of my large SUV, I checked my appearance in a wing mirror. Yes, my quick change now had me sporting an outfit comparable to what e-scooter riders wear nowadays.

"Aw, come on. Couldn't you have waited another few minutes?" I growled at the sky as I stood with one foot on my e-scooter, ready to head off through the park.

The clouds had hung around without looking particularly threatening, and I counted on them staying that way the rest of the evening. Research for my new case was going nowhere in a hurry. A look at the crime scene would be a positive end to the day.

"Well, I'm here now, so I might as well get on with it," I murmured as I felt the first raindrops. Ignoring them, I headed off.

Within a few moments of my entering the park, the rain became heavier. Although still not particularly heavy, the breeze that had sprung up drove the rain almost parallel to the ground. It stung my face, arms, and legs, as I opened the throttle to full power and sped towards a distant part of the now deserted park. The front of my clothes was soaked before I reached the little bridge across the stormwater drain.

Janine's attacker had done his homework well. Either that or he already was well acquainted with the park's layout. This was the perfect spot to stage his attack. Situated in a more deserted corner of the area, the little bridge had waist-high stone-pitched walls along both sides instead of safety rails. Narrow strips of turf ran along either side between the bridge decking and the walls.

A quick peer over one side revealed a small trickle of water from the present rain starting to form in the concrete-lined stormwater drain about three metres below. While it was difficult to find anything good about being bounced off one of the stone walls, it was easy to see how it was preferable to being pitched over the wall to land in the stormwater drain below.

Showers and one particularly heavy downpour over the last few days ensured no evidence of Janine's incident remained. Nevertheless, I will add a multitude of photographs to my case file this evening. Wet is wet, I told myself as I took a final look around the site. Nothing I found changed my original thinking: how could the police dismiss the incident as nothing more than an unfortunate accident?

That is the question I will put to Millhaven's top cop, Ben Richards, over dinner tonight. At least, I will, if we are dining together this evening. A glance at my watch told me it was late. Ben normally had called me by this time to find out what I fancied for dinner, but he hadn't. That's the way my luck with this case is running so far. He probably can't make it for dinner tonight, and I won't be able to quiz him about the police investigation into the incident.

On my way back to my car, I checked the small kiosk at the entrance to the park. I have no idea whether it is privately operated, or remains a local council initiative established as an adjunct to their community fitness program. I wouldn't learn anything about it today. It was closed – not surprising, I suppose, at this hour.

Now, soaked through to the skin and thankful for the hydraulic lift, I loaded my e-scooter back into the car, retrieved a towel kept there for emergencies and spread it over my seat for the drive home. As I drove up my driveway, Ben Richards called to say he was on his way over and would pick up something for dinner. Great! I will just have time for a quick shower before he arrives.

I needn't have bothered rushing about. As I stepped out of the shower, Ben called again. Something had come up at work, and he wouldn't make it tonight. Fine, those leftovers in the fridge will reheat nicely, and an evening alone will allow me to try to make sense of my new case, even if I don't get to ask him about the police investigation.

After printing out all the unenlightening photos I took at the crime scene and adding them to my scant case file, I sat back to ponder what I knew about the investigation I had agreed to undertake for Janine Thomlinson.

"Goodness, was it only a week and a half ago when she first arrived at my city office without an appointment?" I queried the universe as I sat in my home office with her case file open in front of me. So much had happened during those days. It felt like it should be much longer than that since I first spoke to her.

With my feet up on the desk and a glass of red wine beside me, I let my mind roll back to the start of this case.

I well remember the day it all started. It was while I supposedly was in the throes of wrapping up a previous case. Frustration levels were through the roof. The same question kept running through my mind: *How could I think of wrapping up a case when I haven't answered all my own questions about it, never mind my client's?*

My mind insisted on revisiting that not-quite-completed case. That client, Kirsty McGregor, was not only a client but a longtime friend. Having accepted the mystery that remained about her ancestor, Kirsty was moving on with her life. Nevertheless, I continued to fret about a big unanswered question. Despite knowing it was time to accept it, wrap up the case, and move on, I didn't seem able to. With no new cases pending then, I consoled myself with the thought that finalising Kirsty's case offered a tantalising chance to escape to my beach place for maybe a few days.

So much for wishful thinking....

Then, with a little help from Fate, Kirsty's case was wrapped up. But that's when Janine Thomlinson arrived on the scene, and as I sat listening to her telling me of her concerns, I knew my idea of a beach get-away was history.

Chapter 2

I remember so clearly the first time I met Janine and listened to her concerns that appeared the basis for just a routine case. That was before it became something else. Like so many cases, it had begun with the appearance of a stranger at my office.

A tentative knock on my door made me look up from the mess of paper I was trying to shuffle into some semblance of chronological order in a file lying open on my desk. A tall young woman with a shock of copper-coloured hair stood in the doorway.

"Sonoma Whittington…?" she asked nervously.

Closing the file, I stood and motioned for her to enter. Dressed in low-slung designer blue jeans and a dazzlingly white tee shirt, the woman tentatively entered. As she approached, I noticed her enormous blue eyes. The private investigator in me registered this as one v-e-r-y attractive woman.

"My apologies for dropping in like this, Miss Whittington," she began. "I don't have an appointment, but I hoped you might be able to spare me a few minutes."

I allowed her a few moments to settle before trying to make her feel a little more at ease.

"You're timing is good. I'm free for the next hour, so you have my undivided attention. By the way, everyone calls me Sonny. Life's too short to use the rest of it all the time.

Now, who are you, and how can I help you?"

"Thank you, Miss… err, sorry… Sonny. I am Janine Thomlinson … and I might be wasting your time. I don't really know what you do … or for that matter, even if I have a problem to discuss."

"That sounds intriguing. Perhaps, if you tell me why you're here, we might know whether you were right in coming to see me. Now, what's this problem you're not sure you have?"

Becoming more uncomfortable by the moment, her embarrassment was obvious when she finally looked up from wringing hands in her lap. *Man trouble,* I thought – and hoped my smile didn't reflect my thinking.

"This is going to sound ridiculous, but I'm concerned about my husband. I have nothing definite, but things have been a bit strange lately. Before I bore you with my problem, I suppose I should ask whether your work includes investigating husbands' strange behaviour."

Yep, man trouble…

"Janine, nothing you've said so far is ridiculous, or anything I haven't heard before. And, yes, much of my work is brought about by spouses behaving out of character somehow. Sometimes I have the pleasure of telling my client all is well and nothing untoward is happening. But, on other occasions, the client has their suspicions confirmed when I provide them with the evidence of my investigation. So, feel free to discuss whatever is on your mind and let's see where it takes us."

"Well, here goes. I recently noticed my husband, Blake Carter, was going out and coming home at strange times. His comings and goings had changed from what they were in the past and had become more frequent. At first, I told myself it was reasonable in his line of work, but I couldn't convince myself."

"It might sound like an obvious question, but did you talk to your husband about your concerns?"

"I did try to discuss it. He became angry and wouldn't talk about it … told me I was stupid, and he wouldn't put up with being subjected to a third-degree after every time he went out. He accused me of trying to control him, to keep him under my thumb and not let him have a life of his own."

Oh yeah, I can see where this is heading, I thought. Unobtrusively as possible, I reached for the box of tissues I keep under my desk for just such occasions. Any minute now, the tears would start. Hoping to postpone such an occurrence, I scribbled some notes on my pad to allow her a few moments to collect herself. But we couldn't sit there like that forever.

As I looked up from my notes, I cleared my throat to gain her attention. "His comments seem a bit harsh. Has he ever made such remarks in the past?"

"No! No, we've always gotten along well. It's been a happy marriage. I thought it was so, I suppose, that makes his comments feel worse. I wasn't guilty of what he accused me of, not in the least bit. I tried explaining how his change of work hours impacted our lives and how I'd cancelled our acceptance of a couple of invitations to events because it would look odd if I turned up alone. Trying to explain was a waste of time and effort. He became angry and has stayed that way ever since."

"Okay, so what do you think is happening? Is it reasonable to assume his work hours have changed somehow, or do you suspect there's more to the story?"

"Argh… I don't know. He is a personal trainer and works out of one of the gyms in town. It's possible one or some of his clients made bookings at times outside his usual work hours. In his line of work, I suppose he has to be available when the clients want him to be, and not necessarily when it suits him – or me. But why not just tell me about such work commitments?"

"Right, I can see how that might happen. Are there other possible explanations you can think of which might explain the change in his activities?"

"Oh, I don't know what to think. After mulling it over for a few days, I've come up with three possibilities. The first is a change in work hours, as I mentioned. My other two possibilities are: he has become mixed up in something a bit dodgy, or is having an affair."

"All of those are reasonable assumptions. We discussed the possibility of changed work hours, so let's talk about your other two options. Is there some basis for you to think he might be involved in something not quite legal? I find it a curious suspicion without some background to underpin it."

"Again, it sounds ridiculous, but there was something a long time ago – at least, I think it was a long time ago. Please don't ask me when it was, or what happened, because I don't know. I just picked up something somewhere along the way that suggested he had been involved in something dubious. God, it sounds as though I really don't know anything about my husband... and I'm beginning to think that might be true. That's why I'm here this morning."

"Tell me why you think your husband might be involved in something dodgy?"

"He's been so secretive... no, it's more than that. Yes, he is being secretive about where he goes and why, but he's also stopped talking to me. Argh, we still talk, but about nothing. Things like: How was your day? Wasn't that rain heavy today? ...Those sorts of 'nothings'. And, yes, that is a change from how we used to be."

"Hmm... I understand your thinking he might be involved in something shady and doesn't want you to know about it, but what about an affair? Might his behaviour be much the same if he had become involved with another woman?"

Janine shrugged and nodded.

"Okay, then the next question has to be about the state of your marriage. Would you say you were happily married?"

"Definitely; it's been a great marriage, and we have always been close ... until recently. I haven't seen anything to suggest he's found someone else, but I thought it might be another possible explanation for his strange behaviour."

"Right; of the three possibilities – changed work pattern, dodgy business, or an affair – which do you think is the most likely explanation?"

She took to studying her hands in her lap again as she sat silently for a moment before answering. "An affair... Yes, that's the most likely scenario. If I'm right, will you still take the case?"

"If you want me to investigate your husband's changed behaviour, I will look into it for you. Of course, you must understand that the cause could be something altogether different, even something more unpalatable for you to accept. It's up to you to decide if you really want to know and whether you want to engage me to undertake an investigation or not."

"I know I won't rest until I know. So, yes, please, will you take the case?"

After completing the usual initial interview with a new client, I produced a copy of my standard form for her to complete. She looked shattered after casting her eyes over it. I saw her moisten her lips and swallow hard.

"Sonny, I can't answer some of these questions. It's not that I don't want to. I just don't know the answers. Is this information important to whether you'll take the case?"

"No, it's not critical. The form gathers basic information about your husband to help me to know and recognise the man I will be investigating. So, answering any of the questions will help, and there is room on the back page for you to note anything else you think might be helpful to me.

I don't expect you to complete it here and now. Add the form to the other brochures I've given you and fill in as much as you can at home. After you have read everything I've given you, if you return with the form and wish to continue, we will sign a formal contract."

"Tomorrow is a hell of a day for me. Will it matter if I don't bring it back until Monday?"

I assured her Monday would be fine.

"But, if I don't sign a contract until Monday at the earliest, does it mean you won't start work on the case until after that? I'm sorry. I don't want to appear rude, but I am keen to get started as soon as possible."

"Don't worry about it. Just bring back the form on Monday or as soon as it suits you. In the meantime, I will have a quiet poke about to see what I can find."

The relief on her face was something to behold. But it also made me wonder whether there might be more to this story than I'd been told. I hoped the relief I felt about her not getting back to me until Monday was not as evident on my face as her relief was.

There was still some finalising of my work on my friend Kirsty McGregor's case after she found human bones hidden in the old homestead she inherited. If Janine didn't get back to me until Monday, I would be able to work on Kirsty's stuff over the weekend without feeling obligated to start Janine's investigation.

Janine's visit lasted more than the hour I claimed to have spare. It wasn't a problem. Today's agenda was flexible. The only other thing scheduled this morning was to go in search of something for lunch. Later, after a chicken and salad roll and a quick skim of today's newspaper, I spent the afternoon working on the documentation associated with Kirsty's case.

As I recall, everything went to plan until Sunday night. That's when my friend, Emily Ibbotson, who is in charge of the local forensic department, came to dinner and announced a major event in the Kirsty McGregor case would happen at Kirsty's property the following morning. Not only did I want to be there, I needed to attend as I suspected it might go some way to providing the final answers I needed to close Kirsty's case satisfactorily.

There was no way I wouldn't be there, but therein was my problem. Like most people who take care of such tasks in the morning, I expected my new client, Janine Thomlinson, to deliver critical information tomorrow morning to allow a start on her case. … and that's when I would be at Kirsty's Westbrook property. As I wouldn't be in my office in the morning, I needed to find a way around the situation. When Emily left on Sunday night, it was too late to call Janine. After mulling over the problem for a while, I resolved to go into my office early tomorrow to call Janine – hopefully, before she left home to come into my office.

Sticking to my plan for an early start allowed me to avoid the worst of Monday morning's traffic on my way into the city. Hoping it wasn't too early, I called Janine as soon as I was in my office. She took a while to answer and sounded groggy. I was embarrassed. Cursing myself for having woken her, I rushed to apologise.

"No, you didn't wake me. It's the medication I'm given at night. I've been awake for a while, but I don't think I'm functioning yet."

"Who is giving you medication, and why?"

"I intended to call you today to let you know I wouldn't see you until later this week. I'm in hospital, and have been since Friday night. They say, if all goes well, I might be discharged on Wednesday. So, the earliest I might meet with you is Thursday."

"When we next meet is not an issue. But, tell me why you are in hospital … if it is nothing too personal to share with me." Domestic violence, I wondered?

"Oh, it's not personal. Someone knocked me off my bike on Friday night. I know it was deliberate, but the police believe otherwise. It seems you might have something extra to investigate once I escape from here."

"Okay, I'm happy to wait for details until our next meeting. In the meantime, can you give me a basic outline of why you think your accident was deliberate?"

"Because the bloke on the motorbike who rammed me while I was out for my regular Friday evening ride had hazed me for quite a while before he made his move. I think he waited until I was in the right spot before sending me into the stone wall. Of course, the motorbike was nowhere in sight when they found me unconscious, and I was carted off to hospital."

"Hmm… I will be interested to hear all the details. Don't worry about our meeting. It can happen whenever you are up to it."

"Sorry, Sonny; the doctor is here. I have to go. Talk to you again soon."

As it was still too early to head out to Westbrook, I made a coffee, wrote up my notes on the conversation with Janine, and sat back to consider what my new client had shared with me. It was obvious she had no doubts her 'accident' was deliberate. The longer I thought about it, the more inclined I was to agree. My new case showed increasing promise of being quite interesting.

With the problem of a clash between my two cases avoided, I went to Westbrook and spent Tuesday and Wednesday finalising Kirsty's case. Now I could relax while waiting to hear from Janine. Aah, the luxury of spare time to sit and review a case while trying to get my head around all its nuances. I flipped open Janine's case file and flicked through to the investigation spreadsheet I had developed. This was the 'road map' I had created to investigate her original case. I doubted it would have much currency now, given recent developments.

On Wednesday night, I realised the only possible highlights on my Thursday calendar were a half-anticipated meeting with my new client and a visit to the park.

So, what should I tackle first tomorrow? The time for review and planning was over. It was time to start making sense of Janine's case. My concern is for Janine's ongoing safety. Whoever tried to eliminate her must know by now his attempt failed. Is he likely to try again? Probably… and that is all the more reason to achieve traction on this investigation. And, as Ben Richards is back in town tomorrow, we will likely have dinner together tomorrow night. By then, I'll need something substantial to support my concerns, or I won't get much of a hearing from Ben.

The thought of Ben took me back down memory lane. Ben and I go back a long way, to when he was a young constable stationed in Millhaven. We became close friends and were on the verge of becoming something more when he was transferred out of the area. Over the subsequent decade or so, his postings took him all over the state, while I became married and then widowed. Then a case of mine put us in the same town at the same time, and soon after, he was transferred to Millhaven again. Over the years, we have developed a unique way of working together, but Ben is not beyond rubbishing what I do if I can't substantiate my claims with solid evidence.

It's Friday again, and my last chance to talk to people before the weekend. Janine didn't come to see me yesterday, but I did visit the park to familiarise myself with and photograph the crime scene – but I can't see how my photos are likely to be useful.

While there was nothing more to be gained from the crime scene, I had a heap of questions needing answers. Perhaps, there might be people at the park today who could provide at least some of those answers.

After a quick visit to my city office to check emails and messages, I headed across town to the park. I hoped the small kiosk would be open today and I could chat with whoever operated it. And I expected the parking area outside the park to be packed with people embarking on their early morning stroll or jog, or simply stopping at the kiosk for a coffee on their way to work. I struck out.

The car park was empty. But it was 8:30, and most people were back home after their jog or at work by then. Perhaps that was a good thing. I could chat with whoever was in the kiosk without interruption. My luck to date on this case was equivalent to a bald man winning a comb in a raffle.

The park looked deserted, and the shutters were down on the kiosk. I looked for something indicating its opening times but found nothing – not even anything about who operated the place. I stood in front of the kiosk for a moment to consider my options. A distant sound intruded. A mower was working somewhere in the park. Could the person on the mower be much use to me in terms of the information I needed, I wondered as I followed the sound.

It was one of those big industrial mowers with an enclosed cabin arrangement for the operator … who wore hearing protection and was oblivious of my yelling at him. When he finally spotted me bouncing up and down and waving at him not far in front of his mower, he must've thought me a maniac. After turning off the machine, he bounded down to meet me. His look was not encouraging. And his opening words left me in no doubt he was not impressed with my antics to gain his attention.

Once I explained I was trying to gather information about how the park operated, his demeanour changed, and he was up for a chat. We parked our backsides on the grass under a tree, and I launched my fact-finding mission.

"Apologies for interrupting your work, but I intended speaking to whoever was in the kiosk today. It's the second time I've been here, and the place was closed both times. Is it still a going concern, or has it closed down?"

"Good question, but I don't know. It used to open from seven o'clock in the morning until six o'clock in the evening. I'm damned if I know when it's supposed to open now, but I know it's closed more often than it's open. The original intention was for bottled water and energy drinks to be available for those using the park. Then coffee and light snacks were added to the menu for people who dropped in on their way to work and for groups of ladies who strolled around before sitting down to rest for a while. It used to do a roaring trade when it opened regularly. Come to think of it; I don't recall seeing it open for more than a week or so."

"Is it a privately owned facility or council-owned?"

"Not sure; when it first opened, it was a council facility, and someone was employed to run it. Later, it was let out on contract. I heard someone was interested in buying it to run it as a private facility, but I don't know if that happened. Why are you so interested in the kiosk?"

"I'm not. All I wanted was to talk to someone who knew a bit about the park, and I thought someone who worked in the kiosk every day might be the right person to answer some of my questions."

"What sort of questions… and why do you need to know?"

He had become wary. I needed to go carefully if I didn't want to alienate him before finding out what he knew. Sometimes it is safer to answer a question with a question.

"Are you aware of an incident in this park last Friday night?"

"You couldn't help but know about it. The cops were all over the place and asking questions too. I'll tell you the same as I told them: I wasn't in the park when it happened, so I know nothing about it. You don't look like a cop. Why are you interested?"

"I'm a private investigator hired by the victim to investigate her attack."

"The cops said it was an accident. What more is there to investigate?"

"That's what my client wants to know, and that's what I'm hoping to find out. You see, she believes it was a deliberate attack on her life. If she's right, she still might not be safe."

Chapter 3

Suggesting a woman's life might still be in danger appeared to cause the mower man pause for thought. After a moment, his tone told me he might be more inclined to answer my questions.

"Well, like I said, I wasn't here when it happened, but if I can help…."

"Okay, my questions are about the park, not the incident. Given what you said about the kiosk, is it safe to assume it wasn't staffed at the time of the attack?"

"Can't be sure, of course, but I doubt it. As I said, I don't know if it's been open for a while now."

"Right; now a couple of questions about the park that you'll probably be able to answer. Firstly, am I right in thinking motorbikes are not allowed in the park?"

"Yep, that's right… no cars, no motorbikes in the park at any time … that's the rule, and that's how it's always been. Anyway, the actual entrances were altered so it's impossible for motorbikes to enter. There used to be turnstiles at the entrances, but mothers complained because they couldn't bring their prams in. So, the turnstiles were replaced by the 'crooked cattle race' type of arrangement now installed. It's still difficult for big prams, like the ones for twins, but the mothers seem to manage okay. Cyclists soon worked out how to get around the new arrangement. If they are fit or have one of those new lightweight models, they lift them over the railings and then run around and pick them up after they've gone through the entrance. Anyone not up to throwing their bicycle over the railings stands it up on its rear wheel and pushes it through the race ahead of them."

"What about all this new-fangled stuff like e-scooters and e-bikes, are they allowed?"

"So far, they are, but I believe there's been some discussion about it amongst the powers-that-be. So, I wouldn't be surprised if they're banned in the future."

"Here's a tricky one for you: if a person was determined to bring a motorbike into the park with the intention of doing someone else an injury, would it be possible somehow to bring their motorbike into the park? I heard what you said earlier but, if I were really determined to bring a motorbike in, is there any way it might be possible?"

"If you were determined enough, you'd probably find a way."

My mower man, deep in thought, looked off into the distance. After a few moments, he nodded – not at me, but to himself, as though he'd made a decision.

"Now I think on it, bringing a motorbike in here might not be as impossible as I thought. Last Friday evening was it when the accident occurred?"

Rather than interrupt his thought processes, I just nodded confirmation. He grunted and continued.

"Nobody works in the park over the weekend, so nothing was noticed until Monday morning. I noticed something strange when I arrived here a bit after eight o'clock.

A big double gate at the rear of the park allows us to bring in our equipment. It's padlocked all the time, even now while I'm mowing. I have to padlock the gate behind me after I enter."

"So, are you suggesting it might be possible to bring a motorbike in here if you had a key to the padlock on that double gate?"

"It would be, if that just wasn't so impossible. Even I don't have a key to that gate. When I have to work here, before I leave the depot, I have to sign the key out, and sign it back in at the end of the day. They keep a proper register and all that, so they would know who had the key at any particular time."

"But, you think someone managed to circumvent the system last weekend? Am I right?"

While reluctant to share what he knew, or thought he knew, he seemed more uncomfortable about it than aggressive, so I persisted – and possibly struck gold. He spent a few moments studying the toes of his boots before shrugging and looking up at me.

"You have to understand that I didn't think much of it at the time, and nobody asked me anything about bringing a vehicle of any sort into the park. So, I never said anything to anyone. When I arrived here the Monday morning after the incident, I noticed two cop cars in the parking lot out front. I didn't think too much about it because there had been a fair bit of gossip at the depot before I left to come here.

The most interesting thing for me was when I unlocked the double gate. The padlock was all wrong. I was the last person working here that Friday and, according to the rules, I padlocked the gate behind me when I left. I suppose it's just a habit, but I always put the padlock around a certain way. When I arrived on Monday morning, the padlock was wrong. It wasn't how I left it. I had a bit of a look at it but didn't think too much about it – until now. Your question made me revisit what I found that morning. Again, I didn't think it was important at the time, but the surface of the lock was scratched – sort of scored a bit – around the keyhole."

"As though someone had tried to pick the lock…?"

"Yeah, I guess that was sort of what it looked like, and they must have managed to do it, or I wouldn't have found the padlock all wrong when I came in on Monday."

"Did you mention this to anyone?"

"Nah, it never occurred to me, and no one asked."

"Is the same padlock on the gate today?" He nodded. "So, if I had a look at it now, those scratches should still be visible?" There was more nodding in response.

After being given directions to the gate, I asked if he might take me there on his mower. I lucked out. A passenger on his mower was contrary to rules and the safe operation of the machine. He was adamant I must walk to the gate.

So walk, I did… but only after briefly toying with the idea of walking back to my car and driving around the block to the gate. But, as my car and the gate were about equidistant from where I was talking to the mower man, I decided a walk probably would do me good. As I walked, I used my phone to record a few notes from my conversation about the park and the padlock on that gate.

It would be hard not to notice the gouge marks on the padlock. After a few photos of the damage and how the padlock was positioned, I headed back to my car. I hadn't gone far before I kicked myself. There was an important question I neglected to ask my new friend. So-o, I'll just have to interrupt his mowing again. That proved trickier than expected. He had moved to a different area. I let my ears guide me. After quite a bit more foot-slogging, I flagged him down again.

He might not have said 'not you again', but his face certainly expressed the sentiment.

"Apologies for interrupting you again, but there is one more question I forgot to ask before."

He rolled his eyes but motioned for me to go ahead.

"Do you know if there are any CCTV cameras in or around the park?"

"Err… There must be some in the park somewhere. The bloke who had this mowing job before me got the boot for slacking off. It seems he had something else going on in his life at the same time and used to slip away for periods of time most days to attend to whatever it was. His unauthorised activities were captured on camera. I assumed it was by secret cameras somewhere here, but I've never noticed any. I suppose there could be some nearby outside the park that might have captured him coming and going from the park. But again, I don't know if there is, or where they might be."

"Who would know if cameras are located strategically around here and if anything was captured on the Friday night of the incident?"

Although unsure who to approach directly, he gave me the name of the man in charge of the parks and gardens operations and suggested he might be a good place to start. After thanking him and promising not to interrupt him again today, I returned to my car.

Before going up to my office, I visited the bakery a couple of doors down from my building to collect a box of assorted luscious-looking and calorie-packed cakes and today's newspaper. Well, it was mid-morning coffee time… and I needed something to go with coffee. I'm unsure whether it was cakes, but I certainly needed something to get the creative juices flowing. I had to have more than a few scratches on the padlock to show Ben when he arrived tonight. He'll want more before agreeing to talk to somebody at the Council about possible camera footage from the night of the attack.

Armed with coffee, a vanilla slice, and notebook and pencil, I settled into one of the ancient armchairs in the interview corner of my office. What else could I do today to help build a portfolio of evidence before tonight? The vanilla slice had disappeared long before inspiration struck.

"Nick… Yes, Nick Spargo…," I reminded my empty office. The thought of Nick had me out of my armchair and heading for my desk to find his number.

It dialled for quite a while. I was about to end the call when an out-of-breath Nick answered.

"Sounds like I've interrupted something strenuous. Can you talk now, or should I call you later?" I received an ear full of his familiar big, beefy laugh.

"I'd love to use this call as an excuse to stop what I'm doing, but that would show a total lack of self-restraint. Instead, how about you meet me for lunch at that little bistro a few doors from your building? You know the one, the health food place. Is noon okay for you?"

As much as I was tempted to say I couldn't make it, I accepted the invitation. The bistro is one of those that has its menu posted out front for you to read before entering. This place's menu was enough to convince me I didn't need to eat there but, today, I will sacrifice my appetite and taste buds and meet Nick there for lunch.

Nick is the patron saint of all fitness gurus in this area. Not only is he eye candy – a real Adonis – he lectures in physical fitness at the local university campus. Most of the personal trainers in this town owe their qualifications to him. And just for something to do in his spare time, he is part owner of the biggest gym in Millhaven. If he can't tell me something about Blake Carter, I doubt I'll find anyone else who might provide the information I need.

It was far too long since I last spoke to Nick, but we had that kind of friendship. It was always there without us having to be in constant contact. Today was no different. It was as if we spoke just yesterday. While Nick ordered a bowl of some bland-looking vegetable concoction and a startlingly green smoothie, I settled for the safest things I could see on the menu: a gluten burger and mineral water. As soon as we ordered, Nick was straight down to business.

"Now, Sonny, what case am I about to help you with today? It's not that I don't enjoy having lunch with you, but I'm hoping there is a case because I could do some excitement in my life at the moment."

"That sounds a bit worrying. Your life is usually pretty full, and you don't go around looking for excitement. Anyway, I'm not sure that's what I can offer. I'm looking for information about a bloke who inhabits your field of endeavour, supposedly a personal trainer here in Millhaven."

"Supposedly…? You don't sound too sure about him, but I've probably heard of him if he is a trainer, even if I don't know him personally. What's the name of this bloke you're trying to find out about?"

"Blake Carter… I don't know much more about him other than he supposedly is a personal trainer working out of one or more local gyms and possibly has private clients. I believe he was from Tasmania, but I don't know how long ago or whether he obtained his qualifications there or after arriving here. Does the name ring any bells for you?"

"Uhmm… yes … maybe. What's the bloke done, or supposed to have done, to have ignited your interest?"

"Truth is, I don't know yet if he's done anything, but his wife thinks he has. If that's how my investigation pans out, I'd like to put her mind at ease – or otherwise."

"Okay, your bloke, Mr Carter, is a bit of a mystery man as far as I could make out. When he first arrived in town, perhaps about four years ago now, he claimed to have the requisite personal trainer qualifications to be able to work as such. The piece of paper he claimed confirmed the qualification he obtained in Tasmania looked a bit dodgy – or so I was told. Gyms were tightening up on personal trainers at the time. A small number of bogus trainers had caused a few clients to suffer serious injuries. So, when the local gyms started questioning this bloke's piece of paper, they asked the university to test him to enable a cross credit for the qualification in this state. To that end, another university lecturer and I conducted the testing."

"Something tells me Mr Carter wouldn't be happy with his results. What happened?"

"You're right about the 'not happy' bit. As I understand it, initially, he refused to undertake testing, claiming it was an insult to him and the qualification he already held. Long story short, when none of the gyms would employ him, he finally agreed to be tested. I wouldn't say he didn't know anything, but he was awarded a fairly comprehensive fail. After we failed him, he had nothing more to do with the university or the two of us who tested him. A friend suggested that, if he were determined to work in fitness, he should at least undertake a TAFE diploma course."

"Did he do that? I suppose he must've done something to land work as a personal trainer."

"Not so sure about that… After we tested him, I had nothing more to do with him personally. The Millhaven fitness scene was undergoing a bit of an upheaval at the time. Gyms were not paying their staff well, and clients weren't keen to pay the money asked for by personal trainers. Many of our qualified people packed up and headed for the cities where they were guaranteed a better income and the prospect of a brighter future."

"Are you not saying, but hinting, that the industry's dire straits were a stroke of good fortune for Blake Carter – even without a proper qualification?"

"That about sums it up. A few of us more interested in maintaining the industry standards, know or suspect, Carter didn't do any further training but was taken on anyway by a gym in this area."

"So, apart from his dodgy qualification, Mr Carter does not sound like an all-round top bloke. In fact, he sounds more like a shyster. But if he's kept his nose clean, despite everything else, I don't suppose you can hold his personality against him."

"Well, it's that bit about *keeping his nose clean* you might want to look into before you go much further. Before you ask, no, I don't *know* anything. But rumours have floated around the industry on occasion since then. I won't give any of them oxygen today, but, if you do decide to investigate Blake Carter, take care … and start carrying that gun you prefer to leave locked away safely."

"Gyms have become synonymous with drugs in recent times. I take it your warning isn't for me to avoid injury while undertaking some fitness regime, but relates to something more sinister?"

Nick just shrugged and nodded in response. He didn't need to say more. We both understood what was said, although the actual words weren't used. On the way back to my office after a long lunch, Nick's words were on a loop running through my mind. This case was not just about a husband playing away. Over the last hour or so, it had developed worrying overtones. How much of this does my client know?

By the time I was back behind my desk, I knew what I had to do… after checking my case file notes to confirm my suspicions.

Yep, there it was. During Janine's initial visit, she suggested her husband's changed behaviour might be due to one of three possibilities. She favoured the third possibility: an affair. But one of her other suggestions was the possibility he was involved in something illegal. In response to my questioning, she admitted she suspected there was some sort of incident in his background, but it was before she knew him, and he never spoke of it.

Do I need to take a closer look at my client? From the outset, I felt she might be withholding details critical to the case, and that feeling was reinforced after she was attacked. What was she so keen to hide? What was her motivation, and what did she hope to gain? Surely there would be nothing in it for her. Otherwise, it would be pointless to arouse the curiosity of someone like me. It's not the first time I've encountered a similar situation. But, in those cases, the clients created scenarios to rid themselves of their spouses and benefit from them. Their motivation was greed.

That then begged another question: *what did I know about Janine Thomlinson?*

The short answer: next to nothing. And that was despite the family name and business being well-known in the community. Well, by tonight, I had better know a helluva lot more, if I want to talk to Ben Richards about this case. And that dictates what I'll be doing for the rest of today.

My first step is to create a list of sources to research. Janine was a local, probably born and bred here – at least, that was my impression. So, the online archives of Millhaven's local newspaper might be a good source of information. And, Trove, the National Library's online newspaper archive, might turn up information from elsewhere, if my assumption about her origins is incorrect. "Right, let's start local," I told my empty office.

I logged in, typed 'Thomlinson' in the search box … and almost regretted my decision when a long list of hits filled my screen.

"Interesting start…," I told the universe. The list of hits for the Thomlinson name stretched back a long way and long before Janine's lifetime. "So, it looks as though I was right about Janine being a local," I thought aloud.

From the dates involved, I figured the Thomlinsons had been in Millhaven for at least three and maybe four generations. Tempting as it was to start at the earliest entry and move forward, time was not on my side. The headline of one of the hits caught my eye: *Major Changes at Thomlinson's*. Its date suggested it could refer to Janine's father or her grandfather if he lived to a right old age. I printed the article without reading it, before searching for the next interesting-looking one.

Again, it had a huge headline, and this one was recent. Well, recent in the sense that it was written less than three years ago. It followed the previous one to the printer. Then, after printing a copy of the list of hits, I retrieved all the printouts, put my feet up and sat back to learn what I had discovered. With two long articles to read, it seemed logical to prepare myself for the ordeal with coffee and cake.

While standing by the bench in my office's kitchenette waiting for the coffee machine to finish doing its thing, I studied the contents of the box of cakes I bought this morning. "Hmm, maybe a custard tart…," I murmured, before the pounding on my door halted everything. I wasn't expecting anyone. It might be a prospective new client, and it would never do to have them see me messing about with coffee and cake.

"Ben! What are you doing banging on my door at this hour of the day? And why are you in civvies and not in your uniform?"

"If that's how you greet everyone who knocks on your door, it's no wonder you have time to make coffee … and, yes, please, I will have a cup. Oh, and I spy a box from the cake shop." As he inspected the box's contents, he suggested, "Perhaps you could get on with making my coffee while I choose something to have with it."

Apparently, familiarity accompanies long friendships, I mused as I started the coffee machine again and reached for another mug.

"What are you doing roaming the streets of Millhaven today? This is your first day back after a few days away. I expected you to be riveted to your desk trying to catch up."

"No, that's for tomorrow. I returned on the late flight last night after the conference finished earlier than expected, but I'm not expected back in my office until tomorrow. Today allowed me to do a few things I've meant to do for ages."

"Including bumming coffee and cake from me… Never mind, you're here now. So, shall we make ourselves comfortable?" I gestured towards my two ancient lounge chairs.

"Okay, I suppose we should sit there, but I'll never understand why you consider them comfortable."

Our usual opening banter done with, we settled down with our afternoon tea. Although I'm always pleased to spend time with Ben, I had things to do today and hoped he wasn't planning to hang around too long. After a minute or so of munching cake and sipping coffee in companionable silence, I was concerned he might settle in for the rest of the afternoon, if I didn't do something about it. As a first step, I broke the silence.

"Are you planning on coming for dinner tonight?"

"Oh yeah, I meant to call you earlier about dinner. Is Chinese all right tonight?"

Normally, I wouldn't hesitate to agree, but not this time. "Uhmm, no, I think I fancy something a bit more substantial tonight."

His eyebrows shot up in surprise, so I explained about my 'healthy' lunch with Nick and how I'd eaten less than half my gluten burger.

"There was nothing wrong with the burger. It just wasn't my thing and, after a couple of cakes today, I need something solid tonight to settle my stomach. I thought I might escape early this afternoon. So, how about I do us a baked dinner? Would seven o'clock be okay to eat?" He nodded enthusiastically. As soon as he left about ten minutes later, I packed up and headed home.

Once the roast was in the oven, I retired to my home office to spend the next couple of hours researching Janine Thomlinson.

Chapter 4

Whew, Janine Thomlinson was somebody in Millhaven. It appears Blake Carter scored himself a great catch when they married.

Janine's father inherited a well-established, thriving business from her grandfather. The newspaper article about her father, Thomas's revamp of the business after inheriting it, made for interesting reading. He modernised the operation, and the company saw substantial growth and diversification over his time at the helm. As Thomas's only child, Janine inherited quite an empire when her father died during the first year of her marriage.

The other article I printed related to further advancements since Janine took over. It was obvious Janine wasn't just a lucky little rich daughter who landed on her feet. This was a shrewd and talented businesswoman who ran her massive empire with an iron fist while wearing the proverbial kid gloves. It appears the business world was in awe of her. Her employees and much of the community loved her.

After adding a few more notes to my case file, I sat back to ponder what I had learned about the recent years of the Thomlinson family. So far, there was no mention of Janine's mother. While the mother wasn't likely to be of any consequence to my investigation, the little voice in my head warned me not to overlook her. I made a note to research her when I had a spare moment.

For now, my attention focused on Janine and her father, which brought me to the inevitable questions about Janine's marriage. No matter how wonderful or anything else Mr Carter might be, I doubted he measured up to the husband Thomas wanted for his daughter. I reminded myself I knew nothing about Blake Carter other than the less than glowing picture Nick painted of him. And I usually wasn't so quick to make assumptions about people until I got to know them at least a bit better than I did Blake Carter. Still, despite my best efforts, the little I gleaned from Nick had shaped my opinion of Mr Carter.

Should I try for a bit more about Carter before I speak to Ben about my case? I checked the time. I had about half an hour before I needed to return to the kitchen to fuss with dinner. As I hadn't heard from Emily Ibbotson this afternoon, I still didn't know whether I would be feeding two or three tonight. To be safe, prepare vegetables for three, I told myself. The dinner issue settled, I turned my attention to Blake Carter and what Tasmanian newspapers said about him in the past.

Trove's newspaper archives weren't helpful. A search for an online Tasmanian newspapers archive unearthed a project being undertaken by a local family history group. A quick look at their efforts to date told me I had struck out again.

Okay, when all else fails, ask Google what it knows about Mr Carter. I typed in the search request and sent it off to do its thing. A disappointing shortlist of possible hits appeared. A quick look told me none of the three hits was relevant to my research.

"One more attempt before I give up on him tonight," I promised the universe as I returned to the search bar. I typed in my request minus the word 'Tasmania'. This time, Google offered me two possible hits. The first one I looked at was basically an advert dressed up as an article in the local Millhaven paper. It announced that Mr Blake Carter would join the staff at one of the local gyms as an onsite personal trainer. After going on at some length about the advantages of using a personal trainer, the article encouraged existing and prospective gym members to book an assessment session with Blake.

The second hit Google offered me didn't amount to much more than the first one. Again, it was an article from the local paper, but this time it waxed lyrical about engaging Blake Carter as the physical fitness guru for a local football club. If that's the best Google has to offer, I need to devote some heavy thinking to Mr Carter. He has me well and truly intrigued … and my nose is starting to detect something of an odour about the man.

Time had run out. I needed to deal with the vegetables if dinner was to be ready by seven o'clock. Peeling vegetables doesn't require much mental involvement. It was just as well since my mind was preoccupied with Blake Carter. That my research turned up nothing about the man before he arrived in Millhaven concerned me. I didn't want to accept the obvious conclusion, but it tried hard to make me. Was Carter not the man's true identity? It wouldn't be the first time I encountered such a situation, but for some reason, I didn't want it to be a part of Janine's story.

Time slipped away unnoticed until lights coming up my driveway brought me back to reality. Ben arrived a little earlier than anticipated and, as I still hadn't heard from Emily, I wasn't disappointed we would be two for dinner. Just the two of us would allow me to discuss my case with Ben. Not that Emily would be a problem if she were here. It's just that, early in an investigation, it works best for me to discuss things with Ben when we are alone.

Over a pre-dinner wine, I alerted Ben that, after dinner, it would be 'one of those nights'.

"Ah, so you've started a new case. Is this likely to be one I already know about?"

"I'm not sure, and that's part of the problem I want to discuss with you. But dinner is almost ready, so let's leave it until later. In the meantime, you might tell me what you got up to while you were away for the last few days."

We discussed nothing of any consequence until after we had eaten, the dishes were in the dishwasher, and we were settled in the lounge with coffee and port. After a sip or two of port, Ben opened the discussion of my case.

"So, come on, tell me about your case so I can work out how much of my time – and political capital – it might cost me."

"It involves Janine Thomlinson, of the Thomlinson Commercial Enterprises family. Of course, you know the empire I'm talking about. Anyone who has ever lived in Millhaven can't help but know about it. Janine is the lady who owns and currently runs the show. The day after she came to see me about a relatively simple matter, she was involved in an incident that put her in hospital for several days. So now, that simple matter has morphed into something more significant."

"Was the 'incident' you mentioned one the police were involved with, or at least know about?"

"Yep, they supposedly investigated and deemed it an accident."

"Am I to understand your client sees it as something else…?"

"And so do I. Perhaps we should adjourn to my office to review my case file."

As we settled on opposite sides of my desk, Ben sighed and said, "Okay, give me the executive summary, please."

After giving him an overview of my case as I knew it to date, I was ready for the usual interrogation that would follow. Instead, Ben reached over and dragged my case file across the desk to him. While he skimmed the first pages of my notes, I quickly checked something on my computer… but then the interrogation began.

"So, your client claims she was rammed by a motorbike on Friday evening a week ago. What makes you and your client so sure it wasn't an accident? Here in Millhaven, people are always being knocked off bikes, especially at that time of the evening. Was she wearing a high-visibility and reflective vest, and did her bicycle have a light and taillight? Could it have been some form of collision with another bike rider? How much have you discovered about this so-called accident?"

"You – and maybe your officers investigating the incident as well – missed the critical factor about the incident: she was rammed by a *motorbike*, and it happened in a *park*." The confused look on his face told me I might as well have been speaking a foreign language.

"As with most Millhaven parks, and certainly the one in question, vehicle access is banned – not only for cars, but also for motorbikes. As for whether there might have been another bicycle involved, my client is adamant it was a motorbike. I am inclined to believe she would know what hit her."

"Humph… well, maybe the local lads wait until there is no one around much in the evening before taking a few turns around the park on their motorbikes. It might be against the rules, but that doesn't rule it out as being an unfortunate accident. I see her husband was in Tasmania at the time this occurred."

"Except he wasn't… no, okay, I'll rephrase that. Her husband, Blake Carter, did not fly to the Apple Isle last Friday morning as his wife believes. He wasn't booked on any flight, and nor did he have a return flight booked."

"Your notes say he was supposed to be gone for the week. Has he returned? He might not have booked a return flight in advance."

"True… and I admit I don't know exactly what 'a week' means. It could mean he was due back today or, more likely, that he would return sometime over the weekend ready to start work again on Monday. Before you ask, he was not on any flight into Millhaven today. I checked while you were going through my case file."

"Sonny, I find it a bit strange that you are so committed to the concept of a motorbike being involved when you so readily quote the 'no motorbikes in the park' rule to me. Let's rethink the scenario, shall we? Despite the rules, you believe a motorbike was in the park and caused the accident. So, what would have prevented it from entering the park when no one was around after hours?"

I took the next few moments to explain a fully-fenced park, the arrangements at both park entrances, and how they rendered it impossible for a motorbike rider to gain access that way.

"What about another entrance somewhere? Is there another way to access the park besides those two official entrances?"

"Well, yes. At the back of the park, a relatively well-concealed double gate opens into the rear of the area."

"There you are then. Rules might be rules, but a double gate would allow access by a motorbike, wouldn't it? Aw, hell, hang on a minute. That's not the point I was trying to argue here. Okay, I concede a motorbike might have entered the park through the double gates at that time. So where the hell does that leave us with this discussion?"

"It has us overlooking a couple of critical flaws in the assumption, I'm afraid," I conceded.

"Like what? You can't expect me to help you much if you don't give me all the facts."

"That double gate is always padlocked." I slapped down in front of him the photo of the padlock in place on the gate, and then proceeded to explain the rules about the padlock and the key, as my friend on the mower gave me. "That photo shows how the bloke always leaves the padlock positioned after he locks it. That's how it was when he left the park at about two o'clock last Friday afternoon. It wasn't like that when he returned on Monday morning."

"So, he slipped up on Friday and didn't leave as he usually does."

Next, I slapped down on the table in front of him the close-up photo of the face of the padlock, which clearly showed the gouge marks. "Perhaps not…," I quipped. "But perhaps there's another explanation for why the padlock wasn't as he left it."

"Did he make this information available to my officers when they investigated the incident?"

"Apparently not. They were no longer interested in talking to him once they discovered he wasn't near the park when the incident occurred. Anyway, although he noticed and was cranky about the padlock then, he didn't give it more thought until I asked questions today."

"Okay, it looks safe to agree that, at some point, after he left the park last Friday afternoon, someone else who didn't have a key *probably* entered the park via the double gates."

"*Probably*! Aw, come on. There can't be any reason to doubt that was the case."

"You might be right, but we have no evidence to prove it. All we have is evidence the padlock was tampered with sometime around the time of the incident. Much time and effort could be wasted chasing after something we can't substantiate as fact."

"Well, perhaps we can confirm our assumption – okay, suspicion if you prefer. That is, *you* might be able to access evidence to verify if a motorbike entered the park through the double gates that night."

He gave me one of his best sceptical looks, and I knew I was about to receive a torrent of reasons why that wasn't possible. So, I jumped in before he started.

"I understand there might be CCTV cameras either in the park or its vicinity. It was suggested that, if there are cameras in the park itself, they are well concealed for whatever reason."

Ben sat forward on his chair. I knew he was hooked. All I had to do was reel him in before he lost interest. I recounted the story about a bloke being sacked after his inappropriate work practices were captured on camera.

"My friend doesn't know where the cameras are, but believes some are in the area. Furthermore, if they are in the park, he hasn't worked out why Council went to so much trouble to conceal them so well. Was it to monitor park users' behaviour, or to spy on employees?"

"Hmm, that could make it hard to get hold of the recording, and there is no guarantee anything recorded in the twilight of the late afternoon will be worth the trouble of obtaining access. I don't suppose your friend gave you any indication of who might be the keeper of such recordings?"

"No, but he did suggest someone who probably would know." I scribbled a name on a Post-it note and handed it to him. "That's the bloke my friend suggested as a first contact. It goes without saying, I wouldn't get access to such recordings, regardless of my legitimate reason for wanting to look at them. So, to confirm a motorbike was in the park that evening, you will have to prise the recordings away from whoever looks after them."

"There would be no point wasting time trying to talk to somebody over the weekend. Talking to at least this bloke will have to wait until Monday. Do you have anything else for me at this stage?"

"My investigation only started in earnest today, so I have nothing more except the list of the questions I've been compiling about the case. It's frustrating that nothing will be achieved over the weekend unless there's more useful information online."

"Yeah, weekends do tend to get in the way of investigations. As I intend spending a bit of time in my office over the weekend, I'll look at my officers' report on their investigation."

Tiny steps, but more than I had hoped to achieve tonight. Wondering what the police file might contain will keep me curious all weekend.

As I watched Ben drive off, the little voice in my head reminded me patience is not one of my strong points. That voice and I both knew Monday was a long way off. Was there something more I could do tonight or over the weekend to progress my investigation? Although I couldn't think of anything as I stood on the doorstep watching Ben's taillights disappear down the driveway, I knew I would return to my office tonight.

The few minutes it took me to wander back to my office after grabbing a glass of soda water on my way through the kitchen gave me enough time to think of something to research before going to bed. A vague and distant aspect of Janine kept rattling around in the back of my mind. It barged to the front as I walked back into my office: her marriage to Carter. I did not believe for one moment her father approved of Carter.

Thomas Thomlinson was an astute businessman, probably capable of accurately assessing people. Yeah, I might be jumping to conclusions but, from the little I know of Blake Carter – albeit without having laid eyes on him – I doubt he would have impressed Thomas. At that point, something about Janine leapt out at me.

Her marriage! Why didn't my search for Thomlinson information – or on Blake Carter –produce any reference to their marriage? The Thomlinson family's standing in this community almost ensured it would have been the celebrity event of the year. Maybe they married away from Millhaven. If that were the case, why? Was there somewhere else associated with the family where the couple chose to tie the knot? What about Tasmania from where Carter supposedly originates? I turned to Trove for help.

I typed 'Janine Thomlinson' in the search bar and waited. It seemed to take much longer than I expected to find anything. After what was, in reality, no more than a few moments, it produced a short, not particularly helpful, list of hits. All except one were items appearing in the 'social jottings' columns over the years. The exception was the article I found earlier about her improvements to the Thomlinson empire after taking over.

Okay, so that didn't work. What else can I try? I gave Trove three keywords to play with: Thomlinson, Carter, and marriage. After a lengthy search, it found nothing that matched.

"What am I doing wrong?" I demanded of the universe. "There has to be something, unless…."

Unless what…? Now that's a good question. Why didn't their marriage rate a mention in any of the newspapers? … They married in secret? … They married overseas? … They are not married?

That last possibility hit home like a blow from Thor's hammer. If they weren't married, why not? I estimated Janine was in her late twenties or early thirties. About three years ago, when she suggested she had married Blake Carter, Janine would have been well over the age of consent and free to do as she pleased. Or… or …was it possible Thomas forbade it and threatened to disinherit her if she went ahead with the marriage?

Christ, I should not indulge in these guessing games at this hour. I risked keeping myself awake all night with 'what if' scenarios. There is a better way to obtain answers: ask Janine. It's probably not good form for me to annoy my client on the weekend, but it is either that or die of curiosity before I can talk to her on Monday.

A way around my problem occurred to me as I put everything away for the night. I asked Janine to call me when her husband arrived home, or she heard from him. What if he has arrived home, but she hasn't been able to make the call? I could call her and claim to be checking if she was okay and wondered whether her husband had returned. What if he were there and she couldn't talk? Surely we are both intelligent women who can work around such a situation.

Great, I will call her after breakfast, maybe around nine o'clock. Having made the decision didn't guarantee me a good night's sleep, but it improved my chances.

Chapter 5

Wouldn't you know it! Saturday mornings are for sleep-ins, but this one had me awake earlier than on week day mornings. Although I didn't spring out of bed, I struggled to stay there until my usual Saturday get-up time.

I knew I had to keep busy to avoid calling Janine before a respectable hour. So, after doing the laundry and a few other minor domestic chores, I took a quick trip to the newsagents for the weekend papers. It wasn't quite nine o'clock when I returned home. Although I intended a quick scan of the papers first, my office beckoned me. I settled in behind my desk and opened Janine's case file.

Damn, I'm sick of waiting. I keyed Janine's number. She answered after only a few rings.

"Good morning, Sonny. Is everything all right? I wasn't expecting to hear from you. I haven't forgotten to do something you asked for, have I?"

"Apologies for intruding on your Saturday morning, but I just wanted to check you were okay."

She confirmed she was fine but was unsure about the reason for my call, so I rushed on to ease her mind.

"Apart from making sure you were all right, I wondered if your husband had returned or if you had heard from him."

"No… on both counts. I knew he was gone for the week, but I expected he wouldn't return until sometime this weekend. Knowing Blake, he will stretch it out as long as he can before returning to start work again on Monday. I often don't hear from him while he's away on these trips. They spend their time in wilderness-type places where reception is poor or non-existent."

"Okay… well, if he does contact you, or arrives home, please let me know – if you can."

"Yes, I will. And thanks for your concern."

"Oh, one other thing, Janine… if he doesn't return before Monday morning, please let me know."

"Sonny, you are starting to frighten me. Is there something I should know?"

Having blown it, I rushed to reassure her, explaining that she was home alone and I was concerned she might not yet be fully recovered from her attack. After ending the call, it occurred to me. Damn it! I didn't ask her about the marriage, and that was the main reason I couldn't wait to call her.

After adding another note to my case file, I was reviewing the slim file when my phone chirped. Emily.

"Are you working today or sitting around with your feet up?"

"Not working – and at a bit of a loose end. What are you doing today?"

"I came to the lab to finish off some tests I had running overnight, and now that's done, I thought a coffee and chat might be nice."

"Yeah, I could handle that this morning. Come around whenever you're ready."

About half an hour later, Emily pulled up outside. "I brought sustenance," she announced as she came through the front door, and I saw she was carrying a familiar box. "I had to go past the bakers… Aw, no. I *couldn't* go past the bakers without going in to get something to have with our coffee."

Her company was welcome, but I knew my contribution to our chat was scant. Emily noticed as well.

"Sonny, am I keeping you from something you should be doing?" I shook my head in surprise. "You are not your usual self today. What's happened? What's gone wrong?"

"Nothing; well, I don't think it's gone wrong yet. Argh, it's this new case I've started. I can't get a proper handle on it somehow. I feel as though I'm grabbing at smoke. I know it's only been a few days, but I can't get traction, and I feel something I don't know about is happening."

"Do you think your new client is a bit dodgy? You usually sum people up pretty quickly. What's so different with this one?"

"That's the problem. I just don't know. She seems straight up and on the level, but it's just not hanging together for me. It doesn't smell right. While I can't be sure, I don't think she is deliberately withholding information, or telling me porky's, but for some reason, you could drive a truck through what she's told me so far."

"Is this a strictly personal problem, or does it involve illegal activity somehow?"

"The latter, I'm afraid. Her initial approach was for personal reasons, but then it took a turn for the worst. Simply put, she believes – and I agree – the police botched their investigation into a serious incident. And, before you ask, yes, I have discussed it with Ben. I had to. Not only do I need him to access some information for me, I am concerned they might try again after the first attempt on my client's life failed."

In her usual fashion, Emily wanted all the details of the case. I watched her demeanour change as I rolled out the information for her. By the end of my short story, she looked a little concerned. It prompted me to ask, "Have you had something come in from this case?"

"Possibly… but I wasn't directly involved. I did sign off on a report on some tests that might have come from that incident in the park. Either that, or there was another similar incident around the same time."

"Do you remember if the tests produced anything significant?" She shook her head, but I could see she was deep in thought, probably trying to recall details of the report. So I remained silent, allowing her to be the next one to speak.

"Well, we are both sitting here doing nothing," she began slowly. "Why don't we visit my lab to see what those tests produced?"

"Good idea, but it's almost lunchtime. How about we have an early lunch and then visit your lab?"

Soon after one o'clock, Emily unlocked a filing cabinet, withdrew a folder, and opened it on the bench in front of her. I peered over her shoulder but didn't see anything I understood, so I sat back in silence while she scanned the file and was ready to tell me about it.

"Hmm… I'm afraid nothing here will be much use to you. The police sent over a few samples they collected from the incident site. Nothing was relevant to the incident, except for a small sample of blood they collected. Don't get your hopes up. The hospital later confirmed it was the victim's blood. The only other thing tested of any consequence were splinters of material my team collected from the victim's bike. It tested as a form of plastic commonly used in motorbike fairings."

"Colour…?"

"Black…"

"Oh yeah, very useful… most of the motorbikes in Millhaven have black somewhere on their fairings. Given how this case is going, I shouldn't have expected anything more. But I suppose it does confirm there was a vehicle in an area where that type of vehicle shouldn't have been."

Emily had chores to attend to at home, so she dropped me at my place. Before heading off, she indicated she would join Ben and me for dinner tonight. I retreated to my office to make a few notes about the samples the police collected from the scene of Janine's attack, and then took myself out onto the deck to read the weekend papers for the rest of the afternoon.

My fellow diners arrived early, Ben with a selection of pasta dishes and Emily with a container of various gelato flavours and a tub of fruit salad. We adjourned to the back deck with glasses of wine and a few nibbles to fill in a half-hour or so before dinner. Conversation wasn't stilted but was sparse. Each of us seemed to be enjoying the company of our own thoughts rather than communicating with each other.

It was one of those glorious pleasant evenings that lends itself so well to just sitting and thinking. A light breeze barely rustled the leaves, but it was enough to release the delicious perfume of the jasmine and rosemary bushes in my hedge. Without giving them any thought, I watched the squawking tailenders of a flock of black cockatoos heading home to roost for the night. They were nothing more than black silhouette's against a salmon-pink sky.

Before I realised how much time had slipped by as I sat there in a semi-detached way, the sunset had turned to dusk. That gloriously tinted sky already presented a dark backdrop for a lazy moon beginning to poke its head above the distant skyline. I became aware of conversation. At first, it seemed nothing more than a distant buzz, but as I emerged from my reverie, I realised it was me who had been away and not my companions. I sat up and blinked a few times to focus myself in the moment again.

"Hello, welcome back," Emily chirped. "Have you been anywhere good, or were you just snoozing?" Ben's chuckles did nothing to ease my embarrassment.

"Neither… I don't think. Perhaps it was more a case of just switching off for a few moments. Please accept the apologies of an ignorant host. Have I missed anything interesting?"

"Nothing so far, but I just mentioned to Ben about our trip to my lab this afternoon," Emily said and looked over at Ben as though to hand over the conversation to him.

"I didn't go into my office today, so I haven't looked at the report on my officers' investigation into the incident. But the more I hear about this case, the more uncomfortable I become. I suspect I'll be unhappy about what I find in their file tomorrow.

What about you, Sonny? Do you have anything new to report? When I left last night, I suspected you were considering concocting some excuse to talk to your client today." Ben raised his eyebrows in question at me, followed by a hard look as he finished speaking.

"Yeah, I did call her. It didn't add anything significant to my investigation. The only thing to report is that Blake Carter hasn't returned to Millhaven yet, and hasn't contacted his wife since he left here."

"Did your client seem concerned about him?" Emily asked.

"No. She didn't know exactly when he would return, but imagined he wouldn't be back until sometime tomorrow, and then probably as late as possible. She also explained 'no contact' during his absence resulted from the location where they were camped having poor or no phone reception."

"Is she delusional, or just not very bright?" Ben spat at me. "Did she have any concerns about not having heard from him, and without knowing exactly when he might return?"

"Maybe this is a case of ignorance being bliss," I suggested sarcastically. "As much as I hate to admit it, I can't get a handle on this client. I don't know why or what it is about her, but it's as though she is in a cocoon of some sort, and I can't break into it."

"Now I am concerned," Ben quipped. "It never takes you more than five minutes with a new client before you have sussed out what makes them tick. What's your next move?"

"Although I don't hold much hope of digging up anything worthwhile, I'll try to do more research tomorrow. But, unless I've gained a bit more traction on this case after that, come Monday, I'll be demanding Janine comes to see me for a deep and meaningful conversation."

"Okay; I'll check our file tomorrow and share whatever I find with you tomorrow night, so you are well-armed with anything worth knowing before you talk to her."

As he finished speaking, Ben pulled out a pocket notebook and scribbled a note. I was disappointed – or dismayed – that he needed to write himself a reminder to check the police file on Janine's attack. Obviously, I was labouring under the misguided belief my case was important enough for it to occupy the front of his mind and he wouldn't need a reminder.

That was the last discussion of my case before we moved inside, and we were hoeing into bowls of pasta while conversation moved to various inconsequential topics. It's normal for us to linger at the table over dinner, but not tonight. As soon as the pasta was dispatched, we took our bowls of gelato and fruit salad through to the lounge room. I was barely halfway through my dessert when Ben's phone rang.

"Uh huh, to me, that sounds like a call to duty," Emily murmured as Ben took his call out to the back deck. He reappeared a few moments later.

"Sorry, ladies, but I have to love and leave you. The natives of Millhaven are misbehaving again tonight. Emily, do you have someone on roster tonight?"

"Yes, me…"

"Well, hurry up and finish your gelato. You're going to be needed as well. We have to deal with a body washed up on a beach."

I knew it was ridiculous, but the immediate thought that flashed through my mind was that at least it wouldn't turn out to be Janine. After seeing them off, I cleaned up before taking a mug of coffee to my office.

"Why am I here?" I asked the empty room. "I have no idea what I might do."

But, when all else fails, putting your feet up and drinking your coffee seems an appropriate approach. So, that's what I did, and idly read through my case file while I was about it. It only took a handful of moments – and less than a quarter of my coffee – before my thinking refocused. I still knew next to nothing about the Thomlinson family.

To satisfy the little voice in my head, I made one more attempt to find a Thomlinson-Carter marriage mentioned somewhere out there in the ether. The result was predictable: nothing. Don't dwell on it. Leave it and move on seemed like sound advice to give myself. I turned my attention to Janine's parents, particularly her mother. Who was she, and where was she now?

Before starting a trawl through the various states' online marriage indexes, and based on a rough estimate of Janine's age, I took a wild guess at when her parents might have married. Of course, it was too recent to appear in any of the indexes, so I needed to call in the 'Big Guns'. I logged onto Google and typed in the search parameter *Thomas Thomlinson marriage* … and, after second thoughts, added the approximate date range from my earlier calculations.

"Yes! Thank you, Google, my friend. That has to be them – I think."

It was a brief mention in a Melbourne newspaper's social notes. Armed with that tantalising clue, I sent Trove off to find me more information. It found a few hits, and many of the same details appeared in various other resources. I opened the earliest article.

One of a myriad of brief entries in the 'Notices' section of a Melbourne newspaper announced the engagement of Thomas Thomlinson of Millhaven and Amelia Bartlett, the only daughter of Geoffrey Bartlett of Melbourne City. *Melbourne City*…? That sounds as though it should mean something. Was it the equivalent today of mentioning Prahran or even Collins Street to indicate an elevated position in the community? And was it of any importance to my case? Having started down this trail, it felt like being on a narrow road that offered no opportunity to turn around and leave.

The marriage would have paid dividends for both parties. For Amelia, who had lived a privileged lifestyle, Thomas had the money to continue that life for her. Thomas's benefits were a little different. Although a champion of enterprise here in Millhaven and wielding considerable influence over many aspects of this state, Thomas was not from the rarefied world of high society. Amelia would provide his entrée to that.

Well, now I know her name and a bit about her, maybe I should try to find out what happened to her. Although I couldn't remember exactly how or why, I had developed the impression Janine's mother had exited her daughter's life while they were both quite young. Divorce or death…? That question now nagged me. If it were the latter, was it reasonable to assume it happened here in Millhaven and that she is buried here? It was the easiest assumption to pursue, so I brought up an online

Millhaven burials index created by the local family history group.

There she was. Given the way this case was progressing, that was way too easy. Then I remembered Amelia's burial was irrelevant to solving this case. The only thing I gained from discovering the date of her burial was confirmation of my suspicion that Janine had lost her mother when she was quite young, about thirteen or fourteen.

Apart from being at a vulnerable age when her mother died, it doesn't tell me much else. What happened afterwards might be interesting. Was she sent away to boarding school because no one was at home to look after her? How was her relationship with her father before and after her mother's death?

About then, I realised none of that shed any light on possible motivation for the attack on Janine. Rather than sitting in my office wasting time, I should go to bed and try to think of something positive to do tomorrow.

Although I woke at my usual time this morning, for a change, I elected to try thinking about my case while remaining horizontal instead of vertical. By the time I managed to drag myself out of bed, I had a planned schedule of activities for today.

Straight after breakfast, I added a few necessary bits of equipment to my bag, grabbed bottled water and a couple of muesli bars, and drove away. My destination was about half an hour's drive out of town in an area known for large blocks, small acreages, and swanky homes. Well, why not, I asked myself as I turned off the highway. After all, where else would I expect someone as well-heeled as Janine to live?

Janine's place (Thomlinson Estate, the plaque on the high stone-pitched perimeter fence told me) was in keeping with my expectations. Beyond the fence and through sturdy-looking wrought iron gates, an enormous house sat some way back at the apex of a gravelled circular driveway. Surrounded by acres of manicured lawns, patches of bushland and well-tended garden beds, the house commanded views out over the bay in one direction and back over the valley in the opposite direction. As I snapped a handful of photos through the gates, I wondered how many people it took to look after a place like this.

Photographs taken, I stood beside my car and took one long hard look at the place before sliding in behind the wheel and driving back towards the city. My next target was the Tomlinson Enterprise headquarters in part of the industrial area of town. When I finally pulled up out front, I realised it had taken me about forty minutes to drive from the house to the site – and that was on a Sunday morning when traffic was light. It was one hell of a commute to work every day, and the daily trip to and from work would account for quite a bit of time by the end of the week.

The sprawling Tomlinson complex occupied a whole block in the industrial area. Various sheds, workshops and other buildings were packed onto the site to surround what appeared to be an administration building. A substantial security fence surrounded the entire complex. Its gates were closed, and I didn't detect any onsite activity – perhaps not surprising on a Sunday. After taking more photographs, I went home to study my morning's handiwork and hopefully glean something useful from it.

With coffee and a leftover half-stale cake to sustain me, I printed the photographs I had taken and studied them before adding them to my case file. Nothing jumped out to grab my attention, so I sat back with yet another cup of coffee to consider the little I'd learned about Janine Tomlinson. At first glance, it didn't amount to much, but my gut kept telling me I was missing something. So I brought up the photos on my computer and switched them to the big screen.

After a few minutes of careful scrutiny, the only hard fact I'd come up with was that Janine was indeed a wealthy woman. But was that enough to motivate the attack she suffered? In any other case, I might have been tempted to blame such factors. I'm not usually a poor judge of character, and Janine didn't fit the profile. I didn't believe her wealth was the cause of the attack. There had to be something else, something I didn't know about yet. Now that I think about it, Janine almost came across as naïve, unworldly in some way. Does that fit with the image of the dynamic businesswoman she is supposed to be? I tend to think not. But, if that is the case, and I'm not seeing the real Janine, what's her game?

I laughed aloud. I could write a book on what I don't know about this case. I started a mental list of what I didn't know. I knew virtually nothing about Janine despite what I'd like to think. Nothing about her husband. Nothing definite about their lifestyle and nothing about any recent business dealings. The only positive thing to come out of that depressing exercise was the realisation I needed to talk to Janine at some length, and as soon as possible. And that was likely to be problematic.

No doubt, Janine is a busy woman and isn't just sitting around waiting for me to talk to her. While I would prefer to interview her in my city office, that might be difficult to achieve. The alternative is to interview her at her office. An anticipated problem with arranging such a meeting was that I probably would have to make an appointment through her secretary. And, my experience with that is, it would be like trying to book a couple of hours with God.

My many negative thoughts about this case were starting to depress me. I ran up the white flag. Accepting there was nothing else of any value to the case I could do today, after lunch, I curled up with the weekend newspapers, and that's where I stayed until Ben called at about four o'clock.

Chapter 6

Ben arrived earlier than usual and brought a selection of Chinese dishes for dinner. They went into the oven to keep warm while we enjoyed a drink on the back deck.

"I assume you were in your office today," I said. He nodded. "Did you catch up after being away, or will you be chasing your tail all week to achieve it?"

"The case that had me and Emily leave early last night didn't help, but I now have most of it under control again. I did manage to dig out the investigation report on Janine's attack."

His tight jaw told me he was unhappy with whatever he found in the file. Regardless of what it was, and although I felt my stomach starting to tighten, I needed to know what the police investigation found. He suggested I might take our drinks to my office while he slipped out to his car. I cleared my desk while I waited for him to return.

"This is a copy of the officers' brief report on their investigation," he said as he slapped an almost empty folder on the desk in front of him.

After shuffling forward on my chair, I went to reach for it but realised he had kept his hand on it. From past experience, I knew the gesture probably meant I wouldn't get my hands on the folder. He opened the folder and flipped through its contents. From the opposite side of the desk, I thought it contained no more than two or three sheets of paper. Having given the file's contents a cursory glance, he clasped his hands on top of it, no doubt in a deliberate move to prevent me reading it.

"If it is so top secret, perhaps you should close that file before I see what's in it, and we might proceed to eating dinner instead of discussing my case." My tone was a touch more tart than intended, but the sarcasm was intentional.

"Wha…? What are you on about? Yeah, you can read it. Well, you can look at it, but there is nothing worth reading in it.

What happened just then? Did I say something offensive without being aware of it?"

"You're making it obvious it is a top secret, your-eyes-only file, and I must not see its contents. If you don't want me to see what's in it, shove it."

"For Christ's sake, woman, all I did was think for a moment about the poor standard of investigation reflected in this report. Here, read the bloody thing yourself, and then give me your opinion."

The folder slid across the desk at top speed. I caught it as it was about to fly off the edge of the desk and into my lap. Oh yes, more than a few ruffled feathers on the other side of the desk now needing smoothing over. But I could hardly be critical. My own fluffy plumage needed smoothing as well.

His sour humour proved justified. The report comprised only one and a half typed pages and a plastic sleeve containing two photographs. I looked at the photos first. One was a general shot of the crime scene taken from the entrance to the bridge. The other was of Janine's damaged bike.

"Nothing exciting there," I murmured as I slid the photos back into the plastic sleeve.

Then I turned my attention to the report. Reading so little doesn't take long, especially when it says nothing. At the end of it, I looked over at Ben.

He raised his eyebrows at me and demanded, "Well…? What is your learned opinion?"

"Okay, your assessment was right on the money. My file contains more than this, and my investigation hasn't made any progress yet. I assume the two investigating coppers were not mere cadets out on work experience release from the academy?"

"If only that were the case… Those two will be having a long chat with me in the near future. Now, can we put this rubbish aside and look at your file instead?"

"It still won't shed any light on this case, but I did manage a little research over the weekend."

"Has the husband returned?"

"No, not as far as I know anyway. I haven't heard from Janine. I think that's a fair indication he hasn't returned. When I hadn't heard from her, I checked if he was booked on any flights into Millhaven today. Although Janine hadn't called, it was possible he might return on the late flight. I reasoned she might not want to wake me if he were on the late flight and would leave it until tomorrow to call."

"I presume you used that little computer program I know nothing about to check flight bookings. Was he on the late flight?"

"He wasn't."

"If Janine is to call you, why bother checking flights? I'm not being critical. I'm just trying to understand your thinking on this – your train of thought – so I might be able to contribute."

"You're right. I was wasting my time checking flights. Bear with me while I try to explain something I don't understand myself. If he had been on a flight, it would have silenced a half-baked suspicion that's been trying to hijack my attention."

"One of your 'gut feelings', I assume…?"

"Oh, I suppose so. I have a problem with the fact that Blake Carter doesn't seem to have existed prior to his arrival in Millhaven. I can't find anything about him before that. And I suppose I thought that checking flight manifests might produce an 'ah hah' moment. It didn't."

"Right, but I still don't understand what you hoped to prove. Did you prove anything?"

"Of course not, but the truth didn't dawn on me until after I started. I think that, somewhere in the back of my mind, I suspected 'Blake Carter' was not the bloke's real name. Then I realised that, without knowing his alternate name, I wouldn't recognise him if he were listed on a flight."

"How strong is this suspicion of yours about an assumed identity?"

"Dunno… I might be just kidding myself to help cope with my lack of progress."

"The next thing you'll tell me is that you're not sure Janine Thomlinson is who she claims to be."

"Funny you should say that…"

"Geez, Sonny, are you having a mid-life crisis or something? This is not like you. How do you plan to sort all this out – at least to protect your sanity?"

"It all happens tomorrow. I'm not sure how I will achieve it but, tomorrow, Janine and I will be having a long and possibly uncomfortable talk… and it's possible I won't have a client by tomorrow night."

"Maybe it's time you laid out for me all the concerns you're harbouring."

A long time ago, Ben and I developed a unique way of cutting through the fog surrounding an investigation to clarify the real issues. It was one of those sessions he was proposing. I knew I was well and truly 'fogbound', so there was no argument. Afte we had eaten, I refilled our glasses while he dimmed the lights.

"Now, Sonny, let's start with Janine. Why do you hold doubts about your client? What doesn't fit for you?"

Where to start? But I knew how to play this game, so I slumped back in my chair, took a sip of wine, closed my eyes… and let it all roll out however it came to mind.

"Why is Janine a regular user of one of the city parks when she owns hectares of beautiful parkland on the Thomlinson Estate? It's not as though she exercises with friends.

She is a dynamic businesswoman running a major commercial enterprise. Why does she present as almost childlike and naïve? The person I know as my client couldn't run a school tuckshop without succumbing to stress.

What of this Thomlinson/Carter relationship? Carter doesn't appear to have a lot going for him. What does Janine see in him? Does he have hidden talents – a helluva stud perhaps? Why can't I find something – anything – on his background before Millhaven?

How did Janine's father, Thomas Thomlinson, react to his daughter's marrying Carter? His daughter stood to become a wealthy woman. Might he have seen Carter as nothing more than a gold digger and opposed the marriage?"

A long silence followed as I searched my mind for anything else I should mention. There was something, but it was cowering in a dark corner and wouldn't come out for me. At last, I gave up and told Ben that was all I had to offer.

"That's not all there is though, is it? What else niggles you about this case?"

"I don't know. There is something more, but I can't grab hold of it. For a while, I thought it might have something to do with the poor efforts of your officers, but I realised that was a bit unfair. They probably did the best they could with the evidence they had."

As I was about to say something else, I froze. Come on, come on, I kept mentally urging it. It was very near the surface. I couldn't grab hold and drag it out. Ben sat silent and motionless as I grappled with my illusive thought. Then, jackpot….

"Yes. Yes, that's it. The bike … what happened to Janine's bike? Did the cops impound it, or was it returned to her? I don't know why it's important. I just know I need to see that bike."

"Good question – but I don't know the answer. Our file should indicate whether it was retained as evidence but, as you saw, it doesn't mention what happened to it. Hmm… I'm inclined to think it wasn't impounded as evidence. I have the uncomfortable feeling that those two coppers, from the outset, believed it was nothing more than a silly accident, and that's how they treated their investigation.

Why do you think it's important? What do you think it might tell you, especially so long after the event?"

"If I knew, we wouldn't be sitting in semi-darkness playing twenty questions."

The moment was lost, and so was the train of thought. I turned up the lights again on my way to the kitchen to make coffee. A rummage in the fridge produced the wherewithal for a couple of slices of raisin toast to go with it. We took our coffees through to the lounge to wind down before Ben went home.

"Apart from trying to sort out a few things with your client tomorrow, do you have any other plans?" Ben asked.

"Not really; I'm trying not to pre-empt what comes from talking to Janine. Hopefully, I will be able to move forward with a structured investigation plan after that. What about you? Do you think you might have some time to devote to this case?"

"No promises about how much I'll be able to do, but I will talk to the bloke at the Council about CCTV cameras, and I hope to have a chat with the two officers who investigated Janine's attack."

Given his heavy workload and busy schedule, it was more than I hoped for. But I knew a part of his motivation to help with my investigation was because it galled him to have his officers' investigation recorded so far short of professional standards.

At about ten o'clock, I waved Ben off on his way home. I intended to go back to my office and work for a while, until I realised I didn't have anything I could work on. So, after cleaning up the kitchen, I went to bed instead.

My early start this morning might suggest a busy schedule planned for today. In reality, the only thing I hoped to achieve was to interview Janine again. As I climbed the stairs to my office, I thought about my morning. (No one in the know ever takes the lift unless they have a survival kit to keep them alive when the beast gets stuck between floors.)

It was Monday. Logically, as it was a workday, Janine would spend the day at her industrial complex. I tried weighing up my chances of her having some spare time today to spend with me. If I'm honest, my luck will likely be somewhere between zero and none.

After dealing with messages and emails, and sending brochures to prospective clients, I spent a few minutes drawing up a list of the issues and questions I needed to discuss with Janine. The list compiled – for now – it was eight o'clock. Was it too early to call her, or had she already left for work, and I'd missed my opportunity?

"Argh hell, just call her," I said aloud as I checked the time again. "She will either talk to me or she won't."

Janine answered almost immediately, and I dived straight in with an apology for calling so early. She laughed.

"I've been at work since seven o'clock, so I don't consider this too early. Has something happened, Sonny, for you to be calling me?"

She would be free for a couple hours from ten o'clock, and she wanted to know if there was anything else I needed her to bring when she came to my office. I hadn't intended to ask any questions until she sat across the desk from me, but I couldn't help myself.

"Just bring yourself. I do have one quick question now, though. Janine, has your husband returned from his fishing trip?"

"No, and I still haven't heard from him either. I didn't know if I should call you when he didn't return, but you only asked me to call you when he was back … and he still isn't."

Ah, that's better, I told myself. I was beginning to think Janine was the original ice maiden as she hadn't displayed any concern about her husband's non-appearance. It was a relief to hear her voice crack a little as she confirmed he still hadn't returned. I told her not to dwell on it in the interim and that we would discuss it at some length when she came to see me.

Ten o'clock is coffee time in my office, and today I would have a guest – well, a client, that is. I took a quick trip downstairs to the baker's den of temptation and returned to my office with a box of assorted sweet treats. Yes, I only needed a couple of pieces for us to have with our coffee. But I reasoned that, as I didn't know Janine's preferences, I should play it safe and select an assortment. Of course, it meant I'd be left with quite a few pieces for me to deal with afterwards. Oh well, I'm probably up to the task.

As I put the box of cakes on the bench in my minuscule kitchenette, I checked all around the ceiling. I'm almost convinced Ben has a secret camera in my office somewhere.

Whenever I buy cakes, he seems to know and arrives for a free coffee and 'something to go with'.

Back at my desk, I discovered the document I'd ordered from the archives had arrived while I was shopping for cakes. It was a copy of Amelia Tomlinson's will. After printing it, I settled back to study it in detail… and discover whether I'd wasted my money or not. While I doubted it would tell me anything useful regarding my investigation, a little part of me kept hinting – and hoping – that it might contain something worthwhile.

The most obvious fact, even after just a cursory glance, was that Amelia Thomlinson was an independently wealthy woman when she died. The will itself wasn't unduly complicated. Basically, she left her entire estate to her daughter. Perhaps not surprising, I told myself, given Janine was an only child. After reading the will a second time, and then reading *between the lines*, I managed to piece together an interesting story.

It appears that, at some time before her death, Amelia set up a trust fund for Janine. Her will referred to an existing trust fund and confirmed that her husband, Thomas Thomlinson, should continue as sole administrator of the trust fund until their daughter, Janine Thomlinson, reached the age of twenty-five. The will went on to direct what should happen to the fund if Janine was deceased before attaining the required age to take control of the fund. In such a situation, the fund was to be distributed between a number of charitable organisations.

With nothing else of consequence in the will for me to ponder, I sat back to do some basic maths and sort out in my mind what must have happened during the twelve years or so between Amelia's death and Janine's attaining twenty-five years of age. I didn't have to be a genius to work out Janine still did not have control of her trust fund when she married Blake Carter.

Was this an important issue to pursue? By the time Janine arrived for our meeting, I had decided it was important … But only if her father had objected strongly enough to her marrying Carter. As Thomas's role as administrator would have included shelling out funds, whether as a regular allowance or according to some other arrangement, he might have opted to withhold funds or threatened to do so if the marriage went ahead.

Yeah, ascertaining Thomas's position regarding Janine's marriage is definitely something to pursue during our meeting today. I wrote it on my list of questions to put to my client and, as I did so, an even bigger question leapt out. If Janine went ahead and married and Thomas froze the trust fund, how did the young couple support themselves? I doubted Carter was making much as a personal trainer at that stage. And that begs the question of what Janine was doing at the time. IF Carter was a gold digger, and IF Thomas blocked the cash flow, it must have been a significant disappointment for Carter.

As Thomas appears to have been considerate enough to die sometime during the couple's first year of married life, they wouldn't have endured for long any hardship conditions Thomas might have imposed before Janine inherited his estate. Okay, now I need a copy of Thomas's will to find out what would happen with the trust fund if he died before Janine was twenty-five. A few minutes later, I had ordered the requisite copy from the State Archives. It's a pity it won't arrive before I meet with Janine this morning. Although I've ordered the will, should I ask Janine about it anyway? Maybe that's something I'll have to play by ear and use whatever I discover beforehand to help me decide.

Today, Janine was a mixture of fashion trends. Her olive green long-sleeved, soft top was in line with today's fashions, while her skinny black slacks were a relic of yesterday's style. This girl could look stunning in a sack bag! I suggested coffee before we started, and she welcomed the suggestion. Offering a new client coffee always makes me nervous. They invariably want some complicated concoction that would challenge a seasoned barista. But not today; Janine was my kind of girl: "Black with nothing, thanks." I handed her a small plate and directed her to the box of cakes while I made our coffees.

"Ooh, eclairs, my favourites," she cooed as she loaded one onto her plate. While she loaded the second éclair onto another plate for me, I opened the cupboard above our heads and grabbed a couple of paper napkins.

"If we are having eclairs, it goes without saying we are going to need these," I said as I handed her a napkin. Perhaps we might sit at my desk. It will be easier and less messy than balancing things on our knees."

But then all the making-the-client-feel-at-ease ritual was over. It was time to get down to business. What better place to start than with the missing husband?

"Janine, before we move onto other matters I want to discuss today, have you, by any chance, heard from your husband since I spoke to you earlier?" She shook her head and couldn't quite manage a nonchalant shrug. "Is there anyone here or in Tasmania you could contact to find out if everything is okay? What about wives or family members of the friends he is with?" She swallowed hard a couple of times before replying.

"No. I don't know anything about his friends in Tasmania or their families – don't even know their names."

"What about his friends here in Millhaven? Might they have heard from him since he left?" This time I received a resigned look and a shrug.

"I've never met any of his friends, and he doesn't talk about them, so I don't know who to ask?"

"I assume the gym where he works would expect him back by a certain date. Have you considered calling them to find out when they expect him?"

"Sonny, I wouldn't dare, not after his comments about me trying to control his life. He would be furious if he found out I'd been checking up on him."

Well, this is going nowhere in a hurry – but it has told me heaps. Time to move on to other matters. "Okay. Yes, I can see how he might misconstrue your actions. I do have other matters to discuss with you. Is it all right to move on to those?" She almost looked relieved.

Chapter 7

Before we go too much further, can I ask about your bike? What was the damage?"

"I…don't…know…."

"I'm sorry; I was asking about the extent of the damage to your bike, not the motorbike. Was it confined to just a wheel, or was the frame also damaged?"

"No, I understood the question. But the answer is still the same: I don't know. I haven't seen my bike since the attack."

"Do you know what happened to it?"

"Well, I assume it is stashed away somewhere at the park, or maybe the Council's depot, probably in a gardener's shed somewhere."

"So, you didn't get it back. Is it possible the cops impounded it as evidence in the course of their investigation?"

"The police didn't mention it but, as they thought I had an accident, I don't imagine they were interested in keeping the bike."

"When did they interview you?"

"They came to see me in hospital. Nothing made much sense as I was still packed full of drugs, but logic still prevailed. Their message was quite clear. The boys in blue didn't come to interview me so much as to tell me they determined the incident was an accident and that they had completed their investigation. They found nothing to suggest it was a deliberate attack and went so far as to suggest I had a fall while going at full speed. In their opinion, I was going flat-out across the bridge when I fell off and hit my head on the wall. There was no evidence of anyone or anything else being involved."

"Amazing…," I murmured in disbelief as Emily's test results on the evidence sprang to mind. "Do you remain convinced it was deliberate?"

Of course, she was, and yes, in answer to my unspoken question, she did want me to continue investigating. There was no way I was going to drop it anyway, but I gave her the opportunity to end the case. I made a show of scribbling a few notes before asking a series of questions I hoped might wrong-foot her if she had been feeding me a fanciful story.

"How often do you visit that park?"

"Every day, except on the odd occasion… I walk or jog every day, except on Friday evenings when I go for a long bike ride."

"Do you have a set route through the park, and does it always include that area with the bridge over the stormwater drain?"

"The bridge is in a more 'remote' area of the park not used by walkers and runners. That includes me. Most days, I use the same paths as other foot traffic but, when I'm on my bike, I prefer the more remote areas where there is less chance of encountering other people, and it's a more interesting area if you are not footslogging through it."

"Janine, why go to the park at all when you have acres of beautiful parkland you can use on the Thomlinson Estate?"

"Uhmm, that's true, but I don't actually 'live' on the estate. I'm there some weekends and other odd occasions, but it is not my home. Apart from anything else, living there would make my commute to work a daily marathon. I have a unit in the city." She saw my eyebrows rise in surprise and explained. "I bought it when I came home after university and started full-time in the business. I wanted to experience the life most of our employees were living. So, I spread my wings and went out on my own to live on my salary in my own unit."

"Okay, but what happened after you were married? Did you continue to live in the city?"

"Yeah… Well, I couldn't see any reason to change anything."

"Even after your father died and the estate became yours?"

"My unit was closer to our work complex, so I couldn't see any reason to move further away and lengthen my daily travel. I suppose, if I think about it, after that, my time spent on the estate became mainly occasional weekend occurrences and still are."

"What about your husband? How does he feel about living in the city while the estate sits vacant all week?"

"It has been a sore point in the past, but it resolved itself as time went by. Because of the nature of his work, he doesn't have regular weekends like everyone else. So, to compensate for long hours and working on all the normal weekends, he takes days off during the week and spends time at the estate – while I'm at work. It's not such a bad arrangement. Many married couples would love to have a regular short break away from their partners. Although it wasn't planned that way, it does work well for us. I guess it's because we're used to spending time apart that I haven't been too concerned about his nonreturn yet from Tasmania."

I signified my understanding before abandoning discussing their living arrangements and adopting a different tack.

"You told me your husband was from Tasmania. Given that's far from Millhaven, how did you meet?"

"Long story short, he was bumming around the US when I went over to attend a conference and then did the tourist thing for a week afterwards. We met the first day I was there and spent every spare moment together. We stayed in contact after I came home."

"And romance blossomed. Where were you married, here or in Tasmania?"

"Why would you think it might have been Tasmania?"

"Dunno really; I just thought that, if you wanted to avoid the 'celebrity wedding of the year in Millhaven' situation, you might have opted for his home town instead."

"Oh, I see. No, I've never been to Tasmania. We were married in England … away from my father and everybody else who knew us. I was determined that, this time, there would be no interference. It was about as low-key as you can get, with only three strangers in attendance and one of those performed the ceremony."

"While it's none of my business, I do have to ask how your father coped with that."

"Ah… 'Not well' might be the most polite answer. This time, I ensured he was unaware I would be married until I arrived home with Blake in tow. Then life became interesting. As expected, Dad had an instant dislike of Blake, and that never really changed. He even considered sacking me until I told him to go ahead. I was sure our biggest competitor would snap me up."

"How did that go down? I don't imagine it did anything to sweeten the situation. Were you and your father estranged during that last period of his life? It sounds like a sad and difficult time for both of you."

"We managed to come to our senses fairly quickly and, over the next couple of months, our relationship returned to normal, to what it had been before I was married. After all, he didn't want to lose me. I was already starting to take over the reins of the operation, and I was going to inherit the whole enterprise, so it made sense for me to stay on and for us to bury our differences."

"Earlier, you mentioned being determined to avoid interference *this time*. Interference by whom, and in what way?"

"That story's consigned to history now. It goes back to when I was about to start my last year at university. I had just turned twenty and had been in a relationship for about six months with an older man – a bit older, but not too much – and we decided we wanted to get married. Because I was still under age, I needed parental approval. My father didn't refuse. Instead, he asked for time to think about it. What he did was to have my husband-to-be investigated. I resented it at the time.

In hindsight, I realised he saved me a lot of anguish later by refusing his permission. The man in question was a notorious conman well-known to the police, and he was married and living with his wife and a couple of kids. Later, I discovered the man knew that my father would never consent to the marriage and, at the appropriate moment, the swine intended making a magnanimous offer to disappear from my life – for an adequate compensation."

"So, your father paid up?"

"Hell, no. Dad already had been working with the police. When the demand for money came, Dad was wearing a wire, and the cops arrested the man. While I realised my father's actions prevented a terrible situation developing, I didn't need his consent when I wanted to marry Blake. I was older, wiser, and had taken charge of my own life. I was making my own decisions. Still, I didn't trust my father not to interfere. So, our wedding was arranged in secret, and the marriage itself was a covert operation in London."

"If we go back to when he threatened to sack you, how would you have managed – financially, I mean?"

"It wouldn't have been a problem. There was a slight issue I hadn't considered, but it wouldn't have caused much of a problem. When my mother died, she left her entire estate to me. She had been a wealthy woman in her own right before she married my father, and her wealth had increased during the marriage. She set up a trust fund for me when I was about ten. At that time, she was the administrator, but there was no distribution of funds at all. In her will, she appointed my father to administer the trust fund. I was sent to boarding school almost immediately after her death, and later when I went to university, my father paid me a regular small allowance from the trust fund.

When he was threatening to sack me, he also froze my trust fund. I suppose he thought that, if I didn't have a salary coming in, we wouldn't be able to survive, and he hoped to coerce me into toeing the line in that way. His problem was, he forgot I already had quite a deal of capital left to me by my grandmother. Unlike the trust fund, which I couldn't access until I turned twenty-five, I could access my grandmother's money from when I turned twenty-one.

I think, once he realised there was no way he could impose what he wanted, he accepted the situation to a certain extent, and things settled down between us. In case you're wondering, we were close again long before he died."

"While you're probably sick of me asking questions about this, I am starting to feel concerned about your husband's failure to return from Tasmania. I don't wish to concern you, but are you sure there is no one we can ask about where he is or what he might be doing? I'm wondering about the people he works with at the gym or some of his private clients. Might he have mentioned his plans to one of them?"

"Maybe he did, but it would have been unlike him. He's a private person. I think it unlikely he discussed his trip with others. Anyway, I still wouldn't know who to suggest."

"What about the gyms where Blake worked? Wouldn't the managers know when he was expected back at work? If you're hesitant to talk to those people because of potential repercussions when he returns, perhaps I could make enquiries – without mentioning you in any way?"

"Well, I suppose that would be okay, except I don't know where he works. Don't look at me like that. I know it sounds stupid for a wife not to know where a husband works, but all I know is he worked at one gym after we were married but moved on from there. That much I've put together from snippets of phone conversations I've heard, but I've never heard which gyms he works at now."

Janine glanced at her watch. I did likewise. The two hours she had said she had free this morning had just about run out. I needed to consider everything I gained from the interview. It was time to terminate our meeting while ensuring the door remained open for further sessions.

"Goodness, look at the time. I know you're a busy woman with a major enterprise to run. I've taken up a large lump of your time this morning. Thank you for being so patient with me, but it's time you went back to work."

She stood to leave, then appeared to remember something and started digging around in her bag.

"Last night, I remembered this and thought it might be useful." She handed me a photograph. I raised my eyebrows at her in surprise. "Blake hates having his photo taken and will do anything to avoid it. I didn't have a picture of him.

When I went to finalise details for our marriage, I spoke to a woman who later was one of our two witnesses. I happened to mention his aversion and how we wouldn't have a photographic record of the day, although I dearly wanted one. When I returned to collect the copy of our certificate, she handed me an envelope with this photo in it. She somehow managed to take it while Blake watched me sign the register. He doesn't know about it, but it's the only photo I have of him, and I do want it back." I promised to return it undamaged.

I told her I would use whatever resources I had to find out where her husband was and what he was doing, and promised to keep her informed of anything I discovered. Then, I walked her to the door and bid her goodbye. She thanked me, leaving me confused about why she thought she owed me thanks for anything.

On my return from a quick trip to find something for lunch, I booted up the appropriate program on my computer, connected my digital recorder to it, and told it to transcribe this morning's recording. While it went about its thing and I nibbled my lunch, I let my mind roam over everything I'd learned this morning. By the time I'd finished lunch, I wondered if I had learned anything useful at all.

With the transcript of this morning's session on the desk in front of me, I worked my way through it page by page, highlighting key phrases as I went. I soon concluded all I achieved was confirmation of the suspicions I'd held before today's meeting. Only two major issues remained unresolved: the whereabouts of Janine's bike and the whereabouts of Blake Carter.

After giving both matters some thought, I decided it might be possible to pursue both, at least to some extent, this afternoon, and with little preparation required. The only thing I needed to do before I left the office was to call Nick, so I did and was surprised when he answered almost immediately. He welcomed my call as a brief respite from marking papers.

"I'm still working on the case involving Blake Carter and wondered whether you might be able to help me with something else. As you suggested and another has confirmed, Carter might have worked for two gyms in the Millhaven area. Would you know which ones?"

"There are two gyms I would suggest, but I can't be sure about either of them. He might have moved on from them since I last heard of him."

Nick gave me the names of both gyms. One was in the city area, while the other was in one of the northern beach suburbs. In both instances, I needed to speak to the manager and asked Nick for details. I tore the note off the pad in front of me and stuffed it in my bag along with my digital recorder. Then, half believing I was doomed to fail, I headed out in search of information. With three places to visit this afternoon, I spent the trip down to my car working out in which order to see them.

The car park outside the park where Janine's attack took place was deserted when I arrived. I remembered my e-scooter was still rattling around in the cargo compartment, and I gambled on its still having enough charge to take me around the park this afternoon. As I manoeuvred it through the 'cattle race' entrance, I was relieved to hear a mower working somewhere in the distance. It was a long shot that the same man I spoke to previously was on the mower.

It was the same man, and he was mowing in an area close to the bridge where the incident occurred. He didn't look pleased when I flagged him down.

"I'm not going to make a habit of coming to interrupt your work but, following our chat the other day and my subsequent research, there is something I need to check." He heaved a sigh of resignation and gave me a go-ahead gesture. "You might not know, but I wondered if you knew what happened to the victim's bicycle. It hasn't been returned to her and, as the police deemed it an accident, I thought it unlikely they impounded it. The only other option I could think of was that it had been left here at the park. Do you know if it is still here? Maybe locked up in the kiosk or a shed somewhere?"

"There are no sheds in the park, so it rules out that option. As for it being in the kiosk… I doubt that's a possibility. To leave it there, the police needed whoever runs the place to open up for them to put the bike in there. I imagine that would take a while to organise, if it's what they wanted to do. That might not be much help to you, but it's all I can tell you."

On leaving the park, I mentally scratched it off the list as a possible storage place for Janine's bike. That left me with only one other possibility to explore, and I wouldn't be able to do that until tonight – and only if Ben came to dinner.

For no particular reason, I had decided my next port of call would be the gym in the northern suburbs. It appears Monday afternoons were not a popular time for this gym's membership. Only two women worked out on the equipment. The front counter was unmanned, but a bloke sat at a desk in a tiny office off one side of the entrance area. He fitted the description Nick gave me of the manager. So instead of ringing the bell on the reception desk, I knocked on the door to the office. He was reaching for the phone as I did so.

"Who are you looking for?" he demanded gruffly. "Ring the bell on the desk out there if you want to talk to someone."

No surprise that the place wasn't busy with someone so charming at the helm. I stepped into the office. "There's no one out front at the moment, and you're the bloke I came to see. I only want a moment of your time. I came to ask if Blake Carter was here today. He said something about going away for a few days, but I thought he would be back by now."

"You thought wrong. He is not here today."

"When do you expect him back?"

"Good question… and I wish I knew the answer. Now, is there anything else you wanted?"

"Thanks, but no. I guess I'll have to wait to talk to him when he returns."

"Okay… Join the queue. I'm first in line, and you will be a long way back in it. It seems Mr Carter will be busy when he gets back – if he ever plans to return."

I was in no doubt our conversation was over when he picked up the phone on his desk and started keying in numbers. "What a charming and uplifting experience that was," I murmured to the universe as I scrambled back into my car. "Probably hired for his swarthy good looks and not his personality." I continued fuming about the bloke as I drove into the city and found a parking spot close to the next gym I wanted to visit.

Nick described the manager *as a tall, skinny redhead with lots of freckles and a ginger moustache*, and it matched the bloke standing at the reception desk. He was welcoming, and I launched straight into my spiel.

"Good morning … Sally Harding…," I said by way of introduction. "I wonder if I might have a quick word with Blake Carter. Is he in today?"

"Sorry, Love, no, he's not here today. Can I help you at all?"

"Oh, no thanks. I just wanted to ask him about my plan, and I took a punt he might be at work. He hinted he might be going away for a couple of days, and I thought he'd be back. That's okay. When do you expect him to be back at work?"

"Honestly, Miss, I wish I knew. He did take a few days off, but it looks like a few more days than I expected. Did you want to leave a message or anything? I can't give you any guarantees about when he might get it."

"It's not important, but thanks again for your help."

I felt bitchy. "What a bloody waste of a day," I growled. "Nothing achieved in this case so far." But I had to rethink that. I had confirmed Blake Carter was officially 'missing', and I eliminated Janine's place and the park as the location of her damaged bike.

A copy of Thomas's will arrived while I was out. It told me nothing I didn't already know and didn't generate any bright ideas. I revisited my kitchenette for another cake.

The major dose of sugar reactivated my creative juices. The critical missing piece of this puzzle was Carter, not just his present whereabouts, but everything about him. I toyed with the idea of a quick trip to Tasmania. It wasn't as though Janine couldn't afford it, and I promised to make every effort to locate her husband. But practical thinking kicked in quickly.

What would going to Tasmania achieve? I knew nothing about this bloke, not even where to start looking into his background. Tasmania might not be the largest state, but it is too big to tackle without some clues about where to look. I dragged a pad and pencil to me and listed everything I knew about him. The most notable thing about the list I produced was the word 'about'. Carter and Janine were married in England *about* five years ago. Carter was *about* thirty years old, so would have been born in *about* the late 1980s or early 1990s.

It would be helpful to know who his parents were, I mused as I looked at my useless list. A copy of Janine's marriage certificate should provide the names of the groom's parents. I mentally kicked myself for not asking for a copy earlier. Should I risk interrupting her day with another phone call? "Why not?" I almost growled in frustration.

Her phone was engaged, so I left a short but urgent message for her to call me. Patience is not my strong point. There was another call I wanted to make, but it had to wait until after speaking to Janine. The last thing I wanted was for my phone to be engaged when she tried to return my call.

Prowling around my office, I contemplated yet another coffee to help fill in time. Then her call came, only half an hour after I called her, but it felt like I'd spent half the afternoon waiting for it.

Chapter 8

We swapped apologies before I could ask the questions I hoped she could answer.

"Janine, can you give me the names of Blake's parents and do you know if they are still in Tasmania?"

"Uhmm… well, I imagine they are still in Tasmania, but I don't think that information will be much use to you. I don't know their names.…"

I interrupted before she could finish whatever she was about to say. "Haven't you ever heard their names mentioned? What about your marriage certificate? Doesn't that give information about his parents?"

"The reason Blake's never mentioned them is because I don't think he knows who they were. It caused a bit of fuss when we provided information prior to our marriage. It took a bit to convince the authorities he never knew his parents.

My information was sent from here. Blake was already in the UK and completed all his paperwork while he was there. I didn't see any of it beforehand. When I looked at our certificate a couple of days after the wedding, I noticed that the word 'unknown' occupied all the spaces where his parents' details should appear. I thought it must be a mistake and queried him."

"What was his explanation? Surely he knew something about them."

"At only a few months old, he was abandoned on the doorstep of an orphanage. The orphanage needed some paperwork signed by his parents before he could be put up for adoption. So, without the requisite information, he spent his first two or three years in the orphanage before being fostered out. Over the rest of his life, he had a number of foster parents.

As soon as he could, he legally attempted to locate his parents. The authorities told him they had discovered his parents' details.

He was about fifteen when they found the information. But, by then, his parents had been dead for years, probably since not long after they abandoned him. So that was the end of the trail."

"But, although the parents were dead, for the authorities to discover the parents' identities, the authorities must have known his parents' names."

"Ooh, I see what you mean. It hadn't occurred to me before. Initially, he was reluctant to tell me about it. Then, when he did share it, it was just such a sad tale. I didn't want to open old wounds by delving into it further.

Sonny, I'm starting to feel quite concerned. Blake still hasn't returned, and now you are asking me about his parents. Has something happened? If you know something about him, please tell me."

"No, I don't know anything. That's why I'm asking for information. I didn't want to worry you, but I hoped you could provide details of his parents and where and when he was born. Please don't read too much into this. Your case has two streams of investigation: your attack and what's happening with your husband. Try not to worry. I will keep you informed of any developments."

My comments and promises sounded trite even to me. I doubt they did much for Janine. The more I work on this case, the less real everything about it feels. Everything Janine tells me sounds so false, like a weak concocted story. Despite that, a large part of me is starting to warm to her and believes she is on the level and telling it as it is.

"Well, no progress achieved there," I informed the universe. "Now what...?"

The notes scribbled during my call to Janine lacked credibility, but somehow I believed her story was true. I still couldn't decide whether Carter was somehow involved in the attack on his wife or not, but a niggling suspicion remained. I knew the lack of hard information about him was keeping that suspicion alive.

While I didn't want to hare off Tasmania, it was looking increasingly necessary. While thinking about the need to visit Tasmania, I pulled Janine's photograph of Blake from my file. It now lay on top of my notes.

It was a clear shot of Blake looking off into the distance as he stood beside Janine as she signed the register. "Not a bad looking catch," I murmured as I studied his features with a magnifying glass. But something about him looked wrong. What…? I shook my head a couple of times to clear the fog and returned to studying the photo. It didn't help.

Ben called about dinner while I was staring at the photograph. His call ended; I closed my case file and shoved it in my tote bag to take home. There seemed little benefit in sitting in my office any longer. Halfway to the door, my little grey cells finally fired up. I strode back to my desk, pulled out the file and opened it on the desk.

"Yes. At last… That's what's wrong."

The bloke in the photograph – the groom, Blake Carter – did not have the hallmarks of a personal trainer. He looked pudgy. It could be the suit he was wearing, but he didn't have the right build for someone who is into fitness. If England was just one more stop on his bumming around the world expedition, his fitness levels might have deteriorated along the way. But his overall stature appeared more 'bred of a lifetime' than down to being a slack traveller. The two gym managers I'd spoken to, and Nick, were lean, hard-bodied. They oozed fitness.

So the Carter mystery deepens. But does he have anything to do with the attack on Janine? Although my gut suggested I knew better than to ask such an inane question, I wasn't ready to accept that he was involved. After thinking it over for a moment, my brain finally found top gear. There was another way.

After consulting my contacts list, I dialled the number. It kept dialling. I was about to end it when a familiar voice answered.

"James, this is Sonny Whittington. How are you? It feels like ages since we last spoke. I take it you are still in the investigations business?"

Tasmanian private investigator, James Rothwell, and I go back a long way. While I was still learning to be a private investigator, I undertook some Queensland research for him. Our paths crossed on frequent occasions after that. We became good friends as well as colleagues. To date, the ledger showed I had undertaken quite a bit more research for James than he had done for me. Maybe this call will help balance the books a bit.

The usual catch-up stuff done, I moved on to the reason for my call and a long and apologetic explanation of my problem. Relating the 'facts' of my case to James Rothwell sounded even more ridiculous and fanciful in the telling. Professional that he is, James listened politely without interrupting until I finished outlining my problem.

"Stop apologising, Sonny. This sounds fascinating. I've just finished a case and don't have another one pending. So, tell me what you'd like me to do, and I'll crack on with it."

After scanning Janine's wedding photo and adjusting the image in Photoshop, I emailed James the amended image, along with all my notes on Blake Carter. I felt pleased with myself until I realised how late it was. If I didn't get a move on, I would find Ben waiting outside my front door with our dinner going cold. I shoved the file in my bag and raced down to my car. The good thing about leaving so late was, I had missed the afternoon peak hour traffic.

Nevertheless, Ben almost followed me up the driveway when I arrived home. As he brought fish and chips, it was as well there was no delay in getting it onto plates and sitting down to eat. No 'shop' talk intruded during the meal. Then, the food dispatched, we took the last of the bottle of chilled white wine out onto the back deck. Now it was time to talk 'shop', after doing the usual how-was-your-day stuff first. Ben looked weary, so I let him go first.

"The Millhaven natives were restless over the weekend. We had almost the full range of crimes to deal with. That's probably why Emily isn't joining us tonight. So much was sent to forensics over the weekend. Her whole team has been working flat out. She's probably still in her lab tonight. What about your day?"

"More questions, no answers… every day of this case has been the same so far."

"Did you manage to question Janine further as you planned?"

"Yeah, twice today – once in my office and once over the phone – and all I gained were more questions. No, there was something else. She brought me a photo of the missing husband. I don't suppose your day allowed you time to think about Janine's case?"

"I intended to talk to the two officers who investigated the attack but, like everyone else, they were fully occupied with stuff from over the weekend. I did talk to the bloke at the Parks and Gardens depot about CCTV cameras. He gave me the contact details of the right person to give me the information I wanted. I've set up a meeting for first thing tomorrow morning. Will you be too busy to come along?"

We both knew he was joking. Of course, I would go with him to talk to whoever might shed some light on what happened to my client that evening. I wanted to show him Carter's photo, so we adjourned to my office. While he studied the image, I asked him about Janine's bike.

"Although I'm sure you haven't had time to look into it, I thought I'd ask anyway. Have you been able to shed any light on what happened to Janine's bike? She doesn't have it, and my friend on the mower at the park doesn't know where it might be unless the cops took it with them. My gut tells me your blokes took it, but I can't think why they would. As they were so dismissive of the incident, I doubt they needed to impound the bike."

"Yep, agreed… and, yes, I did check. It is not recorded as being in the vehicle compound, and it hasn't been entered in the evidence register. So, I don't know where the damned thing is, and I want to know."

"Something just occurred to me. It relates to the cops' investigation of the incident. They were adamant it was an accident, and even went so far as to suggest Janine was going too fast, fell off and banged her head. According to her version of a visit to the hospital by the officers, that story of why she ended up in hospital is their preferred version."

"Okay, well, I don't know yet how they arrived at that conclusion. Apart from sounding a bit odd, what about their version bothers you?"

"If she fell off and it was nothing more than a simple accident, why were shards of plastic material taken from Janine's bike sent to the forensics lab for testing?"

"Are you sure? Sorry; I know that was a stupid question, but…"

"Emily showed me the report of tests on the material. It was black and was consistent with the material used in the fabrication of motorbike fairings. But, it didn't suggest any particular make or model."

He pulled a notebook out of his pocket and scribbled a note. "Regardless of whatever else those officers have scheduled for tomorrow, they will be in my office first thing. What else do you have to tell me about?"

"Nothing to concern you, I don't think. Most of my efforts have focused on trying to get a handle on Blake Carter – and it's like clutching at smoke. He doesn't seem to have existed before working in Millhaven gyms. I need to find evidence of him in Tasmania before then. I sent everything I have about him, including a copy of that photo, to a colleague in the Apple Isle to see if he can track down anything for me. A copy of what I sent is in that file if you're interested."

Of course, he was. So, while Ben pored over my file, I devoted some serious thought to *where to next* with my case.

"Do you believe any of this?" he demanded as he pushed my file across the desk to me.

"I admit it appears too far-fetched to be true, but whether I believe it is unimportant. I'm convinced Janine believes it because that's what her husband told her. Until I prove at least some of it is rubbish, there is no chance of convincing her to question anything she's been told. Even the fact he is AWOL hasn't shaken her faith in him, although she does admit to being 'a bit concerned'."

"Ain't love grand?" he snarled and gave a dismissive shake of his head.

"Beyond my *ken*, I'm afraid but, in Janine's case, it might be both blind and stupid." But that aside, I needed information on another matter. "Ben, does someone have to be officially reported as missing, or identified as a definite suspect in a case, before the police can obtain a warrant to check his finances, phone calls, and everything else?"

"More or less, but why do you ask?"

"Obviously, Blake Carter hasn't been reported as missing, but I think he might be. I wonder whether his phone and financials might shed some light on what's going on. I know he's not a suspect in Janine's attack as he allegedly wasn't here then, but it seems too 'convenient' for him to be away at exactly the right time."

"And the coincidence makes him a possible suspect?"

"That's about what I am suggesting, but that doesn't help me. It's what you think about such a coincidence that matters."

"We have applied for a warrant but are unlikely to receive a response until some time tomorrow. For now, all I can do is to try to track down Janine's missing bike, and see what we can find out about those CCTV cameras in or around the park."

"Well, that's more than I can do. Until and unless I find something more to work with, my case appears to be stalled. I am keen to hear what comes out of your chat with the officers who investigated Janine's incident, but admit I'm half prepared for it to produce nothing useful."

With little else about the case to discuss, Ben didn't hang around, resulting in a relatively early night. Most nights, I would think an early night a blessing as it allowed me time alone to think about my current case. Tonight, it felt like wasting valuable time. It didn't matter how hard I thought about it, or how creative I tried to be, Janine's case was stalled.

Rather than go to bed and wait hours for sleep to come, I poured myself a nightcap, dimmed the lights in the lounge room, and ran over in my mind everything I knew or thought about this case. Nothing happened, except I must've fallen asleep in my chair at some point.

My eyes snapped open. Where am I? What was that noise? Groggy and with my eyes still unfocused, I strode over to check the front door was locked. Then did a slow prowl through the house, checking windows and doors. Nothing untoward discovered anywhere. I was returning to the kitchen when I realised something wasn't quite right.

The neighbour's dog was barking so hard it was just about turning itself inside out. It's not a dog that barks at nothing. Whatever woke me is likely what caught its attention. Without turning on any additional lights, I tiptoed to the bedroom and gently slid open the wardrobe door. Shoving shoes out of the way and running my hand around on the floor, I found the edge of the carpet square and forced my fingers under it.

I stopped and waited, straining my ears for any unusual sounds. All I heard was the wild pounding of my elevated pulse. I returned my attention to the job I had started and dragged my hand across the patch of cold steel until I found my target. Doing things in the dark is not easy, but practice over an extended period makes certain functions second nature. Within moments I had the floor safe open. My hand scrabbled around in its contents. Mission accomplished… After putting everything back in place, I sat in total darkness on the edge of my bed and considered my situation.

For a few moments, I just sat there listening. The neighbour's dog continued to bark while I rummaged in my wardrobe, but its ferocity had subsided. It still offered a few solitary yelps, but it sounded as though the cause of its annoyance had departed or was in the process of doing so. My Glock lying in my lap felt heavy but reassuring as I ran my hand over it.

"Probably won't need you," I whispered to the weapon as I felt myself relaxing and my pulse rate dropping.

Was I jumping at shadows? If I had reacted to something that wasn't there, the neighbour's dog must've been spooked by the same 'something that wasn't there'. I sat there in the dark for a good few minutes. My house wasn't in total darkness. The dimmed lights in the lounge room still cast a subdued glow over that room and, to a lesser extent, the kitchen. With a firm grip on my Glock, I padded out to the lounge and turned off the lights.

Now what? The little voice in my head was yelling at me. It was only one o'clock. Still a few hours before daylight started making an appearance. I stood there in the now darkened lounge room weighing up my options. There weren't many to consider: continue to sit in the dark in the lounge room until first light, or go to bed and try to sleep. I didn't need to belong to Mensa to work out the latter was the only intelligent option. So, after hanging about in the lounge for another couple of minutes, I went to bed.

Sleep did eventually come, although I don't know when. All I know is it felt as though I spent a long time in the darkness, staring at the ceiling before it arrived.

Late to bed, poor sleep, and having slept-in, had me in a less than sparkling mood this morning, but somehow I had to kick it up a notch. At 8.30 I was going with Ben to meet the bloke at the Council to talk about CCTV cameras. Everything transpired against me, not the least of which was being forced to crawl along in peak-hour traffic when I knew I was cutting it fine to meet Ben on time. Then, when I arrived, parking spots close to our venue were at a premium.

As he strode off toward the Council building, Ben growled, "Come on, we shouldn't be more than a minute or so late."

After giving us directions, the young woman in reception alerted the relevant staff member that we were on our way up. I was surprised by the youth of the man who ushered us into his room. It was an office-cum-workroom with a desk and filing cabinets in one corner, and the remainder of the space taken up with computers, screens, and a workbench covered in bits of electronic gear and what looked like parts of cameras.

I don't know what I expected from our visit, but I hoped for more than we achieved. In truth, something would come from it – but not today. In keeping with my mood this morning, leaving empty-handed had me even crankier than when I arrived. As we strode back to our cars, one aspect of the meeting did give me a giggle. I shared it with Ben.

"He might look as though he is just out of High School, but I have to admire his guts and determination. Not too many would stand up to Millhaven's top cop the way he did. There was no way you would winkle the location of those cameras out of him."

"Bloody cheek! I have a good mind to speak to his superiors," Ben growled.

"…Not until after we check those recordings he promised to have ready for us tomorrow. And, who knows, a word to his superiors about how he refused to divulge security information might even earn him a promotion or a pay rise."

"Are you going back to your office?" I nodded. "Good; stop by the baker's before you go upstairs, and I will join you for coffee at about ten o'clock."

Oh good; just what I needed: Ben bumming free coffee and cake and cluttering up my office. But why not? He might as well. I have nothing else to do this morning.

Chapter 9

As there hadn't been time to call in at my office before meeting Ben this morning, all the usual daily admin chores still awaited attention when I arrived at about 9:30.

I filled the coffee machine while my computer booted up. I suspected today would be a high coffee consumption day. Somehow I managed to refrain from making myself a coffee straight away. Ben would appear in under half an hour, and we would have coffee then. Instead, I switched my attention to dealing with messages and emails that arrived overnight.

Ben arrived as I dispatched a brochure and other information to the last email inquirer. Desperate for caffeine by then, as soon as he walked in, I bolted for my kitchenette. While I dealt with the machine and set out mugs and plates, he examined the contents of the box of today's baker's fare. Neither of us appeared too keen on conversation as we sat in my ancient lounge chairs, sipping coffee and munching cakes. He eventually stirred himself and broke the silence.

"Those two officers who investigated the incident in the park were due to see me at nine o'clock. I thought of something I wanted to check before they arrived, so I couldn't hang about after we finished at the Council."

"Did you learn anything from your chat with them, or are they sticking to the story they had in their report?"

"It was both interesting and disappointing. I have to admit...."

My phone chirped, cutting short whatever Ben was about to tell me. I cursed under my breath and was about to let it go through to voicemail until I checked the caller ID.

"Janine, this is an unexpected call. Has your husband returned?"

"What? No… and that's not why I called. Sonny, I'm out at the estate, and I think something strange might have happened out here." She sounded stressed, maybe even scared.

"Take a deep breath. Try to calm down, and tell me why you think something has happened."

"Sonny, I don't know what to… I'm sorry this is going to sound stupid, but something is not right out here. My security guard is out prowling the grounds now, and he felt it necessary to carry his weapon. What should I do? I'm not just losing the plot. Something has happened out here."

"Right… first, you must call your security guard back into the house. The pair of you must stay together. Don't touch anything; even if you already have touched something, don't touch it again. Don't open or shut any doors or windows. Go to your security control centre and stay there."

"I was just going to make both of us a coffee. Is that okay?"

"No. Don't touch or move anything. Stay in the security control centre and bring that guard back in there with you. We're on our way." I ended the call and shouted at Ben, who was still sipping coffee and eating cake.

"On your feet, Ben… something has happened at the Thomlinson Estate, and Janine sounds terrified. Should we take separate cars?" I asked as I strode into my office's kitchenette and flung open a cupboard door.

"Doesn't she have a security guard of some sort? What are you doing?"

"Yes, and he is now armed and searching the grounds. Come on… or stay here if you prefer, but I'm going to the estate. And, as for what am I doing, I'll be armed too."

Slamming the safe closed, I set the combination, closed the cupboard, and turned to leave. Ben was on his feet and standing near the door.

"We'll take my vehicle. I'll use lights and siren until we are through the main city traffic area. Then, we will go dark and silent for the last part of the run to the estate... Don't want to scare off anyone still lurking about."

It's normally about a fifteen minutes run from the city heart to the estate. With Ben at the wheel, it didn't take anything like that long, but it felt like half an hour. I called Janine to tell her we were on our way, and described Ben's car so we didn't encounter a hostile reception.

The huge wrought iron gates swung open as we approached from the street. We drove straight in and up to the front door. I heard the gates clang closed behind us when we were only a few metres onto the estate. As we scrambled from the car, the big timber front door opened a fraction. Janine peered around it. She shouted for us to come in and slammed the door behind us. I heard locks and invisible bolts thud into place. I did the fastest version of introducing Ben and Janine before she led us off to the security control centre.

"This is Brett," she announced as we entered. "He's the security guard on duty today. He came on at midnight." Then she went to introduce me, but I stopped her and introduced myself without giving him any more than my name.

"Hi, Brett, I'm Sonny." He looked as though he was going to salute but settled for a nod instead. "And this is…," I said as I went to introduce Ben. I didn't need to say more.

"Sir… it's great to have you here. I hope I'm not wasting your time." Ben looked a bit bemused. The guard continued. "Brett Galbraith, Sir, on special training at the moment."

"Yes, I recognised you, but was a bit taken aback to find you here. Okay, everybody, let's get down to the hard part, shall we? Who saw, heard, or did what, when? Let's start with you, Brett. When did you come on duty?"

"Midnight, Sir; two of us are doing twelve-hour shifts while one of our guards is off sick for a few days."

Janine confirmed she had arrived only a few minutes before she called me. I was intrigued. Today is a work day. As she doesn't visit the estate often, why was she here today? But I didn't need to ask. She continued to explain.

"This is going to sound rubbish, but something told me I needed to be here. The thought – idea, or whatever it was –

nagged me from the moment I was out of bed this morning. By the time I had breakfast, I knew I had to come. So, I left a message for my assistant to cancel all my appointments for today and drove out here."

Ben took charge again. "So, Brett, at what point did you first suspect something was not quite right? Maybe start from when your shift started and walk us through until you discovered something was wrong."

"Okay. I arrived at midnight, said a few words to the guard I relieved, and then sat down to sign-in and go through the logbook entries from the previous shift. Nothing had happened; everything had been quiet. Then I checked the entire perimeter via the monitors and found nothing untoward anywhere outside. Once that was done, I left the control centre to undertake a routine patrol of the interior of the building, checking all the doors and windows before returning to the control centre.

By then, it was coming up to two o'clock. I usually have a coffee about then. So, after one more check of all monitors, I went to the little kitchen next door, made a coffee, and brought it back here. I had just sat down when I heard a noise, one of those noises that don't belong. It sounded as though it came from outside but close to the building. I checked all monitors again and used the pan cameras to check the surrounding area. Nothing came up on any of the monitors, but I knew I'd heard something that wasn't supposed to be there. I patrolled the interior of the house again, checking all the doors and windows and making sure everything was secure. Nothing was out of place. Everything was as it should be. My coffee was lukewarm by then, but I drank it anyway.

And that's about as much as I remember until about half an hour before Miss Thomlinson called to tell me she'd be arriving in about five minutes."

"When you say that's 'as much as you remember'," Ben began slowly, deep in thought, "what do you mean? Are you suggesting that nothing happened between sometime after two o'clock and Miss Thomlinson's arrival?"

"Not exactly, no. I don't know what happened between when I drank the coffee and I found myself so groggy after waking up at this table. It took me a minute or two to focus and be able to stand. As my first priority, I rushed to check all monitors. When I realised I didn't have a clue what happened during all those hours, I ran the recordings back to two o'clock and reviewed them for the period I'd been out to it. That's when I knew we had a problem – *I* had a problem.

As soon as I spotted the problem on one of the recordings, I did an immediate patrol of the interior of the building. There were no signs of entry, forced or otherwise. I was almost back of the control centre when Miss Thomlinson called, so I ran back here to open the gates for her."

"Miss Thomlinson, what happened when you arrived? Talk us through events from when you drove onto the property, please," Ben asked.

"Well, as Brett said, he opened the gates just as I turned off the road. I drove straight through and into my garage."

"Stop there, please," Ben interrupted. "I assume your garage is normally locked." Janine nodded. "So, did that trigger an alarm or something in here when you unlocked the garage?"

Brett jumped in before Janine could answer. "No, that's not how the protocol works. When Miss Thomlinson lets me know she is coming, I open the gates for her about when I expect her to arrive. I turn off the alarm and unlock the garage before opening it for her. That way, she can drive straight in and close the roller door behind her without being exposed to anything lurking on the grounds."

"I see… and that's exactly what happened this morning?" Ben checked. Both Brett and Janine nodded in response.

Ben paced along in front of the row of monitors, checking each one as he went. At the end of the row, he stopped and stood deep in thought for a few moments. Not wanting to distract him, the three of us standing at the table remained silent. Then, abruptly, Ben was in interrogation mode again.

"Anything else happened after Miss Thomlinson arrived?"

"Uhmm… I told her something was wrong with one of the recordings and gave her a rundown on everything since I came on duty. That's when she called someone. I think that was you, Sonny," Brett told us.

"Right; you say you believe something is wrong with one of the recordings. What's your best guess at what that might be?" Ben asked Brett.

"From what I've seen, I think someone took a camera off-line and did something to a part of the recording just before that happened. Basically, someone changed a camera setting."

"Who has the authority – and knows how – to change the cameras?"

"We three security guards and Miss Thomlinson… oh, and also Mr Carter."

"You said you immediately did a patrol of all the windows and doors and were just finishing that exercise when Miss Thomlinson called. Did you go into every room or just check all the external entry points?"

"Just the external entry points… nobody else was in the house at the time and, if there was no evidence of entry, there still wouldn't be anyone in the house."

"Sonny, perhaps you and Miss Thomlinson might run a check on all of the rooms while I have a chat with Brett," Ben requested.

"But what are we looking for?" Janine asked. "If no one's been in the house, what are we likely to find?"

Ben's jaw started to tighten. So, I bustled Janine out of the control centre. I explained we probably wouldn't find anything, but it was as well to check everything was as it should be. She hesitated but didn't argue. I told her to lead the way. Then, as an afterthought, I suggested we start with any rooms that were considered hers and her husband's.

She led me to a self-contained suite of rooms comprising bedroom, sitting room, ensuite facilities, and a small area containing a microwave, sink, and fridge.

"This is my apartment. It was much bigger, but I didn't need all the rooms. So, we divided it and made half of it into an apartment for Blake. Everything looks normal in here. Do we just have to check that nothing's been disturbed?"

"More or less. You should have a quick look in cupboards and drawers to be quite sure there hasn't been any intrusion. When you've done that, we'll go next door to your husband's apartment."

A couple of minutes later, she opened the door to a mirror-image apartment and announced, "This is Blake's pad… No, this doesn't seem right. Someone's been in here."

Nothing caught my attention, but I was standing behind Janine to peer over her shoulder. I moved to stand beside her for a better view.

"Point out to me what you think is not right. As I've never seen this area before, it looks okay to me. I can see that drawer is not closed properly and one cupboard door is gaping a bit, and another one over there is almost fully open. Now, this is a bloke's room. Would he leave it tidier than this when he left on Friday?"

"Well, I haven't been in here since he left for Tasmania, but he is a bit fastidious about things – almost OCD about everything being in its place and absolutely tidy. That's part of the reason he ended up with his own apartment. He used to follow me around, closing things behind me and turning lights off, even though I had just left it that way because I went to get something and would be back in a few moments. It drove me mad. My father suggested giving him a space of his own. I didn't want to create any problems about what I gave him, so I made sure his apartment was exactly the same as mine."

There was no way I would mention the two separate bedrooms… But both looked like they were in use. Interesting, and something I will mention to Ben later.

We rushed through the rest of our tour of inspection and found nothing untoward anywhere other than in Blake's apartment. Our mission accomplished, we headed back to the control centre, where Ben and Brett were deep in conversation. I knocked before sticking my head around the door. over at Ben. He gave me a nod of approval and took the bag from me.

Distraction over, Ben refocused on the camera and its recording. His questioning of Brett resumed, but he had another important question to ask first.

"Are the gates open?" Brett looked surprised and shook his head. "Okay, open them, please. A team of police specialists and one from forensics will be here shortly. They will want to fingerprint just about everything that stands still long enough and collect any other relevant evidence. After they leave, you will be able to resume normal operations but, until they do, don't touch anything you don't need to.

Now about this camera interference… which camera was it? I mean, what area did it cover?"

"…An area along the front of the house that includes the garages."

"Humour me for a moment. If someone had managed to enter, say, through one of the garages, would it have triggered an alarm?" Brett nodded. "Okay, let's assume someone had come into the garage and triggered an alarm… where can they go from there?"

"A door from each of the garages opens into the house. Once they are in the house, they can go anywhere in here – including this control centre. But, the moment they opened a door from either of the garages, it would have triggered another alarm… unless they had a key, of course."

"How would you identify the site of the alarm?"

"It lights up on this console's schematic and also gives the location in a warning text."

"And you heard no alarms at all this morning?"

"Well, no… but, as I said earlier, I must have fallen asleep, and when I woke up, I felt as though I'd been out to it for a while."

"How do you feel now?"

"Honestly, apart from embarrassed, not so great. I feel as though I'm hungover."

Two things that happened almost simultaneously brought the questioning to an end. Three vehicles carrying the investigation officers arrived, and Janine's phone played its tune. Ben went to meet his team and brief them on the case. Janine left the control centre to take her call and wandered back in a couple of minutes later. She waited for Ben to return to the control centre while his team unpacked their gear.

"Do you need me to hang around any longer? It's just that something has come up at work and I do need to be there to deal with it."

Ben told her she was free to leave but that he probably would want to speak to her again later. I saw my chance and took it.

"Ben, if Janine will give me a lift back to my office, I'll leave with her if that's okay with you." He signified his approval. "Thanks, but I need a quick word before we leave."

He followed me out of the control centre and a little way along the hall before I felt it safe enough to talk. "There's nothing more I can do here for now, and I don't think it's a good idea for Janine to drive out of here alone. Remember, I am armed. As soon as you can get away from here, come and have a chat with me. I might have something interesting to throw into the mix, but I need to run it past you."

Janine didn't object to being asked to drop me at my office but appeared a bit surprised by my request. As usual, there was nowhere near my building where she could pull over to let me out. "Take the alley and drive around behind the building. There's a parking area there for tenants. You'll have plenty of room to turn around after you drop me off. I'd invite you up for a coffee, but I imagine you have more pressing matters demanding your attention."

"Thanks; I'm not quite sure what is happening, but I had better go and sort it out. Please keep me informed of anything you discover about the incident at the estate."

I agreed, and she drove off. I didn't think it wise to tell her I expected to be speaking to her again quite soon… probably just as soon as Ben and I conferred on my suspicions.

After picking up a newspaper and two chicken and salad rolls for lunch, I hauled myself up the stairs to my office. After stashing the rolls in my fridge, my priority was the coffee machine. I topped it up again and checked my cake supply. I felt sure Ben and I would be lunching together today. Then, after again checking emails and messages, I pulled out my phone and flicked through to the covert photos I took in Blake Carter's apartment on the estate.

"Definitely not just someone being untidy," I murmured to the universe as I printed two copies of the photos, one for my file and one I was sure Ben would want.

While that happened, I dragged over a pad and pencil and started jotting down notes from this morning's time at the Thomlinson Estate. The more notes I made, the stronger my suspicions became. And, yes, I knew what Ben will say when I shared them with him: *Who else do you have in the frame for Janine's attack?* And he would be well justified to ask.

Was I being too blinkered in my approach to this case? Had I fallen into the trap of believing the old adage about 'the husband did it'? In this case, in the absence of a butler to blame, of course, it must be the husband. If only life was so simple, and you didn't have to worry about having evidence to prove it. I sat back to ponder that train of thought. I hadn't considered anyone other than Janine's husband, Blake Carter. But who else was there to think about?

Maybe, if I could at least get a handle on Carter, I might be able to rule him in or out. In reality, I suspected getting to know Blake Carter, who might not be directly responsible, might lead me to his other friends and associates, who were the culprits. The man really is a ghost. Even those who knew him, like the gym managers who employed Carter, knew nothing about him. It might be a hell of a long shot, but I hope James Rothwell is able to dig up something – anything – that proves this bloke was born and had a life like the rest of us on this planet.

The time for soul-searching was over. Ben arrived… And yes, he was starving and had I thought to organize anything for lunch?

Chapter 10

We made ourselves comfortable with salad rolls and coffee, and observed the generally unspoken rule that there be no 'shop' talk while we're eating. But, to hell with it today. I've wasted enough time on this case already.

"Anything interesting happen after Janine and I left the estate this morning?" I asked between bites of my roll.

"After moving Brett out of the control centre so the team could work in there, I chatted further with him. What was your assessment of the security guard and his story?"

"For me, a few things don't add up. I'm not suggesting any of Brett's report was fabricated. It's just that some parts of it don't make sense to me. I think he was pretty shaken by this morning's incident, and the evidence does support the notion of an incident. But, his story falters in that he was out cold for several hours during the time it occurred... and he feels compromised by it."

"What do you make of that part of his story, that he was out to it?"

"Don't laugh, but I suspect he was drugged. He doesn't strike me as the sort of officer who would fall asleep on the job. His embarrassment seems to support that. While I know it seems impossible, I think that's what happened today. But don't ask me how it could have happened. I haven't a clue, but my gut supports the theory."

"I'll wait for the results of the tests on his coffee mug before I form any definite opinion, but I think we might be on the same wavelength with this one. He admitted he was feeling groggy, a bit hungover. That wouldn't be the case if he had just been asleep. He's a good officer, and I can imagine how he feels about being asleep on duty."

"As you say, we don't know anything without the results from the lab. For the moment, let's stick with our assumption he was drugged. When did it happen? How could it happen?"

"Everything is so tightly regimented in that room, but I think it's that strict routine that somehow allowed it to happen."

"Yeah, I picked up on that. From when he arrived, everything he did followed a strict routine that filled in the first two hours of his shift. Then, still in accordance with his set routine, he made a coffee. The timing of the so called *noise outside* was perfect." As I spoke, I ran my mind back over Brett's report of the sequence of events. It also brought to mind the noise outside my house this morning.

"That noise made him abandon his coffee and charge about checking doors and windows." Ben was staring off into the distance as he spoke. I suspected he was indulging in the same mental rewind I was.

"Okay, we know Brett's coffee was unattended in the control room, but someone needed to be already in the building to be able to tamper with it. According to how the security system is supposed to work, two alarms should have sounded before then if someone entered the place."

"Maybe only one alarm... There wouldn't have been a second alarm if the intruder had a key to open the door from the garage. While the possibility of such a key introduces another can of worms, it doesn't explain why there was no alarm if/when someone entered the garage. Regardless, Brett would have been awake to hear the alarm – but he didn't." Ben hadn't mentioned anything that hadn't occurred to me, but it just gave voice to the questions occupying my mind.

"Agreed, Ben, but why not? Was there something wrong with the system? Is it possible to jam the system somehow? If so, who would know and be able to do it?"

Ben slumped back and stretched his legs out in front of him. "I need more caffeine and sugar if you want me to come up with answers to those questions."

I made fresh coffees and took them and the box of cakes to my desk. "If you want fuel for thought, you'll need to come over here to have it."

After a wistful sigh, he struggled out of his lounge chair and sauntered over to my desk. I grabbed the printouts of this morning's photos and spread out one set on the desk in front of him. He gave each one a quick scan before looking at me. Although he said nothing, it was clear he was waiting for me to explain. So, I did. At least, I tried to.

"Before I tell you about the photos, I want to chuck in another wild idea so we can deal with it before we turn our attention to hard evidence." He gave me an eye roll and told me to get on with it. "What if the intruder wasn't an intruder as such? What if it was Blake Carter who actually was in the house this morning? And, all right, it sounds ridiculous, but if it wasn't Blake Carter himself, was it someone else he put up to it?"

"Of course, you have something to support this wild idea of yours, I assume. It's not just your gut telling you fairy stories to make you feel better, is it?"

"Anything is possible today… Those photos in front of you were taken in Blake Carter's apartment, which is adjacent to his wife's suite. We found nothing out of the ordinary in any other room when we checked them as you requested. It was the only area where things weren't quite right, according to Janine. She claims her husband is meticulous about keeping his area tidy. How things appear in those photos would not be acceptable to him at all, although, to me, it didn't look all that bad."

"You're right about it not looking too bad, but to someone a bit fastidious – OCD even – it wouldn't be acceptable. What are your thoughts about it?" Ben's question started me thinking.

"Nothing definite at this stage, but I feel whoever was last in that room was in a hurry to not be there for long. I have no ideas about whether they were searching the place, or were there to collect something."

"Such as if Blake had come home to collect a few things, or maybe something specific – like something that was important for some reason?" I nodded in response.

Then, we sat silent for a while as we both tried to marshal our thoughts into something resembling intelligent thinking. My scribbled notes I stared at didn't help, and I suspect my photos Ben stared at didn't do much for him either. Suddenly, the little voice in my head nudged me. There was something important in this case I had missed from the outset.

"*Where is Blake Carter's car?*" I yelled. "Janine and I checked the garages. It's not there. Where did he leave from when he supposedly flew to Tasmania last Friday, the unit in the city or the estate? If he drove himself to the airport, his car should still be there somewhere. If he took a taxi, his car would still be at either the unit or the estate, and we know it's not at the estate. Perhaps I need a further conversation with Janine."

"A mate is the head of security at the airport. I'll give him a call to see if his men could carry out a check on the parking areas, particularly the long-term areas. I'd better check his registration first."

After working his phone with what seemed unnecessary vigour, I heard him curse. It didn't sound like good news, but I pursued it anyway.

"There are no vehicles registered to Blake Carter. Not for one minute do I believe he doesn't have one."

"He might drive one, but not necessarily own it. Remember, Janine is the one with all the dollars. Maybe she owns whatever he drives, and it's registered in her name." Before I had finished speaking, he was attacking his phone again.

"Damn… there are two cars registered to Janine." I held my hand out for his phone to see what he found.

"The top one is the vehicle she was driving today. The other one sounds like a more 'blokey' model and might be what he drives." The vehicle in question was one of those huge, fuel-guzzling utilities.

"Worth a try, I suppose," Ben said as he flicked through his contacts list. I dealt with the lunchtime plates and mugs while he made the call.

Another call came in for him as I finished in the kitchen. He went outside to answer it. I took advantage of the opportunity to call Janine. She was a while answering. I was about to end the call when she did.

"Hi, Sonny, what's been happening?" Her question had me wrong-footed for a moment, so my reply was a little guarded.

"Nothing new since the last time we spoke, but I have a couple of questions about when your husband went to Tasmania." She told me to 'ask away'. "That Friday morning before he left, was he at your unit in the city, or out at the estate?"

"Uhmm… At the unit, I suppose… Yeah. Yeah, I think he was in town."

"Do you remember how he went to the airport? Did he drive out in his own vehicle, or use a taxi?"

"Not sure, but he might have driven himself to the airport. Then he would have to leave his car in the car park for a week. I don't think he would be happy about that. I wouldn't have been happy about it either, unless it was left under cover in the long-term area. So-o… no, maybe he didn't drive himself to the airport. Maybe he did catch a cab after all. Is it important? I could ask the security guards to check if his car is at the estate."

"No, it's not important at this time. Don't bother the security guards. It was just something that I realised I hadn't checked with you earlier."

The call ended. I stood there staring at the phone still in my hand. Ben came back into my office and found me that way.

"Is everything okay? You look a little strange. What happened while I was outside? Talk to me, Sonny."

"I'm not sure everything is okay. While you were on your phone call, I called Janine to ask about Blake's car and whether he drove himself to the airport. I also asked her whether he was at the unit or the estate before he left that morning. Now, I really am worried about my client."

"Why? For God's sake, Sonny, sit down and talk to me about that call."

He was right, I needed to talk it through with him, but first, I needed to get my head around it. It took me a few moments to sort out what I needed to say and how to say it.

"At some point earlier in this case, I suggested that Janine didn't come across as the sort of person she was supposed to be. Her demeanour and personality were far too naïve to belong to this high-flying giant of Millhaven's corporate world. When she answered my call just now, it was as though we hadn't been together this morning. Okay, she only asked what had been happening. But, I would have expected her to ask something more pointed about the morning's activities."

"As you said, she has a busy commercial enterprise to run, and your call might have caught her in the middle of trying to sort out something else."

"That much I could accept, but it was her reaction to the rest of the questions that alarmed me. She was vague. She wasn't sure where Carter was before he left for the airport but managed to convince herself he was at the unit in the city. When I asked how he went to the airport, her answer told me she didn't have a clue, but she eventually decided he must've caught a taxi.

Then, the clincher was when she offered to check if his car was in the garage at the estate. Together, we checked both garages this morning. Only her car was there. Carter's garage was empty. Somehow, it was as though this morning had never happened. It is not normal, and it's not naïveté. This is something more serious."

"While I agree something serious could be amiss, you've spent more time with the woman than I have. What's your thinking on all of this?"

"Good question, and I wish I knew the answer. I thought something was wrong from the word go, but that appears to have escalated today. I don't know what it is, but I'm wondering…. Could it be drugs, do you think? I don't mean she is using drugs. At least, I don't think I do. Is she being fed them covertly? How long before you get the results back on the security guard's coffee mug?"

"That's a question better put to Emily, but I expect something by the end of the day. Are you suggesting Janine might be being fed the same drug as was used on the security guard?"

"I don't know. But no, I don't think so. Whatever it is, it doesn't knock her out. It just makes her dopey, vague and forgetful."

"We need another chat with her, both of us together, but it might be best after we have the results from that coffee mug. Coming up with a reason for an urgent meeting won't be a problem. Let's see how she is when we talk to her. If she still doesn't seem to be on the same planet, and depending on the results from the coffee mug, I should be able to apply for a blood test.

If she calls you any time this afternoon, let me know. In the meantime, I need to go back to my office to deal with a couple of things. If nothing comes up before then, I'll see you for dinner tonight. It might be useful if Emily could be there as well."

"While Emily might be otherwise occupied today, I'll try calling her to suggest we might like to talk to her this evening. If she is as busy as I think she is, leaving a message might be the best I can do."

Ben left and, after spending some time tidying my case file, I realised most of the afternoon had disappeared. Although I'd lost count of how many I'd had today, I made yet another coffee and took it to my desk before I tried calling Emily. She didn't answer. Rather than leave a message, I decided to try again in a few minutes.

I sat back in my chair, closed my eyes, and tried to sort through everything that happened today. None of it made sense. I was starting to feel uneasy about everything to do with this case. My phone jarred me back to reality. Emily.

"Sorry I didn't answer before. I was with Ben and couldn't take the call. He seemed quite insistent I should join you for dinner this evening. Any ideas why?"

"My call was for much the same reason. I hoped you might have some free time so we could talk over a few things with you. If you were with Ben earlier, did you give him the results of the tests on that coffee mug from this morning?"

"Yep, that's why I went to his office. I knew he was in a hurry to have the results, so I took them over. Were you involved in that incident as well?"

"It links to my current case and adds new dimensions to what I thought I was investigating. I don't know whether you can tell me or not, but a simple yes or no would do. Was the coffee in that mug drugged?"

"Oh, definitely; I'm surprised the person who drank it isn't still out to it. Gotta go, but I will see you around seven o'clock for dinner. I've already told Ben I will be there."

I might be trusting my memory a bit but, when Ben showed me the information on the two cars registered to Janine, I made a mental note of the details of the one I thought was Blake's. Although Ben had asked the airport security people to check their carpark area for the vehicle in question, I was impatient. With nothing else I could do at the office, I decided a quick trip through the airport's carparks might be something useful to do on my way home. After scribbling down what I remembered of the car's registration and checking everything was in my case file as it should be, I headed for the airport.

Traffic in the airport precinct was light. Arrivals on the three o'clock flight had long departed the airport, and the next flight wouldn't arrive for another hour. The lack of traffic meant my driving slowly through the place was bound to attract some attention, but no point worrying about it until it happened. The long-term undercover car park was my prime target. I drove into the general area and pulled up close behind a small sedan stopped at the ticket vending machine at the entrance.

When the boom went up to let her through, I stayed close, tucked in behind, and managed to be through safely before the boom came down again. I drove up and down the rows of cars parked in the area I wanted to search. On occasion, this section of the car park is fully occupied. Today, it was less than half full, and the cars were spread out.

Having yielded no result, I drove out into the short-term car parking area again and cruised the lines of parked cars. Satisfied Carter's car wasn't in the carpark; my next challenge was to exit the place – without the appropriate bit of paper to raise the boom and let me out. I slipped into a spare space close to the exit and sat there with the motor idling.

With no flights due in for a while, it was unlikely any cars would be leaving this car park anytime soon. That left me with two options: sit and wait for the best part of an hour for someone to drive out of here, or go and find a security officer and try to explain how I 'lost my ticket'. The latter held no appeal whatsoever. After about five minutes, I was seriously considering that option when my luck changed.

A young woman walked into the parking area. Her uniform suggested she worked for one of the facilities within the terminal building. I watched her slide into a small sedan, not unlike the one I'd followed into the place. In a repeat performance of my entry, I snuggled up close and personal to the rear end of her vehicle and exited the car park with her when the boom went up.

About twenty minutes later, I unlocked my front door. Dumping my bag on the kitchen bench on my way through, I headed for a shower in the hope it would make me feel more intelligent by the time the others arrived for dinner. A quick shower doesn't provide much time for thinking, but it did allow for something rattling around in the distant reaches of my mind to take on a little more clarity. When the others arrived, it still remained a long way from a definite idea.

Ben brought great looking steaks to barbeque and a couple of salads to go with them. Emily managed to pick-up a tub of fruit salad and a tub of gelato on her way over. I threw three potatoes into the oven for jacket-baked potatoes to go with the steaks. Then, with our drinks in hand and a plate of cheese and crackers, we adjourned to my back deck. Tonight, there was no waiting until after dinner to talk 'shop'.

Emily provided information on the drug she had found in the security guard's coffee mug. It was obvious whoever spiked the coffee didn't fancy a murder wrap hanging over their head, but it also suggested they knew what they were doing. They knew exactly how much would knock out the guard without being fatal. Only one set of fingerprints was on the mug, the security guard's.

The timings of the various phases of the morning's incident were recounted for Emily's benefit before being discussed at some length. Part way through our discussion, Ben lit the barbeque to warm up in readiness for the steaks. While Ben fiddled with the barbeque, Emily cocked her head to one side and raised a questioning eyebrow at me.

"Sonny, you're a bit quiet. It's unlike you when we are discussing a case involving us all. What's wrong with you tonight?"

"Nothing really; I've been comparing what has been said with what I thought I knew. I hoped something would jump out at me."

"Did it?" Ben demanded.

"Not sure yet, but I'll let it develop until after dinner before I throw it out there for discussion." No one argued with me, and as it was almost time to eat anyway, we did that.

As soon as the table was cleared, we took our fruit salad and gelato through to the lounge room and settled down for what I knew would become an intense discussion. After the usual faffing about getting settled and complaining of having eaten too much, I could tell Ben was becoming impatient to move on to more meaningful dialogue. At the first lull in the conversation, he started us in the direction he wanted.

"Right, Sonny, has that idea you were playing with taken on any substance yet?"

After a moment's hesitation, I took a deep breath and thought, what the hell? Here goes; nothing to lose.

Chapter 11

"I've had a problem with the sequence of key events in the incident at the Thomlinson Estate. According to the guard, he made coffee, heard a noise outside, checked all the windows and doors, returned to the control centre, drank his coffee and passed out. From his other information about the security system, I have a problem with his account of what happened."

"In what way?" Ben demanded. "Are you suggesting he was being creative rather than truthful?"

"No. I think he provided an accurate account of what he knows."

"Then what are you on about, Sonny? That's either how it happened or it's not. Why question his account of what happened?" Ben's impatience was approaching critical levels. It was time to float my theory – carefully.

"As Brett, the security guard, explained, an alarm would have sounded at the moment of any unauthorised entry, and a further alarm would have triggered if they had entered the house via the garage. He heard no alarms.

If we assume the system was functioning properly at the time, but no alarms were raised by unauthorised entry, an alternative could be that the intruder was already in the house. If a trespasser was already inside, he could roam around the house without triggering alarms. If that were the situation, the intruder only needed to wait until the security guard left the control room before dashing down to spike his coffee."

"Realistic, at first glance, your theory has a major flaw," Ben began. "At some point, the intruder (as you call him) had to enter the building to be there at the time in question. When and how did he enter the building – without triggering an alarm?"

"That's what bothers me about my theory. It's not only 'the how' the intruder entered the house. It's 'the when' that might be crucial. If he entered through the garage, one or two alarms would have sounded, depending on whether he had a key to the internal door or not. Regardless of how, when, or where he entered, he should have triggered an alarm … unless an accessible entry point was left open and with its alarm disabled."

Emily sat forward in her chair while continuing to stare at some undefined point on the carpet. Without lifting her eyes, she began speaking tentatively.

"I guess that begs the question of when it might have happened. If your theory holds true… might the intruder have entered at some unknown time in the past… and been holed up in the building the whole time? Wouldn't this person raise some sort of alarm anyway? I don't know how the system installed there works. But, if the house was supposed to be empty, and somebody was roaming around inside, wouldn't security be alerted somehow?"

"Good question, Emily," Ben said and looked thoughtful. "We didn't check the log book for any alarms recorded over the previous day or so. Your theory allows for someone to have entered the house at any time prior to this morning. Sonny, do you have any further thoughts on this scenario?"

"I'm not sure… There are a couple of other things that I suspect might be relevant to this morning's incident. But, so far, I can't see how, and I don't have any evidence to support them."

"Well, we have nothing concrete, so put it all out there and let's think about it," Emily suggested.

"Yeah," Ben agreed. "If we throw all our ideas out there now, even if they're only wild speculation, they might help prove or disprove at least some of your theory. So, come on, what are these couple of things you are holding back?"

"They are speculative, but, okay, here goes anyway. Blake Carter, where is he? Where has he been for the last week and a half, and why hasn't he contacted his wife? I haven't found anyone in Millhaven who knows anything about him or who his friends and associates might be. The not knowing has niggled me since the start of my case. But, this morning, finding his room the only place in the house showing any evidence of disturbance has strengthened my suspicions.

The other thing that has me on edge is a big one. It's Janine herself. From the outset, I felt the person I was dealing with was inconsistent with the businesswoman she is reported to be. And she was a bit strange this morning when we were at the estate, but I put it down to her feeling rattled by what happened to the security guard.

Then this afternoon, I became really concerned for her and her welfare. She appeared to have no recollection of this morning's visit. Worse than that, perhaps, when I asked her basic questions about her husband's trip to Tasmania and his vehicle, she was vague, struggled to answer, and gave only speculative suggestions. It's as though she is not with it at the moment – or something worse."

"Do you think it's a sign of drug use?" Emily asked. "Perhaps the stress of this morning's incident, added to her already worried state about her missing husband, might have encouraged increased usage. It wouldn't be unusual in a habitual user."

"No, I don't think so. While I can't prove it one way or the other, I don't believe she is a user. I suppose common sense tells me that if she were, she would not be capable of running her commercial enterprise as well as she does. So, if we assume she is not a drug user – not intentionally anyway – where does that leave us? I know it leaves me concerned about her mental state and general welfare."

"So, Ben, what's the possible next move on this one?" Emily asked.

"First thing tomorrow morning, I'm going to have another chat with Brett and go through entries in the logbook over the last few days. Beyond that, I don't have much idea. I've requested warrants to look into a few things. Hopefully, they will be through by tomorrow, and I'll be able to dig around a bit more than I can at the moment. And, if the bloke from the

Council doesn't call to say he has the recordings from the CCTV cameras for the night of Janine's attack ready for me to collect, I will be demanding to know why."

Nobody wanted another coffee, but we all opted for another glass of port. As I refilled our glasses, I wondered if I'd achieved anything tonight, and whether mentioning my speculative theory was a wise move. It hadn't produced anything for me to go on with, and I was concerned the others might waste valuable time trying to prove or disprove its possibility. I suspected a dollop of tonight's sleep time would be spent reviewing all we discussed about the case.

It felt as though I had only just closed my eyes when my phone woke me this morning.

"I forgot to ask last night, and while I know it's a silly question, did you want to go out to the Thomlinson Estate with me today?" Ben asked.

He was right. It was not only silly, but an unnecessary question. Of course, I wanted to accompany him to the estate… and to check the log book myself… and to hear what Brett had to say. Ben said he would pick me up in half an hour.

"Half an hour…" I yelped after he ended the call. I was still in bed.

About forty minutes later, I was showered and dressed and gulping down the last of a piece of toast when he drove up my driveway. I tipped my mug of coffee into an insulated travel mug, grabbed my bag, and slid into the passenger's seat as soon as he pulled up. He eyed my coffee with disdain.

"I didn't get you out of bed this morning, did I? Didn't ruin your beauty sleep?"

"What are you on about? No, of course not. I just hadn't finished breakfast when you arrived, that's all." The lie rolled off my tongue so easily I shocked myself.

As we turned onto the road to the estate, Ben called the control room to announce our impending arrival. The wrought iron gates swung open as we drove up, and we continued unhindered to park at the front door. Brett opened the front door for us as Ben killed the engine.

"This is a surprise," he said as we trooped inside. "Nothing has gone awry with the investigation, I hope. I don't think I'm up for more drama at the moment. Follow me. You'll need to talk to me in the control room so I can keep an eye on the monitors at the same time… unless, of course, you have something specific, other than talking to me, you need to do while you are here." Ben assured him the control centre would be fine. We followed him along the hallway.

We were barely in the centre when Ben asked if he could have a look at the logbook before we left.

"Yeah, sure; help yourself. There's been nothing interesting entered since yesterday."

A phone call cut short anything else he might have intended to say. I kept half an ear on his conversation. "No, Miss, no further problems … "Yes. Miss, everything has been quiet. No need for you to be concerned. Yes, I will let you know if anything else happens."

It wasn't too difficult to work out that the 'Miss' he was speaking with was Janine. I kept my eyes on the logbook I scanned with Ben while Brett was engaged on his phone call. As soon as his call ended, he came and stood beside us.

"Apologies for the interruption. It was the boss making sure nothing else had happened since yesterday's incident. Did you find what you were looking for?"

"Eh? Oh, no, we weren't looking for anything in particular. It was more a case of looking for anything else out of the ordinary that might have happened in the preceding few days. Are you aware of anything?" Ben asked. "Even if it wasn't anything serious or didn't cause concern at the time. Has anything at all of interest happened, perhaps over the last couple of weeks?"

Brett was shaking his head. "No, nothing has happened on my shifts. I'm sure if anything happened on the other shifts, I would have heard about it – and it would have been logged. I assume you have more questions. Would you like a coffee or something before we start?"

I followed Ben's example and shook my head. We settled around the desk. Amid the scraping of chairs, a stray thought slammed in from left field. As Brett slid onto his chair, I asked my question.

"Is the third member of your team still sick?"

"Yeah... We thought he would be back yesterday, but it seems he hasn't recovered sufficiently yet. He's been given another week off. It's not a problem for me. This job isn't hard work and, as I don't have anyone else to worry about, the long shifts aren't a problem for me – unlike Stan. Stan is the other guard doing twelve-hour shifts with me. He has a couple of young kids, one in kindergarten and the other one has just started school. And his wife works part-time. I think, for him, the long shifts have thrown everything at home into chaos."

"It must be difficult for them." I hoped I sounded more sympathetic than I felt. "He wouldn't be too happy about facing another week of long shifts."

"Argh, he's not complaining too much. The extra money in his pay packet is useful. They are buying their own home."

But I had run out of questions and light conversation to fill in time, so I was pleased when Ben completed his detailed scan of the logbook and slammed it closed. It was my cue to sit back and let Ben take over.

"As you suggested, Brett, there doesn't appear to be anything worth noting happened over the last couple of weeks. But I'm not sure I understand what types of events you're required to log."

"Uhmm… Sorry, Sir, but I'm not sure what you mean?"

"Okay… What about the arrival of a family member to spend a couple of days – say, the weekend? Are their arrivals and departures something you are required to log?"

"While I don't think it is a requirement as such, I would log it. I'm not sure about the other two. Although, now you mention it, I don't remember seeing any such comments in the logbooks – other than my entries, that is."

"I see. Now, cast your mind back to a week ago last Friday. What shift were you on then? I assume it was before you started the twelve-hour shifts."

"That's correct, and I would have come on at… Oh, wait a minute. No, that's not quite right. Just let me check something."

Brett spun the logbook around to face him and flipped back several pages until he found the page he was looking for. He tapped it with his index finger as he read that day's entries.

"Yeah, now I remember. That was the day Stan got crook at work and had to have the next two days off. I was supposed to come on duty at 4.00PM, but Stan called me at lunchtime and asked me to come straight in as he had become quite ill. It was just after one o'clock when I arrived. Stan looked a bit green by then. We exchanged a few words, and he went home. It seems the chicken he had for dinner the previous night was off, and he ended up in bed with food poisoning for a couple of days."

"Apart from his bad chicken dinner, did he have anything else to report about his shift before he left?"

Not five minutes ago, Ben had finished scrutinising the logbook. I was sure he would have paid particular attention to that day's entries and found nothing as I had done.

"No, but he probably wasn't thinking straight, or too interested in anything other than going home to bed," Brett continued. "In all honesty, on most days, there isn't anything to report apart from the occasional visit by one of the family, or the gardener had mowed the grass. We record even such insignificant matters just to record something for the shift."

As soon as Brett finished speaking, I jumped in with a question that had just occurred to me.

"Brett, I know you have all this technology monitoring the perimeter of the property and all the windows and doors, but as part of your duties, are you expected actually to go outside and patrol the area? I mean, apart from the cameras, are you expected to have actual feet on the grounds on any regular basis?"

"It's not a requirement. In fact, I think it might be discouraged because, if we're out there wandering around, we can't see what the monitors might be seeing in other places. I suppose our job description might be to stay put and watch the world from in here."

"What about if you heard a strange noise out there somewhere? Or you noticed something strange on one of the monitors but couldn't quite work out what it was? Would you go outside to investigate whatever it was?"

"I'm pretty sure that is discouraged, if not forbidden. If I went outside, I could be attacked and disabled – or worse – and that would leave the place unguarded. There are protocols we have to follow in the case of a possible unknown intrusion, and the overarching rule is: *call the police to investigate*."

Ben decided to take over the questioning again. "Has there ever been occasion to call the police?"

"Well, as you probably are aware, I haven't been here long, but I'm unaware of anyone calling the police in the past, and I haven't had any temptation to do so."

"So, you don't go outside at all, not to patrol the grounds or for any other reason?"

Brett started shaking his head but stopped abruptly as though something had just occurred to him.

"Uhmm… well, this is a bit like telling tales out of school but, on occasion, Stan does go outside. Not on day shift, of course, but sometimes on the other two shifts, he has a wander around outside. When he is almost falling asleep on duty in here, a stroll in the night air helps keep him awake."

"And those nocturnal outdoor ventures are not logged, I suppose…?" Ben suggested.

Looking a bit uncomfortable, Brett shook his head. "They might not be a regular thing, just occasional. As it is against the rules, he doesn't log them. I only know about them because, sometimes during the handover of shifts, he mentions something about the weather, how clear the sky was that night, or how the grass needed mowing again already. The only way he would know those things is if he went outside… And, he did tell me once that when he can't stay awake, he takes a walk outside."

"Okay, let's return to that Friday a week and a half ago when you were called in just after lunch because Stan went home sick. Other than what is in the log book, did he make any comments to you about that morning?"

"Like what? No, there was nothing other than he hadn't been able to venture too far from the toilet all morning."

There was a pause while Ben considered what he still needed to know. It was my opportunity to jump in again.

"These days, many security systems, like the one I have installed at home, have a remote gadget to disarm the system before you drive into your garage or unlock your door. Does this system have similar remotes?"

"Ye-e-s, there are two remotes. Miss Thomlinson has had one since the system was installed, of course, and she obtained one for her husband after they were married… no, that's not right. If I remember correctly, I was told it was after her father died when she organized one for Mr Carter. I believe those gadgets caused a few problems in the early days of the system. It seems that whenever one was used, it disarmed the entire system.

The two remotes they have now only disarm whatever they are pointed at. Everything else remains armed."

"Are the remotes used much?"

"Miss Thomlinson's hasn't been used in my time here. Well, not that I'm aware of anyway. As I think I told you earlier, Miss Thomlinson always asks the guard on duty to disarm the locations she needs to enter. Apart from anything else, it's one way of letting the guard know someone will be on the premises for a while."

"What about Mr Carter? Does he use his much?"

"He only used it once when I was on duty, but I believe he uses his remote a bit. It's as though… argh, no… sorry; it's none of my business."

"Make it your business, Officer Galbraith," Ben ordered. "Everything and anything is relevant to our investigation. So, what were you about to say?"

"Right, sorry, Sir. It's as though sometimes he wants his comings and goings and presence here to be covert. At other times, he seems perfectly happy to set off every alarm possible without a second thought. He never thinks to advise the guard he is coming, or to ask for certain areas to be disarmed."

"Let's return to the matter of Stan's taking a stroll outside to keep himself awake." Ben noticed Brett's discomfort and rushed on to reassure him. "No, don't be concerned about it. When Stan goes for an outdoor walk at night, would he lock the front door behind him as he goes out, or would he just pull it to?

Regardless, he would have to disarm the door that was his exit point before he went out, and that particular portal would remain unalarmed until he came back in and reset it. Is that a fair observation?"

"That's about the way it would happen. But I've never asked him about it, and he has never volunteered details of what he does or how he does it."

"And, I take it none of the guards have a remote they can use – even as an emergency measure?"

"No, Sir."

My turn; jump in quick, I told myself, before you forget what you were going to ask.

"Brett, this might sound a silly question, but humour me. If, as you suggested, Mr Carter arrived covertly at some time, and then during your shift, you heard strange unexplained and unexpected noises from somewhere in the house, what would you do?"

"It happened on the shift handover to me one night early in my time here. I became alarmed and indicated the noises to Stan, who just grinned at me. He said it happened from time to time. When it did, he told me the best thing to do was to check the camera scanning Mr Carter's garage. Stan said, like as not, I would find Mr Carter's car had arrived without anyone knowing, and we shouldn't worry about the noises unless his car wasn't here."

"Good to know. Thanks, Brett." I said, and felt the speculative scenario I had suggested to Ben earlier gained quite a deal of credence thanks to our conversation with Brett.

"Ever have it, or anything like it, happen on your shift?" Ben asked.

"Nothing out of the ordinary had happened at all until yesterday morning. It's just one dead boring shift after another."

"How much longer will you be in this job?" Ben asked.

"I was told I should spend about three months in each position I accepted. That means I should spend another month here, but I have applied for a position with a different security firm that patrols commercial premises mainly in the industrial area. If that works out all right, I'll stay with them until my six months are up, and I have to come back in for my review. If I get sick of it before my time is up, I've thought about a short stint as a cash security escort guard. Anyway, I'm here until I hear back about the other position."

A few minutes later, Ben and I drove out of the Thomlinson Estate, and I watched in the wing mirror as the gates closed behind us. He dropped me at my office building. Before driving off, he said he would return in a few minutes... and perhaps I could check my cake supply in the meantime. If this keeps up, I will have to buy more coffee as well.

Chapter 12

Although I had little time before Ben returned, I tried to develop an idea rattling around in my head into something more substantial before then. While I didn't achieve as much as I'd hoped, I did have a basic concept to run past him.

"Ben, I have the outline of a plan I'd like to implement as soon as possible. I feel more is going on at the Thomlinson Estate than meets the eye. I'm not questioning Brett's story, but I can't shake the idea that someone, other than the security guards, spent time in the house during the last week or so."

"It's a possibility, I agree, but that's about it as much credibility as I'll give it. I can't comprehend how the guards wouldn't be aware of someone else's presence in a supposedly empty house at any given time. Perhaps you should share your plan with me before developing it further."

"The only thing preventing development of the plan is the implementation. It is simple enough: I would slip into the house and take up residence in one of those suites of rooms and keep a watching brief over the place. For it to work as I think it should, I need to move into the house without even the guards being aware of my presence. And yes, I know that's just about impossible, as would their remaining unaware of my presence be difficult to achieve."

"Forget the words 'difficult to achieve', and try substituting 'impossible'. If you were able to slip in undetected, how long might this on-site vigil last? Even if it were only for twenty-four hours, you would still need to eat, use the toilet, and maybe take a shower. How do you conceal any of that? There's a possibility nothing would occur for days, weeks, or at all.

If you hope I'll approve this harebrained idea, forget it. And, if you thought I'd help you achieve it, the answer is …

NO … Don't do it. Don't even try implementing anything so ridiculous."

There was nothing surprising about Ben's response. I knew the concept wasn't sufficiently developed before I presented it. But, discussing it allowed me to come up with an alternative idea. Using the time it took to make fresh coffee, I mentally polished my second proposal to the point I felt safe to present it to Ben.

"Okay, I accept your comments about the impossibility of my sneaking into the house and staying there unnoticed for any period of time. You might find another idea more acceptable."

"Spit it out, and I will soon tell you whether I think it's acceptable or practicable."

"Your enthusiasm is not exactly overwhelming. My alternative plan is to place the Thomlinson Estate under surveillance – not during the day, only at times during the night. I haven't quite worked out the finer details yet, but it would mean I'd be working for some period every night."

"What would you hope to achieve? And how and where are you going to carry out this surveillance? The answer to that might well influence my response to your suggestion."

"Some finer details still need to be ironed out. My thinking is that it would have to be from outside the estate's perimeter so as not to trigger any alarms. It would be simple visual surveillance, so I need to find an easily accessible vantage point from which to watch the front of the house."

"Why just the front of the house…? What if the action occurs at the back of the house, or somewhere down one side? You could spend a lot of time sitting out there in the dark while who knows what is going on inside the house. All right, all right. Don't look at me like that.

I can't stop you keeping the house under surveillance from outside somewhere in the public area – unless someone from inside the house complains. Do I support your proposal? Not really; in my opinion, it's about as foolish as the first proposal you put forward. But, as I said, I can't stop you giving yourself sleepless nights with little prospect of achieving anything worthwhile.

Hang on a minute. Before we finish discussing your proposal, explain what it is you hope to achieve."

"Being able to identify some definite anticipated outcome would be wonderful. I suppose the most I can hope for is to see some form of unauthorised activity around the house or, perhaps, some activity by a security guard that might allow undetected entry."

"You are aware, I assume, that pipe dreams generally end in disappointment. But, as I said before, it's your plan and your decision. I shall be interested to hear what comes of it. Anyway, it's time I was back in my office. Unless I hear something to the contrary from you in the meantime, I'll see you at dinner tonight."

No point in trying to explain to Ben that I wasn't about to embark half-cocked on some heavy surveillance program. There was much to do before I could implement it, apart from reconnoitring the area for a suitable vantage point. A couple of potential clients arriving without appointments after lunch kept me busy in my office for most of the afternoon. By the time I left for home, nothing further had been achieved regarding my plan to monitor the Thomlinson Estate. I made a mental note to check the area around the estate instead of going directly to my office in the morning.

We would be three for dinner tonight. As I climbed into my car to go home, for a brief moment, I toyed with the idea of cooking dinner. My phone saved me from such rash notions. Ben called to ask if Emily was joining us for dinner. When I confirmed she was, he said he planned to pick up roast dinners and was just checking how many to order.

Although it wasn't early when I left my city office, it was early enough to miss the worst of the peak hour commute at the end of the day. As I turned onto my driveway, my neighbour was checking her letterbox. I gave her a wave. She indicated she wanted to talk to me and raced over to tap on my window.

"I just wanted to apologise for my dog," she began. "I don't know what's gotten into him over the last few days. He never barks at night, but lately, something has stirred him up a couple of times. I'm sorry he's kept you awake, but I don't know what is causing him to play up like he is."

After giving her what I hoped was my most reassuring smile, I told her I hadn't been bothered by her dog and made some inane suggestion about a possible new cat in the area. It didn't seem pertinent to tell her I suspected her dog's barking might be providing me with not only advanced warning but also possible added safety. Nevertheless, her comments gave me something to think about as I dumped my bag on the desk in my home office and turned on my computer. I didn't have any research in mind but hoped something might have come from my Tasmanian colleague.

A car crunched up my gravel driveway as I waited for my computer to boot up. Emily had arrived. I checked the time. Something must be amiss. It is much too early for Emily to be out of her lab and here for dinner. If there was news from Tasmania, it could wait until later. I raced to open the front door.

"It's early. I know, but I hoped you wouldn't mind. I really could do with a quiet glass of wine. If you are in the middle of doing something, I'll just take my 'friend' here out onto the deck and leave you to get on with it." She brandished a bottle of condensate-cloaked white wine in my direction.

"Come in… and perhaps you could introduce me to your new 'friend' as soon as I bring a couple of glasses to join you on the back deck."

With the ice bucket tucked under my arm, two glasses in one hand and a plate of crackers and cheese in the other, I marched out onto the back deck to find Emily slumped in a chair and staring into the distance. My stomach tightened. I had never seen Emily like this before. I spoke to her as I approached.

"You might get the top of that thing while I deposit all this stuff on the table." I filled our glasses before collapsing into a chair opposite her. "Big day, was it, or has there been some specific disaster? Anything I can do to help?"

"Wine and a quiet time with good friends might help. Sorry, I know I'm not much company at the moment. Maybe I'll come good as the night wears on."

The best approach was to allow Emily to dictate how this evening should proceed. She wasn't keen on conversation, and I was happy spending time with my own thoughts, so we sat in silence for a few minutes. I hoped some quiet time alone with my thoughts might generate inspiration about how to progress Janine's case. It seemed my muse had taken the afternoon off, and it was almost a relief when Emily broke the silence.

"Have I offended you in some way?" She asked quietly.

"Offended me...? What gave you that idea? If you mean because we are sitting here in silence, I thought that's what you wanted – time to unwind. It wasn't a problem for me to just sit here without indulging in conversation. It allowed me to think about my current case. So, I'll ask you again, why do you think you might have offended me?"

"Oh, I don't mean right now. It's just that you've been working on this case for a while now – a few days anyway – and haven't involved me in any way. You haven't come to me for help or discussed the case with me. I thought I must be on the outer."

"Either you're in a worse state than I thought, or one of us is losing our marbles. If you think back, you did help with my case. Remember the bits of plastic you analysed from the crime scene. As for helping with anything else, it would be great if I had something you could help with. My current case is significant for its complete and utter lack of progress. Now, what else is eating at you right now?"

"Why do you think there's something else?"

"From what Ben says about the current crime rate, you and your staff have been rushed off your feet. I imagine you're exhausted. So, unless I had something specific to your line of work for you to help me with, I would be reluctant to bother you when you are so busy.

Anyway, it's irrelevant. My case is going nowhere in a great rush. It currently has me parked at the proverbial brick wall, and as of when I left my office in the city, it showed no sign of going anywhere anytime soon."

"This doesn't sound like you at all. Do you want to talk about it? Maybe if we talk through it, some possibilities might emerge."

I checked the time. Ben would arrive at any minute. While it would be good to talk with Emily, having Ben come in the middle of our think-tank wouldn't do us any good.

"Perhaps after dinner might be the best time to discuss it. Who knows, Ben might have discovered something today that helps us formulate a new plan of action. In the meantime, tell me how things are going in the forensics department."

"Nothing exciting; routine work, and plenty of it over the last couple of weeks. Argh… it's not the workload that's bothering me. We are always busy, and that's how I like it, but I think I might have a staff problem that's causing me some concern."

"Is it none of my business, or would you like to discuss it?"

"It's probably a bit like your case. I think I have a problem, but I can't pin it down… can't find the evidence I need to be sure one way or the other. But, if my suspicions are right, it's a major problem with enormous implications."

"We might need to park this discussion for now. I think I heard Ben arrive."

The table was set for dinner by the time Ben walked in. We wasted no time putting it on plates and onto the table. Once the roast with all the trimmings was dispatched, my fridge/freezer provided the remnants of a tub of ice cream and a container of fruit salad for dessert. We adjourned to the lounge room to do them justice.

Conversation was sparse until after the desserts disappeared. Then, while I made coffee and poured glasses of port, I heard chatter starting to flow in the lounge. When I rejoined them, I discovered conversation had been inconsequential. The moment I sat down, it took on a more serious note.

"So, Sonny, did any progress worth mentioning on your case happen after I left you this morning?" Ben asked. I shook my head.

"No … *nada*… not a thing; I'm beginning to think I should give this game away. How long have I been on this case? And I'm still no further advanced than the day after I started it."

"That's unlike you," Emily said. "I suppose every investigator, at some point, comes up against a case they can't crack, or it seems that way. What's your problem with this one? Is it just the age-old question of *who dunnit*?"

"*Who done what* is more like the real question. And that begs two more questions: who is the *who* involved, and is there even a *what*? I still haven't determined exactly what I am investigating. Yes, there is the incident involving Janine, and now there is a missing husband. Is that the extent of it? Or is there something bigger and more sinister behind it? A clue to any of that would be useful."

My explanation provided the only levity of the night. It was one of the gloomiest occasions we've spent as a trio. Ben seemed preoccupied all evening and looked exhausted, but I was more concerned about Emily. She appeared close to being burnt out and heading for a meltdown. Maybe that might be nothing more than a negative assessment resulting from my own state of mind.

"Well, what a cheery lot we are tonight," I chirped. "You could have more fun at a wake than being here tonight."

"Yeah, I know what you mean," Emily agreed. "I don't recall too many other occasions when all three of us struggled at the same time to make sense of the world. Ben, I do have a possible situation that has potential ramifications for your operations.

Please be aware anything I tell you now is off the record. So far, I haven't taken this anywhere else."

"Sounds intriguing; perhaps you should share your… suspicions?… with me. You never know. We might be able to put whatever it is to rest here and now. That would be something positive to come out of today," Ben encouraged Emily.

"You nailed it. At this stage, they are only suspicions. Argh… hell, let's just get it out there. I suspect I might have a rogue in my team. As I said, I can't be sure – yet. But, if I'm right, it might throw some of our lab's analyses into question. And, in the interests of full disclosure, such as it can be at this stage, it might also impact your current case, Sonny."

"I don't know how it could impact my current case. Even I don't know what my current case is about. Don't let me put you off. Spit it out so I can feel really depressed about life."

While I tried to control the squirming mass in the pit of my stomach, I watched Ben, in slow motion, put down his coffee mug and hunch forward in his chair. With his elbows planted firmly on his thighs and his chin resting in his hands, he appeared to consider Emily's statement before speaking. After a few moments, he cleared his throat and looked directly at Emily.

"As Sonny suggested, spit it out, please, so we know what we might be dealing with. Do we or don't we don't have a problem to worry us?" Emily nodded but took her time before speaking.

"Sonny, we checked the file on Janine's incident. It all seemed pretty straightforward. Some bits of plastic came in for analysis and were identified as coming from a motorbike fairing. So, yep, straightforward, nothing more to see here…."

"But now, you don't think so. Is that what you're suggesting?" I almost feared asking the question in case I gave it veracity.

"I don't know why, but something drew me back to that file. Early this morning, while I waited for some tests to finish running, I pulled the file again. I still didn't see anything wrong, but my antennas were twitching – suggesting I should look into it further. Anyway, long story short, I cross-checked what was in the file with some of our other records, including the Receipt of Evidence Log.

The investigating officer's list of evidence submitted included more than the bits of plastic analysed. Before the place became busy for the day, I searched the lab for the other items on the officer's list. I still haven't found those other items submitted. And before you ask, no, I don't know what they were. They were simply listed as *unknown object (metal)* and *unknown object (possibly plastic)*.

I checked various other records we keep that relate to evidence entering the lab, but I haven't found those objects and still don't know anything more about them."

"…Other than they haven't been analysed?" Ben asked.

"Yep, there's nothing to prove they ever existed, other than their appearance on the investigating officer's list of material submitted," Emily confirmed.

"Okay, from my point of view, that is worrying," I began tentatively. "But that's a long way from suggesting a rogue in your forensics team. Those objects might have been quite small, easily overlooked, and possibly even thrown out. I can understand your fear it casts doubts over the efficiency of the forensic laboratory and your team, but I don't think you have enough to call-out a rogue operator. I assume you haven't yet spoken to the person in question?"

"No, of course not, but I did start checking on the files relating to recent work carried out." Emily became even more agitated as she admitted checking those other files. It seemed Ben picked up on it as well.

"So, what did you find, if anything? Is checking just the cases worked on by that particular team member going to provide sufficient evidence to ease your mind? Should you, perhaps, cast your net a bit wider?" Ben asked. "With reference to an adage, if there is one rotten apple in the barrel, might it have contaminated others in the barrel as well?"

"Of course, I haven't overlooked that possibility. I made this bloke's cases a priority because, as you suggest, it's difficult to 'cast my net wider' when all the potential suspects are working around me. With so much crime happening at the moment, and so much material coming into the lab, there is no opportunity to schedule time off for anyone. Even weekends have us operating with a full house."

Further discussion of Emily's problem descended into generalities but, after another couple of minutes, Ben's phone interrupted us. He took the callout on the back deck and wasn't gone long. When he returned, the set of his jaw told me the call had not been good news.

"Gotta go," he announced as he downed the last of his glass of port. "Emily, you will probably need to be involved as well, or at least call in one of your team. It appears the Millhaven natives are hell-bent on havoc again tonight. As Ben finished speaking, Emily's phone played its tune.

A few minutes later, I was alone in the kitchen, stacking the dishwasher. I hadn't planned on an early night, but wasn't disappointed to be handed one. As soon as I could escape the kitchen, I went to my office. I had serious planning to do. Despite Ben's comments and the apparent impossibility of it all, I still wanted, somehow, to spend time covertly in that huge house on the Thomlinson Estate.

After struggling to develop a plan for what I now call 'Mission Impossible', at about eleven o'clock, I gave up and went to bed. While my mind went to bed with me, we didn't share the same idea about sleep being essential. I tossed and turned for quite some time.

I was still waiting for sleep to claim me at about 12:30AM when my neighbour's dog embarked on another of his frenzied barking episodes.

Chapter 13

Wide awake after leaping out of bed, in one bound, I was down on my haunches to retrieve my Glock from the floor safe in the wardrobe. Now what, I asked myself. I don't fancy taking on an intruder in my bedroom. I was at the door before another thought stopped me.

A potential future newspaper headline flashed across my thinking: *Private Investigator wearing only Tee shirt and nickers takes on armed intruder.* Not great for my professional image, I realised, and backtracked to the wardrobe to pull on a pair of shorts.

"Right, now let's see what's happening outside that's so offensive to Rusty nextdoor," I murmured. After easing out of my bedroom and into the hallway, I hesitated.

Where to go? To the lounge room or the back deck? I hadn't heard any noise tonight to alert me to an intruder's presence. The only warning was Rusty's barking. It sounded as though the dog was in his backyard. Right then, my back deck might be my best vantage point.

Easing open the backdoor, I slid out and stood still, enveloped in the intense blackness of the night, as I allowed my eyes a moment to adjust. I was too late. As soon as I heard Rusty's performance reduced to a last couple of yips, I knew they were to see off the already-departing unwelcome visitor.

Too wide awake and pumped-up to go back to bed, I slipped back inside, locked the door, and made my way through to the lounge room. Dark corners were hard to come by in the living area, thanks to all the bright LEDs lighting up that part of the house. I selected a chair in the darkest spot. No point in advertising my presence if I do have a visitor.

All was quiet. No unusual sounds disturbed the night, and Rusty appeared to have come to his senses and gone back to bed … Good for Rusty! I took a moment to consider whether Rusty's behaviour was a help or a hindrance. Might it be better to allow the intruder to go about his intended business and take him down in the act, rather than to keep frightening him off only to have him return? I think I would prefer to know what his endgame is rather than being kept wondering about it.

While I might not have gone back to bed, I did fall asleep at some point during the remainder of the night. I woke this morning still in the lounge chair and with my Glock lying in my lap. Every part of me was stiff and complained bitterly as I tried to extricate myself from the chair. It was only the sound of car doors slamming across the neighbourhood that woke me when residents were heading off to work.

Regardless of how much sleep I managed in that chair, as I dragged myself into the kitchen, I knew it wasn't enough. I tried to brighten my outlook with the thought that, as my current case was going nowhere and I had no appointments booked for today, at some time during the day, I would be able to escape home for a nap. The only good thing about this morning so far was that it was now so late, I had missed this morning's peak hour traffic into the city.

It was just as well I arrived at my office when I did. I barely had time to dump my bag before my phone demanded attention. It was James Rothwell, my Tasmanian colleague. My pulse stepped up a gear. Could I be so lucky as to have him share Blake Carter's background with me? My excitement was tempered by his opening remarks, but they offered a glimmer of hope.

"Your Blake Carter is a bit of a mystery man, but I might have picked up a possible lead last thing yesterday. I'm not confident about it, but I'll follow it through to see where it leads. Anyway, I thought you might be anxious to know how I was getting on, so this call is only to let you know I am working on it. Stay tuned. I'll let you know if my lead comes to anything."

The way this case is shaping up, James's lead is bound to lead to a dead end. I counselled myself not to hope for a worthwhile discovery. I felt guilty about giving James a job that would take up so much of his time with little prospect of achieving a successful outcome.

Nothing other than calls from a couple of potential clients wanting to make appointments marred my time in the office. I struggled to keep my eyes open, so after a late lunch, I went home and fell asleep on the couch on the back deck. Goodness knows how long I might have slept if Ben hadn't called at about five o'clock. He would be working tonight and wouldn't be coming for dinner. A few minutes later, Emily called to say she also couldn't make it this evening.

No one for dinner tonight suited me fine. After having slept well this afternoon, I decided to reheat leftovers for dinner before having a shot at another short nap before going to keep watch on the Thomlinson Estate for a few hours. Well, that was the plan, except I didn't wake from my 'short nap' until after three o'clock. Nevertheless, I was in position by four o'clock and managed a couple of hours of surveillance before it became too light for my presence to go unnoticed.

During my watch, nothing happened. No one came or went, and nothing else of any consequence occurred. After a boring and less than successful couple of hours, I went home at first light to have a shower and breakfast before going to my office in the city.

As I reversed out of my garage, I noticed my neighbour waving frantically to attract my attention.

"Sorry; I know you probably are in a hurry to go to work, but I just wanted to apologise again for my dog's barking last night. I can't work out what's wrong with him. He doesn't normally bark at night. It seemed as though he was going to behave himself last night. Then, at about 4.30 this morning, he started that terrible barking again. I've no idea what might be happening to set him off, particularly at that hour of the morning."

Having delivered her apology, my neighbour also left for work. In the couple of minutes between receiving the apology and her driving off, I pretended to have forgotten something. After scratching around in my car as though I was looking for something, I went back inside and waited until my neighbour was out of sight. Once she was gone, I went back outside to prowl around my yard. My neighbour might be at a loss as to what could be upsetting her dog, but I was reasonably convinced an intruder was to blame.

There it was, evidence someone had been stumbling about in the dark in my backyard… but when? As the day wore on, the more I thought about the 'evidence' I found, the less certain I became about its relevance. A few odd marks don't really scream 'intruder'.

Apart from an appointment with a potential client at mid-morning, I had the rest of the day free to devote to devising a plan to deal with unwanted nighttime visitors to my house, and working out how to keep tabs on what was happening on the Thomlinson Estate.

"That bloody dog is not helping," I confided to my empty office. "I'm sure all the racket it makes is scaring off would-be intruders." Is that a good thing or not, I wondered. After several moments' consideration, I decided I would prefer the dog didn't frighten them off. Whoever they are, they seem determined to pay me a visit. It's time I confronted them and sorted out their end game. As I plan to have the Thomlinson Estate under surveillance from about 1.00AM, there is nothing I can do if they try again tonight.

A late afternoon call from Ben told me I would be eating alone again tonight. Both he and Emily would be working a crime scene. I was polite enough not to cheer, but it suited me not to have others around tonight. His other piece of news also fitted my plans. It had become time for the security guards at the estate to swap rosters. Instead of coming on duty at midnight, Brett would now start at midday. That meant Stan, the other security guard, would be working the twelve-hour shift from midnight.

It might not seem much to become excited about, but it couldn't have worked out better for me. After talking to Brett, I had pegged Stan as a potential weakness in the security system at the Thomlinson Estate. Although Brett was careful not to criticise his fellow worker, his mention of Stan's nighttime strolls in the grounds interested me. With Stan now working the nighttime shift, I will see what he gets up to and whether everything remains as secure as it is supposed to be.

"Argh hell, not again," I muttered as I drove up my driveway. My neighbour came around the hedge separating our properties and followed me to my garage. I parked outside and got out to speak to her.

"I know it must feel like I'm making a habit of this, but I have some news I wanted to share with you. For the next week or so, you'll be able to sleep in peace without being woken by Rusty's barking. First thing tomorrow morning, he is going into the kennels for a lovely little holiday.

My husband is attending a work-related conference in Western Australia for a couple of days. I've decided to go with him. We'll stay on afterwards for a few days for a holiday. So, while we are away, Rusty also will have a holiday away from home."

Things are falling into place for me this afternoon. A nap, a quick snack, and I'll be on surveillance by about one o'clock. Things couldn't work out better for me … unless my unwanted visitor chooses to come calling tonight while I'm not home. Damn, there's always a flaw, even in the best developed plans – but at least Rusty will still be at home tonight.

Right on schedule, at a few minutes before one o'clock, I took up my vantage position to watch the Thomlinson house, and discovered my plan was almost blown before the night even started. Brett was still there. He should have left at midnight, leaving Stan on duty until midday. I thought Brett was about to leave when he stepped out of the front door. Then, although outside, he appeared to be talking to someone just inside the door, but that person was blocked from view by the partially opened door.

"Please leave, Brett," I muttered under my breath. I wanted to see what Stan gets up to when he is alone on night shift. He was unlikely to get up to anything with Brett hanging around.

Then, after his brief conversation with the unseen person, Brett went back inside, closing the door behind him. Had something happened? Had the roster changed again? Was Brett going to do night shift, and Stan should be on his way home? After about another ten minutes, the situation was resolved. Brett reappeared. This time, after a momentary pause on the top step, he continued to his vehicle.

During Brett's brief pause after exiting the house, some unseen person (presumably Stan) closed the door behind Brett. In the time it took for Brett to stride to his car, scramble into it, settle himself and start to move off, the estate's big wrought iron gates magically swung open. I watched Brett drive out, and those gates glide closed behind him.

"God, what am I doing?" I murmured. "I've been here no time, and already I'm questioning Stan's integrity." While I sent Stan a mental apology, I quietly told myself I would reserve my judgement for a later date… at least until after I had some evidence to support it.

A few boring hours followed, during which I managed to consume all the muesli bars, water, and coffee I had brought. There was nothing else to do but sit there watching nothing happening. I was pleased to see the sky lightening as dawn crept over Millhaven. While it would be possible to continue surveillance for a bit longer before my presence became noticeable, my bladder was cramping after so much water and coffee. My immediate concern was finding a toilet.

Out of sorts and with nothing to show for my surveillance, I drove home. As I drove up my driveway, a thought slammed in from left field. Had someone taken advantage of my absence this morning? Instead of opening the garage, I pulled up out front of the house. It wasn't until after a thorough inspection of my yard produced no new evidence of intruders that I went inside in search of a toilet and breakfast – and definitely in that order.

Despite my early start this morning, it was ten o'clock before I picked up my bag and headed to my car. Anticipating an undisturbed day in the office, I was surprised by a phone call soon after I had dumped my bag and started the coffee machine. It was Janine. At first, I thought she sounded tentative. But after only moments into her call, I realised she was anxious, maybe even frightened.

"Slow down. Slow down, Janine. Keep calm. Just try to explain what has upset you. Have you heard from Blake?"

"Blake? No, it's not Blake."

"What do you mean by 'it's not Blake'? Who is it you are talking about?"

"I don't know who it is, but I think someone might be watching my unit. And I'm not sure, but I think whoever it is might be following me."

"Do you think it might be the police? It wouldn't surprise me if they decided to keep an eye on you to ensure you didn't meet with any further mishaps."

She didn't think it was the police. She reasoned the police would have told her if they were keeping an eye on her, rather than let their presence frighten her. She had a point.

"Leave it with me, Janine. I will look into it. I will check if it is police officers keeping an eye on you. Before I do that, please clarify a couple of things for me.

You said you thought someone was following you. Were you followed to work, or has someone been hanging around where you work?"

"I think someone did follow me to work. My office is in the back of the building, and I can't see out front. My windows only allow me to see what's happening on-site. Any unauthorised people coming onto the site would soon be asked why they were there. I could ask my secretary if she's noticed anyone hanging about. Should I do that?"

"No, let's not upset her until we know what's going on. Okay, I'll look into it straight away, but I'll also follow you home this afternoon. Give me a call a few minutes before you are about to leave your office. I'll call you back as soon as I'm in position to follow you. Are you happy with that arrangement?"

"Uhmm… Yes, I suppose so. I usually leave here about six o'clock, but I'll call you about fifteen minutes before I'm ready to leave today."

As soon as the call ended, I tried Ben's number. It was engaged. While I waited an appropriate period of time before trying his number again, I revisited the coffee machine. Armed with a steaming cup of coffee, I tried Ben's number again. This time he answered immediately.

"Do you have officers watching Janine Thomlinson's unit in the city, or anyone following her?"

"Should I have?"

"It is a bit worrying if you don't. She believes someone is watching her unit and might be following her. I've arranged to follow her home from work this afternoon to see if I can pick up on anyone lurking about. Would it be safer if she moved onto the estate until we get to the bottom of this mess?"

A long pause followed. I couldn't work out why. I believed my question was fairly straightforward. So, why didn't Ben answer it? Only one way to find out, so I asked him.

"Am I to assume you think she would be safer at the estate than in her unit?" he asked.

"I don't know, that's why I asked you," I snapped.

"The advantage of the estate is all of the security measures in place out there. But, on the other hand, and given what happened to Brett, perhaps she's safer not being there. Do you have anything further to offer? We still haven't found anything to base an opinion on. The motivation behind the attack on Janine remains a mystery, and we still don't know anything about Blake Carter or his mysterious disappearance. If I weigh up the safety afforded by the Estate against that of the unit in the city, they tend to balance out one another."

After a moment's pause, Ben continued. "If I have time, I'll give it some thought this afternoon, but my initial inclination is to leave things as they are until we find out more. If you follow her home this afternoon and maybe undertake some extra surveillance, we might be in a better position to decide where she will be safest. Perhaps it might be best to give dinner together a miss tonight so you can be out and about."

While I knew he was right, I took a moment to consider the implications. There was no getting around it. Between following Janine home, keeping an eye on what was happening around her apartment and carrying out surveillance on the Thomlinson Estate, I was going to be out and about for the whole night starting from about six o'clock. The prospect didn't thrill me, but it is part of what I do, so there's no point in getting uptight about it.

Where to from here? My investigation is going nowhere. I have no leads to follow-up, and no ideas about what else to do. As Emily suggested, all investigators probably have at least one case they can't solve, and this one is shaping up to be mine. I slumped back in my chair and put my feet up as I prepared to do some heavy-duty thinking about Janine's case.

My thinking came to an abrupt end rather sooner than I anticipated. A thought flashed in from left field and had me scrambling for my phone. I keyed Janine's number. A strange female voice answered. Janine's secretary informed me her boss had just slipped out to make a cup of coffee, but she could see her coming back now. So, if I wouldn't mind holding…. Of course, I wouldn't mind holding – but not for too long. This was urgent, something I should have dealt with before now.

"Sonny, has there been a development? Has something serious happened? I was told you said it was urgent that you speak to me."

"With everything else that's been happening, Janine, I haven't asked you about something critical to my investigation.

While it might feel as though I'm invading your privacy, I need to know about bank accounts or other sources of your money that your husband can access. Is it possible for you to tell me?"

Silence flooded down the line to meet me. After allowing her a couple of moments, I again asked the question but in a slightly different manner.

"Okay, I can understand you might be reluctant to share such information, but it is important to you and your case. If you haven't already done it in the last day or so, please check on activity on any and all sources of funding your husband might have accessed over the last couple of weeks. I can't stress enough how important this might be. So, while it might appear an unpalatable task for you to undertake, it must be done and done now."

She assured me she wasn't questioning my request but was taken aback by it and admitted it was something she hadn't thought about. After confirming our earlier arrangement for me to follow her home this evening, the call ended.

Apart from adding a few more notes to the Thomlinson file, nothing else happened for the rest of the afternoon. At about 5.30, I slipped out to buy a fish and salad dinner box as a substitute for dinner at home and, on the way back to my office, picked up a couple of muesli bars to sustain me through the late shift. I had little hope of spending any time at home tonight and wished I'd had the forethought to fit in a nap sometime this afternoon. I was organising my coffee and water supplies for tonight when Janine called.

"I'm almost finished for the day. How much time should I allow you to be in place before I leave?"

"Just give me fifteen minutes, and then go ahead and get ready to leave. I'll call you when I'm in position and have checked for anyone or anything unusual hanging around out front."

Traffic exiting the city at this hour of the day is at its worst. With few exceptions, everyone is on the way home at the end of their working day and is in a hurry to get there. As a result, my trip out to the Thomlinson Industries site took twenty minutes. The bonus now was the street out front was almost deserted. I made a show of looking for a particular address. I slowly picked my way along the road before making a U-turn to park on the same side as Janine's office building.

To maintain the pretence of being lost, I made an exaggerated performance of scanning all the names of the fronts of the buildings in the area and then consulted a map. So far, nothing gave me any cause for concern.

I called Janine. Two minutes later, I watched the gates swing open. Janine's car slid out and onto the road. Patience, I told myself as I waited to see if Janine's appearance caused any reaction as she drove away.

Chapter 14

Out of habit, I switched on my digital recorder and plugged in my earbuds. As Janine drove away from her complex, I started my recording by quoting the date and time and noting the commencement of Janine's trip home to her unit.

As soon as she passed it, a small dark blue van swung away from the kerb on the opposite side of the street, executed a tight U-turn, and fell in behind Janine's vehicle. I recorded the van's registration number and general description.

"Ye-es! So the game begins…," I murmured and thumped the steering wheel as I prepared to follow the van as soon as a sufficient gap developed behind it.

When it was far enough ahead for me to join the cavalcade without arousing suspicion, I reached to start my car. My hand froze on its way to the ignition. Another vehicle had entered the scene.

It eased down the driveway from behind a panel & paint workshop and sat idling, waiting at the kerb for the two vehicles to pass. As soon as the blue van was a short distance ahead, the sedan fell in behind it. Again, for the benefit of my recording, I recited the car's registration number, make, and light grey colour. Once more, I waited for an appropriate gap behind the sedan before I hit the ignition and pulled out into the traffic. Now we were four vehicles in convoy.

"This is interesting," I muttered. "Two vehicles to consider and nothing to indicate which one might be my mark."

Although I liked the look of the blue van and leant towards it as the target vehicle, nothing suggested it would be the van and not the sedan. There was nothing for it but to stay in the queue. It was unlikely both vehicles were following Janine, I told myself but, if they were, all three of us could end up parked somewhere close to Janine's unit. I considered whether it might be prudent to alert Ben to Janine's possible tail. That was until common sense intervened, and I realised there was nothing to suggest either of the cars ahead of me was tailing Janine.

Our four-car procession continued unchanged until we reached the main crossroads at the city gates. I gave my recorder a running commentary as we approached the lights. My theory looked disproved when the blue van eased into the left turning lane and came to a halt as it waited for through traffic to clear. In compliance with the *Turn at Any Time When Safe* sign, the blue van waited for the end of the through traffic before swinging in behind them and heading west of the city.

"Right… It seems I got that wrong," I muttered. "Scratch the blue van," I told myself – and my recorder – as I sat at the lights.

So, is the grey sedan now my target vehicle? I knew there was more than a chance it had no connection with Janine whatsoever, and the fact it was travelling close behind her car might be nothing more than coincidence. The lights at this intersection seem to be set on frustratingly long sequences. This evening, that didn't bother me so much. It allowed me time to plan my next move.

I knew there was every chance the sedan might turn off the highway into the city at any of the myriad side streets along the way to Janine's unit. I opted to trust my gut. By the time the lights changed, I knew what I would do and where I would do it. Our cavalcade of now three vehicles was blessed with a green light, and we continued towards the city for about two hundred metres to the next set of lights.

Those lights turned red as we approached. I slipped into the right-hand lane and, at the lights, waited for a green arrow to turn right onto a side street. I trusted my instinct that Janine and her tail would continue along the highway to Janine's unit block in the city. If you know the suburbs well enough, they provide a shorter route into the city heart and are devoid of such delays as traffic lights, school zones, and peak hour traffic.

My 'backroads' way should have me at our destination before Janine arrived.

While Janine and her tail would have crawled along in peak hour traffic into the city, I had an almost unhindered run to Janine's street. After finding no sign of the grey sedan, I pulled into a parking bay further along and across from Janine's block of units... and right out front of one of my favourite eating places. Not wanting to be seen and unsure how long before Janine would arrive home, I hurried into the restaurant as soon as I parked.

Yang, the owner, checked his watch. "Sonny, welcome. Isn't this a little early for you?" I shrugged and gave him my best smile. "What can we get you? ...Or are you working?" He gave me a considered look. "Yeah, you look as though you are working."

"Sorry, Yang. Yes, I am working tonight. For now, all I need is the use of one of those front tables and a long glass of soda water. I might have time to eat something later."

"Anything I can do to help... like watch for someone or something?"

Good old Yang; he never gives up. He considers himself something of a sleuth since he helped me with a case a few years ago and would dearly love to be involved again.

As I settled myself at the front table affording the best view of the street, I saw a waiter heading for my table. Yang, on his way to the bar to fetch my soda water, shook his head at the waiter, who promptly veered off to tidy one of the other unoccupied tables. I checked my watch and was surprised at how much time had elapsed since my arrival. Surveillance takes as long as it takes, I reminded myself as I strained my eyes and craned my neck forward to ensure I didn't miss anything happening on the street.

I didn't have to wait long before Janine's car came along the street and turned onto the driveway to the unit block's basement carpark. I craned my neck forward a little further and, moments later, the grey sedan crawled along the street and pulled into a parking spot opposite the unit block.

Okay, so she was right about having a tail. Let's see if we can work out who it might be. The problem was, the sedan driver was mimicking me. He, too, just sat there watching, but he was watching the units across the road, while I was intent on watching him. I saw him lift and focus a camera fitted with a long lens. Best I call in someone with authority to ask this bloke a few difficult questions.

I keyed Ben's number and hoped he would answer. He did, but it took him a while. "Is this important," he demanded by way of greeting. "I'm a bit busy right now."

"Well, that's fine, but I thought you might be interested to know that the bloke who tailed Janine home from work is now parked across the street from her unit and is practising his photography skills."

"Maybe I'm not as busy as I thought I was. What's the address?"

"The unit block is 9 Richmond Street… front right-hand corner unit on the first floor is Janine's unit." As I finished speaking, I thought I heard a car door slam.

"Keep an eye on him. I'll be there as soon as I can."

That must be the easiest job Ben has ever given me to do. The bloke in that car doesn't look like he is going anywhere anytime soon, so it wasn't his car door I heard. That then begs a question. If he is going to sit there taking photos in his vehicle, what's it all about? And, there is another more worrying question: Who is behind all this? I didn't have long to ponder any of that before other events captured my interest.

Richmond Street is only a couple of blocks from the police precinct, so I wasn't surprised to see Ben's SUV turn onto the street soon after my call to him ended. Simultaneously, a patrol car entered from the other end. The two vehicles came together in a pincer movement, blocking the grey sedan in against the kerb.

As the patrol car turned onto the street, the bloke in the sedan spotted it in his mirror. Deciding it prudent to be elsewhere, he hit the ignition and attempted to pull out from the kerb. That's when he discovered Ben's big, boxy SUV blocking his exit. A moment later, the patrol car was in place to complete the blockade.

Unhappy with his situation, the driver of the sedan attempted a desperate and futile escape. He flung open his door and was halfway out of the car when Ben barrelled into the car's door. The sedan driver screamed as his car door slammed against his leg, pinning it between the door and the car's body. The officers from the patrol car soon had the hapless bloke out of the sedan, handcuffed, and bundled into the back of the patrol vehicle.

Ben flicked me a mock salute before scrambling back into his vehicle and following the patrol car to the police precinct. Moments after he drove off, my phone played its tune: Ben.

"It will take a few minutes to process this bloke before we interview him. If you're interested and want to observe the interview, allow us a few minutes and then come in. I'll warn the desk you're coming. You'll be able to listen in from the observation cubbyhole off the side of the interview room and watch proceedings through its one-way glass partition." I assured him I would be there, and the called ended.

Yang drifted over to my table. "All is okay?" he asked.

"Yes thanks, Yang. Everything is good and mission accomplished."

"You would like to eat now?"

So far, it was a quiet night for the restaurant. I knew he hoped I might indulge in more than a soda water while I was there. I donned my most apologetic expression and gave a half-hearted shake of my head. A party of four arrived before I could say more. I waited until they moved off to their table before slipping a couple of notes into Yang's hand.

"To pay for the soda water, and the hire of your table, thanks, Yang. Depending on how the rest of my night pans out, I could return later for a meal." I remained hopeful of fitting in a meal break before starting tonight's Thomlinson Estate surveillance.

Although my instructions were to wait a few minutes before going to the police precinct, I wanted to be in position from the start of the interview and not miss a word of it... and I didn't care how long I might have to hang around in the observation cubbyhole. As I exited the restaurant, the grey sedan was being winched onto a police flat-bed trailer. No doubt, it would be taken to the forensics building in the police's seized vehicles compound. While I wasn't interested in the fate of the vehicle, I was concerned about the bloke's camera.

By the time I walked up to the officer on duty at the front desk, the suggested 'few minutes' had elapsed, and I was taken straight through to my observation location. The young officer told me they had almost finished processing the man and would bring him into the interview room shortly.

Good… that allows me a few minutes to consider whether I'm bold enough to record the interview (probably not supposed to), or to restrict myself to taking shorthand notes of the more important bits. Who was I kidding? The whole interview is likely to be interesting and important to my case. I have no desire to be taking down shorthand when I should be watching how the bloke physically responds to questioning.

Having opened a new file in readiness, I placed my recorder on the bench in front of me. The little voice in my head told me that was not such a good look. I retrieved a notebook from my bag, opened and positioned it so a few pages fell across the recorder, concealing it from view but unlikely to hamper recording.

About five minutes after I was shown to my observation post, the door to the interview room opened. I sat forward on my chair and leaned in close to the glass panel. A uniformed officer led the suspect in and seated him at the table. Ben and one of the detectives followed and occupied the chairs on the opposite side of the table. After the brief requisite palaver prior to commencing an interview, Ben opened the questioning.

"So, Mr Hutton, suppose you start by telling us why you were parked on Richmond Street this evening."

"Why am I here? What am I supposed to have done? Do I need a solicitor to be here?" Hutton responded. I saw Ben haul himself up straight in his chair.

"Mr Hutton, let me explain something. This is a police interview. How police interviews work is, the police ask the questions, and the person on your side of the table answers them. So, now you know how this is supposed to progress, we will start again – and this time, we will ask the questions, and you will answer them. Now that's all clear, do you have any questions before you begin? No?... Good, then let's get on with it."

My focus was on Mr Hutton, as I now knew his name to be. I was watching for body language. So far, I'm disappointed. The most I had seen from him was a poor attempt at a confused look. My gut told me Mr Hutton was not a first-time police interviewee. He looked far too composed – too relaxed – to be genuinely perplexed about why he'd been dragged in for questioning. On the other hand, Ben's body language told me he was fast losing patience with the suspect. I watched him straighten the papers in his file before again starting to ask his questions.

"Right then, Mr Hutton, why were you parked on Richmond Street this evening?"

"Ah, well, that's a long story. I mean, it's part of the long story."

"I don't know about you, Mr Hutton, but we have plenty of time – all night if necessary. So, please share your story with us, starting with why you were parked on Richmond Street this evening."

"Well, yes, that is part of the longer story. Okay, I'm training to become a private investigator. This was one of the tests I had to do. Ooh, is dragging me in here a part of that test?"

"Mr Hutton, your presence here has nothing to do with any test," Ben snarled. "I would suggest you move on with the story you were about to tell us."

The suspect appeared a little more uncomfortable and unsure of himself. I sat forward again. This could become interesting, I thought, before Hutton found his voice again after a couple of false starts.

"Er… yeah, as I said, I'm doing this course, and we have to do this test on 'surveillance'. I decided to have a go at it today. Maybe it would be a practice run but, if it went okay, I'd finish it off and send it away, and that would be another test completed. Looks like it's only going to be a practice run after all. Even before you blokes ruined things for me, it wasn't going all that great anyway."

"Why not? What went wrong?" the detective asked.

"And who did you have under surveillance?" Ben added. "Tell us what you needed to do to complete this test."

"We had to choose someone and follow them for at least five hours, but they recommended we do it for about eight hours if possible. Then, when we were 'on the job' and doing the surveillance, we had to record everything that happened. I mean, we had to record everything the person we were following did. Once the surveillance finished, we had to write a report and submit it to be marked."

Without looking up from the notes he was scribbling, Ben asked, "How did you choose who you would keep under surveillance for a number of hours?"

"Who you chose was your decision. I thought choosing someone well-known from the community would be the way to go, so I chose that Thomlinson woman. She is a big name around here, and I thought her life would probably give me a few things to record. That's one of the reasons I think this was just a practice run. I got it wrong. There was stuff-all to record."

This is rubbish. That's not how such a module is supposed to be completed. I sent a message to Ben: *ask him for the full name of the module, the title of the training course, and who the training provider is.*

Ben's phone was face-down on the table. I saw him turn the phone over and glance at my message before turning it back again. His action didn't reassure me. He needed to ask those questions to establish the integrity of the information he was being given. I had a few moments of concern about whether my message would be ignored. Ben appeared deep in thought as he leafed through the paper in his file before deciding it was time to get back to business again. Then, he switched his attention to the detective sitting beside him and away from Mr Hutton.

"What do you think? It sounds interesting, doesn't it? We should look into this course. It could be useful, maybe what we need." The detective appeared to consider it a good thing and added enthusiastic comments to support Ben's suggestion.

"The course sounds pretty good, actually… Well, this particular module does anyway. Yeah, we might have to look into what the course covers," Ben continued before making a performance of consulting his notebook and again addressing Mr Hutton.

"This course you're doing, Mr Hutton, is it through a university?"

"University…? God no; it's a training program, not a university course."

"Oh, I see. What's the full name of this training program, and the proper name for this surveillance module you are undertaking?"

Hutton stuttered and stammered but managed to rattle off a convincing line of rubbish. Ben wasn't done yet. He moved on to deliver the killer punch.

"How is the program delivered? Do you have to go to lectures, classes, or something on a regular basis?"

"No. No, it's all online. You just do it in your own time, bit by bit, whenever you can."

"Sounds even better…." Ben said, giving the detective a nod of approval. "Mr Hutton, what's the name of the training organisation you're doing this course through, and where are they located?" Hutton said he couldn't remember the exact name of the organisation but provided a spurious sounding name

"Thanks," Ben said with feigned enthusiasm. "Are they in Queensland, or do they at least have an office in the state?"

"Yeah, they're based in Brisbane… Ah, well, I think it's Brisbane, but it might be down towards the Gold Coast area."

Time to send Ben another text, a short, single-worded one: *Bullshit*. His response also was a single word: *Yep*. His attention then returned to the suspect.

"So, what I managed to distil from what you've told us so far is that you had chosen Ms Thomlinson as a person to have under surveillance for a number of hours this evening. As part of that surveillance, you followed her from her workplace to her residence in a block of units on Richmond Street. Does that about sum it up?" Hutton confirmed Ben's version of it, and Ben continued.

"Okay, then perhaps you could tell me why you were photographing those units – and what else you photographed in the course of this surveillance. And, as part of this module, are you required to keep a photographic record of your surveillance?"

"Uhmm, not really; as I said before, we had to do the surveillance, record times and places, and stuff, and then put it in a report. I just thought I might give my report a bit of extra weight if I included photographs of what I did."

"I assume Ms Thomlinson was unaware of your surveillance activities and had not given permission for you to follow or photograph her. Is that correct?"

"Well, no… You're not supposed to tell them you're following them. That would be like staging it, rather than doing it the proper way where the target doesn't know about it."

"In our world, Mr Hutton, following someone and taking photos of them – spying on them – is called *stalking*. For the moment, Mr Hutton, you will be charged with stalking Ms Thomlinson. But we're not convinced you were working alone, and we're not buying any of that rubbish about undertaking a private investigator's course.

Our investigations will continue, and you can expect to be interviewed further over the coming days. It's likely that, as a result of the outcome of our investigations, your charges may be upgraded to those of a more serious nature." Soon after that, Mr Hutton was taken away and formally charged.

Stunned, I turned off my recorder and dropped it in my bag. Why hadn't Ben asked the really big question: who was Hutton working for? Why hadn't he pushed that aspect? It didn't make any sense to me, given what we already know about the Thomlinson case. I intended to demand answers as soon as he reappeared – and he probably knew I would. That's why he didn't come into the observation room. Instead, a young uniformed officer came to escort me to my car.

I knew I wouldn't see Ben again tonight. He will deliberately avoid me and the pointed discussion he knows I will initiate. The question for me now is what to do with the rest of my time before beginning tonight's surveillance of the Thomlinson Estate. It was heading for ten o'clock, and not worth going home for a couple of hours or so before starting work. As I climbed into my car, I wondered what time Yang closed his kitchen on a quiet week night. I might as well try finding something to eat to help fill in time.

Chapter 15

Yang's trade had improved during my absence. A number of diners were on their way out when I arrived, and three tables remained occupied. I remembered the restaurant was family-owned. The kitchen was staffed by family members, and the place stayed open for as long as a customer wanted something to eat. The restaurant was a favourite of workers in the city heart's retail sector. After the shops closed at nine o'clock, a few workers often drifted into the restaurant for a drink, a snack, or a late evening meal.

When I entered, Yang was busy with diners settling their tabs. I gestured towards the table I occupied earlier. He nodded, and I slid onto a chair at the table. A waiter was at my elbow almost before I had dropped my bag. I waved away the offered menu and ordered my favourite and a glass of white wine to wash it down. He apologised for what he called 'a possible short delay'. It seems the table of eight behind me had just ordered, and the kitchen was missing one staff member tonight.

A short delay would suit me fine. A long one would be even better. I was in no hurry to leave. There was plenty of time before I started surveillance, and I had plenty of thinking to do. Waiting for my meal to arrive allowed me to review this evening's activities. I was still feeling offside with Ben about the way he ended his interview of Fred Hutton. All the other stuff resulted in charges being laid, but it didn't tell us who Hutton was working for or what his endgame was.

It was eleven o'clock. The last of the other diners were settling their tab. It was time for me to do likewise and leave Yang and his family to close up for the night. As I strolled to my car, I managed to persuade myself it wasn't too early to be in position for tonight's surveillance. If the change of shifts on the Thomlinson Estate happened as Brett had indicated, Stan should arrive sometime between eleven and twelve o'clock for a debrief before taking over at midnight. It might be interesting to see if that holds true tonight.

At just after 11.30PM, I was in position for tonight's vigil. Only one car was parked out front of the house. I assumed it was Brett's. It was 11.55 before the gates swung open. Stan drove in. I told my recorder about it, and then waited to see how long it would be before Brett left. It was a little over half an hour later before Brett drove off.

I expected that would be the last activity for the next few hours. Unless Stan chose to wander outside at some point during his shift or an uninvited visitor arrived, I would be counting stars to fill in time. I poured myself a coffee from my thermos and leaned back against my gnarly tree trunk backrest that was so uncomfortable, it was guaranteed to keep me awake. Another day had ended in my investigation of Janine's case, and I doubted I was any closer to understanding it. As nothing was likely to happen on the estate for the next few hours, it was an ideal opportunity to devote serious thought to how to progress her case.

Just before 3.00AM, a car's headlights lit up the estate's wrought iron gates as it swung off the road towards the house. I grabbed my camera and checked the settings were okay before firing off a couple of shots. I knew the images would be useless as the vehicle behind those lights was not close enough to the gates to be visible from my vantage point. As I waited for the car to drive up to the gates, I wondered what Stan could see on the control centre monitors. Would the camera show him the source of those headlights before it reached the gates? The question proved irrelevant. A few moments later, the headlights swung in an arc away from the gates and disappeared.

"Interesting…," I murmured. I reviewed the images I had taken. "Yep, as expected, no use whatsoever." After a moment's thought, I wasn't so sure they were useless, and I had conjured up a couple of questions to ponder.

Two possible explanations for the headlights: (1) the vehicle was just using the driveway to make a U-turn, or (2) someone was checking out the place. Why were they checking out the place?… or were they trying to unnerve the security officer on duty? My gut was in favour of the latter possibility, but my head couldn't see the logic in that. Headlights at the gate – even the vehicle itself – wouldn't cause concern. At best, it might create a few moments of interest in an otherwise boring night.

I tried persuading myself it was someone using the driveway to turn around. I didn't succeed. The lights had remained stationary for too long for that. Another thought drifted in from nowhere. Was it possible it wasn't someone scoping the place but simply checking which guard was on duty tonight? The headlights had extended far enough through the gates to light up the guards' carpark. The area was only dimly lit, but it would have been enough to enable anyone interested to identify the car parked there.

Although feeling a bit drowsy before the headlights appeared, I was now wide awake, and my mind had clicked into top gear. Why would it matter who was on duty? Would they have preferred it to be Stan or Brett? … And am I barking up a completely wrong tree? Too many questions, the little voice in my head told me and demanded I focus my thinking.

Another thought managed to swim through the soup that constituted my thinking: was it likely Stan would take a stroll outside to clear his head and wake himself up sometime in the next hour or so? The 'witching hour' for nightshift workers is just before first light. Depending on the climate and time of the year, that's likely to be around 4.00AM. The fight to stay awake disappears as the sky first begins to lighten. If a stroll outside the house had become habitual for Stan, it would likely happen in the next hour. I kept my camera in my lap, ready for action if he did.

I sat forward and picked-up my camera. "It is 4.05AM," I told my recorder as I checked the time, "and the front door has partially opened."

As I watched, my breathing rapid and shallow, the door eased to about halfway open. A couple of seconds later, a man in a security guard's uniform emerged and took a few hesitant steps out to the edge of the doorstep. I shot a couple of photos and waited. Would he descend the three steps and go for a stroll in the yard? I assumed that man, who I didn't recognise, was Stan.

He appeared hesitant but, after a moment of indecision, he stepped down onto the next step… another couple of shots for my file. The front door remained open behind him. Again he paused on that step. Then it seemed as though, having made up his mind, he continued down the stairs to stand on the path at the bottom of the steps. I wondered if he was smoking. It might be contrary to rules to smoke in the house and, if he felt in need of a cigarette, had he come outside to indulge? Later, when I examined the series of images I took, no cigarette was evident in any of them.

Then, to my surprise, he didn't take a stroll around the garden. Instead, he climbed the stairs again and paused briefly on the top step before going back inside and closing the front door behind him.

"Odd… Definitely odd…," I muttered before telling my recorder it was now 4.21AM.

Why come outside to just stand on the stairs for a few minutes? I continued to consider his motive as I watched the sky lightening above me. No explanation or any other bright idea occurred to me by the time I left for home a few minutes before five o'clock. Another idea was taking shape by the time I drove into my garage. Had Stan come outside to check the surroundings after the cameras picked up those headlights at the gates? Or…what if Stan had come outside to wait for someone – or something?

I mulled it over all through breakfast. By the time I was down to the dregs of my coffee, I had decided one thing: Stan had not come outside to take in the night air. He was waiting.

Whether it was for someone or something remained a mystery, but his demeanour certainly suggested he was waiting.

Okay, if I accept that premise, who or what was he expecting and why? My first thought was that he expected the vehicle with the headlights to enter through the gates. After worrying that idea for a while, I dismissed it. If he expected the car, or someone from the vehicle, to enter via the gates, he would need to be in the control centre to open the gates, not wandering around outside – *unless they had a remote to open the gates.* But the gates didn't open. Nobody entered.

So, what have I achieved? Other than almost killing myself with mental exhaustion. Last night achieved nothing. That realisation did not augur well for a good day ahead. My frustration was at a critical level, and today's calendar offered no prospect of achieving anything to alleviate the situation. Surely I must catch a break soon, but there's nothing to indicate it will be today.

It was after nine o'clock when I climbed the stairs to my office and made a beeline for the coffee machine. I was sipping coffee at my desk when my phone chirped. My stomach tightened. The caller was Janine. Had something happened at Janine's unit while I sat watching nothing happening at the Thomlinson Estate?

"Good morning, Janine. Has something happened? Has Blake returned?" There was a long pause before she answered. I wondered if she was not alone.

"No, Sonny, nothing has changed. He hasn't come home, and there still hasn't been any contact." Her tone was hard. I could almost feel the acid dripping off her words. "Sonny, I'm almost at the point where I don't want him to come home. I don't even want to hear from him or know if he's all right. That's partly why I called. Would you have any spare time to see me today?"

"If you can get away, I'm free now and will be for the rest of the morning."

My stomach became a squirming mass as I contemplated what might've prompted today's visit. Before she arrived though, I wanted to look at last night's photos. I put them up on the big screen to see the finer details. Ten minutes later, I hadn't given them more than a cursory inspection but killed the images when I heard Janine arrive. Rather than waste time on niceties, I took charge as soon as we were seated in my interview corner.

"Janine, did something happen last night to prompt this visit today?" She shook her head. "Okay, so tell me why you needed to talk to me so soon after our last conversation."

"Well, last night, I spent a lot of time thinking. A lot of what I've said was rubbish, but I did make one decision, and that's why I'm here.

I don't want you to waste time trying to locate my husband or to find out what he's doing – or with whom. I would prefer for you to concentrate on why someone would try to kill me. I don't know how your investigations work, but is what I've asked for possible?"

"Of course, it's possible, and it is your right to set the guidelines for the investigation. It might still be a bit premature to do so, but I will share something with you. While my investigation will continue according to your instructions, I suspect the outcome will tell us not only who tried to kill you, but also something about what your husband is up to."

It took her a while to digest my comments. At last, she raised her troubled eyes to meet mine.

"Why is this happening to me, Sonny? What have I done to deserve whatever's going on? Argh, I suppose the real question is, how do I make it go away – all of it? I just want my life back the way it was… even though I realise it wasn't so great anyway.

How blind have I been? I've always considered myself to be relatively bright, but it's taken me this long to realise that, for all these years, I've had a shitty marriage. Well, now I'm not even sure it deserves to be called a marriage. Maybe 'existence' is a better word to describe it."

"Whoa… hang on. What's this all about? How did you arrive at that conclusion?"

"Don't ask, because I don't know. The last couple of days have felt as though I was waking from a long, deep sleep – or maybe a nightmare. Then yesterday, when you told me to check all my bank accounts, it felt as though my mind demanded to know why I hadn't already done that."

"And did you check all those accounts?"

"Yeah… And no, the results were not good. Some funds have been disappearing from one account for a while. Another account shows more recent anomalies – major anomalies."

"Do you want me to take this to the police, or will you do it?"

"Not yet; we will carry out a forensic investigation first. At this stage, I'd be jumping to conclusions. Best to be sure of the facts before we do anything."

"But, in the meantime…? Don't you risk funds continuing to be siphoned off?"

"That won't be possible. A few safety measures have been put in place to prevent further intrusion, and will also show who and when any attempts are made."

"Good. Have funds disappeared since your husband supposedly went on his Tasmanian odyssey?" She nodded. "Much gone missing?" I asked, not expecting an answer, but I received another nod. "Any chance of tracing the money or its whereabouts?"

"A couple of us spent much of last night on it. We dug up a fair bit of evidence and implemented actions to recover some of it."

"Janine, if you know where it went, and unless I'm mistaken, you have a good idea how it got there. Isn't that enough for you to take it to the police?"

"Perhaps… but I would prefer to recover as much of the missing money as possible before I do that. I'm sorry, Sonny. I know I'm being obtuse about all this, but it's best to keep it that way for the moment." She paused for a moment before continuing. "If I might change the subject, did anything come of your decision to follow me home last night?"

"That was to be the subject of this morning's call, but you called me first. Yes, you were followed home, but there is no need to be concerned. He is in jail and unlikely to be out and about for some time to come. I don't know all the details of the person involved, but I hope to learn more today.

There is something else I wanted to talk to you about, the estate's security guards. Does the security firm allocate the guards from their ranks, or are you involved in selecting those for the estate?"

"Previously, the man who started the security firm was a friend of my father. Dad trusted him to allocate us the best operators he had. Then, a short while after Dad died, his friend also passed away, and his son took over the firm. Since then, I've had occasion to speak to him about the quality of the guards on a couple of occasions. I have to admit now that I don't spend much time on the estate, I don't know too much about the current guards. Is there a problem I should be aware of? Apart from what happened to Brett the other night, I mean."

"Hmmm… perhaps, as with your disappearing money, my best answer might be: *the jury is still out on that one.* I don't think there is reason for concern but, like you, I want to make sure before I say so."

With nothing else she wanted to discuss, she prepared to leave. I stopped her.

"Please keep me informed regarding your disappearing money and the initiatives you have put in place. I will inform you of anything we discover." She shook my hand and headed for the door.

I checked the time. It was 10.30AM and, despite two coffees already this morning, I was fading fast. I was heading to the kitchen to make another one when a knock made me detour to answer the door. A potential client had arrived without an appointment. I spent the next fifteen minutes explaining my services to her. She left with a handful of information, including my brochure and list of fees, but I still had no idea about her problem.

"Back to the coffee machine," I muttered after closing the door behind her. Again I was foiled in my quest for coffee. Ben arrived.

"Coffee would be good," he said as he marched in.

"Funny you should say that… Don't ask. Coffee I can manage, but don't expect anything to have with it."

"Well, that's disappointing, but I'll settle for coffee."

"What brings you to my office today, apart from free coffee, I mean?"

"As I was on my way back to my office, the Tech guys called to say they had finished the job I asked them to do for me. Do you want to view the CCTV footage I received from the Council?"

Honestly, this man is capable of the most inane questions at times. Did he really expect me to turn down the invitation? "Do you want to forego coffee to head back to your office now?" I asked instead of answering his question.

"Uhmm… no, let's have coffee. I was told it would be ready in about half an hour. After I'm back in my office, I should make a couple of phone calls before we look at the CCTV stuff."

Neither of us was inclined to dawdle over coffee. As soon as he emptied his mug, Ben was on his feet and heading for the door. He stopped when about halfway there. "Plan to be in my office in about half an hour. That should give me time to make those calls and for the Tech guys to deliver the footage."

"Okay, I'll join you in about half an hour."

"Oh, and perhaps you had better pick up something for our lunches on your way over."

Then he was gone, and I was left feeling shellshocked but aware I had little time to waste. After rinsing our mugs and checking everything was in order in my office, I grabbed my bag and left. After collecting a couple of fish and salad lunchboxes from the little place on the ground floor, I set off on foot for the police precinct. The queue ahead of me to buy lunch delayed my arrival at Ben's office, but he was still finishing a phone call. He beckoned me to come in and sit down.

As soon as the call ended, he suggested, "Let's eat first and then watch what the Council has given us. The Council copied the stuff we asked for onto another tape. I asked the Tech boys to convert it to a format I can play through my computer." He held up a memory stick for me to see. "According to the bloke at the Council, the images in this footage have been taken from three cameras in the park, one covering each of the entrances and one from the area around the rear double gates. Footage from a camera outside the park but trained on the carpark area has also been included."

"Plenty for us to look at then?" I mumbled through a mouthful of fish.

It's a miracle we didn't suffer indigestion for the rest of the afternoon after bolting down our lunches in minimal time. But, at last, the time had come. Ben inserted the memory stick in his computer, and an image from within the park soon filled his big screen. The logical thing to do would be to sit back, relax, and watch the images as they rolled by. Somehow, neither of us seemed capable of that as we sat rigidly focused and tense on the edge of our seats.

Chapter 16

A procession of images rolled across the screen. I was surprised at the clarity and detail the camera had recorded. A minute into the footage, we confirmed it was taken from somewhere near the main entrance. The camera panned across an area that took in the entrance and the kiosk and then across the park as far as the picnic tables. It didn't extend in the direction of, or as far as, the site of Janine's incident.

I sat almost mesmerised as the images of the park rolled by before returning to the entrance and the kiosk again. The coverage continued to loop over the same area for at least another ten minutes before I felt myself relax and settle back on my chair. The images were great but contained nothing of interest. No one was captured entering, and few already in the park roamed into the area covered by this camera.

Then, a two-second blank ran across the screen before more images appeared. We soon realised this was the footage from the camera near the second entrance. Again, it panned across a fair area of the park, overlapping the area covered by the previous camera at one point. But it didn't take in the little bridge we wanted to see. As with the first footage, these images also contained few people. After a few more minutes, the footage ended abruptly and, for a couple of seconds, the screen again was blank.

Ben hit pause on his computer and the startlingly white screen persisted. "I need a coffee before we tackle the next bit," he announced.

Coffee sounded like a great idea. Apart from anything else, it would give my eyes a rest and a chance to refocus. After staring at the screen for so long, they felt as though they were huge and bulging like the comedian Marty Feldman's. Taking a comfort break and making coffee took about ten minutes, during which time Ben and I never exchanged a single word. I had no idea what occupied Ben's mind, but mine was becoming crowded with negative thoughts.

All the footage we had viewed had not given us a single item of interest. Although the park wasn't closed at that hour on the Friday night in question, it was obvious few people were there at the time. I kept reminding myself we knew people were there. Janine was there, as well as the joggers who later found her. Perhaps it was nothing more than bad luck that others who were in the park that evening were enjoying parts of the park not covered by the cameras. Try as I might, I am not a big believer in coincidence, and I remained unconvinced as we carried our coffees back to Ben's office to watch the rest of the footage.

Moments after we resumed our seats, images again scrolled across the big screen. I expected the next lot of footage to be from the camera covering the area around the rear double gates, but whether by design or otherwise, they weren't. The next footage was from the camera covering the carpark out front of the park. I didn't hold much hope of seeing anything useful in it. Would a bloke on a motorbike who harboured ill intent be bold enough to approach the park through such a public area?

I thought he might be more inclined to approach the double gates at the rear of the park via the network of surrounding suburban streets, one of which ran behind the park. A motorbike on that street at that hour of a Friday evening probably wouldn't arouse too much interest. But I kept my thoughts to myself and patiently watched the images slide past.

After about ten minutes of this segment, I saw Ben check the time. A couple of minutes later, and before we had reached the end of the carpark segment, he paused the footage again.

"Sorry, Sonny, I've just remembered I have a video conference due to start in about five minutes. It's likely to keep me tied up for a couple of hours. Although we haven't found anything useful so far, I'm keen to check the rest of the footage we received."

"Yep, okay. I suppose it will keep until you are available to put it up on the screen again."

"Well, no. I was going to suggest you go through all of the recordings for any clues in the rest of this extract as well as the stuff we've already seen. It's always possible there is a clue there that we haven't found yet."

"I don't think it would be appropriate for me to remove your copy from the police precinct, and I don't think I want to spend the afternoon here."

"No, that wasn't the idea," he said, pulling open his desk drawer. "I had the Tech boys make two copies. Here… this one is yours. Take it with you and see if you can find anything worthwhile on any of it. Send me a message if you find something."

It was the best news I'd had in an otherwise 'nothing' sort of day. Rather than watch the footage in my office, I opted to study it in the comfort of my home office – where I was less likely to be interrupted. I walked back to my office, grabbed Janine's file and a couple of other things I wanted, and went home.

While my computer booted up, I poured myself a long glass of soda water, added a dash of lime juice, and took it back to my office. My computer waited for me to insert the memory stick and start the recording again. I raced through the first two segments Ben and I had watched before resuming normal speed and restarting the segment from the carpark camera. As we hadn't watched this part through to its end, in a commitment to thoroughness, this time, I watched it until the screen went blank at the end of the segment.

"Nothing new came out of that," I told my office as I took a break for a few moments before pressing PLAY to watch the last of the CCTV extracts. I was about to watch the recording from the camera at the double gates. If nothing showed up in this segment, we would remain unable to verify Janine's claim there was a motorbike in the park that evening.

"That motorbike has to be on here somewhere, and it has to appear in this last segment. The only way it could enter the park was through the double gates," I muttered as I reminded myself of the 'facts'. The images had barely started rolling across my big screen when something caught my eye.

After rewinding a short distance, I told it to play again, but this time at a slower speed. It was a false alarm. Someone's dog bounded past the gates. Although my pulse settled back to a normal rhythm, I kept the recording playing at the slower speed. It was quite some way into the recording before my pulse spiked again.

A motorbike came into view. It stopped at the gates, and the rider threw it onto its side stand as he dismounted. The camera's images were so clear, it was almost like watching through the bushes as it played out in front of me.

The camera followed the rider as he approached the gates and set about the business of picking the lock and removing it. He swung the gates about half open, remounted his bike and rode through. He was so confident, he didn't even stop to pull the gates closed behind him before roaring off into the park and out of range of the camera. I paused the recording at that point to think about what I had just watched. At least we now had evidence of a motorbike in the park that Friday evening. But, as the bike hadn't appeared in any of the other footage, these images of it didn't help support Janine's account of the incident.

"Keep watching," I told myself. "There is still more footage to see. The bike might appear again." It was a bit like waiting for the other shoe to drop as the tape crept forward. I was beginning to feel disheartened. "It has to reappear," I reminded myself. "The only way it can leave the park is through that gate. The camera must pick the biker up again as he leaves."

Just as I was explaining my rationale to the universe, that motorbike flitted across the screen again. I rewound to a point just before the bike reappeared and watched it again. It was a brief glimpse at best, as though the bike flew through the edge of the camera's range for no more than a split second. A minute or so later, there was another brief glimpse of it travelling in another direction. Moments later, the camera again caught the bike for a few seconds –travelling in a different direction than in the previous images.

"What the hell is he doing?" I asked my empty office. With no reply received, I continued watching the recording in silence. It was some time before the bike made another appearance.

My phone played its tune. I paused the recording while I checked the caller ID. Ben.

"I take it your video conference has ended."

"Yes, just now. So what have you found… or is the rest of the footage the same as the stuff we watched earlier?"

"No, not at all. We do have evidence of a motorbike in the park that evening. I haven't finished viewing the last of the segments yet, so it might still provide something more."

"I should be able to escape from here in about half an hour. I'll come straight to your place so we can go through the whole lot again."

That was not what I wanted to hear. I aimed to view the CCTV footage and then sleep until about ten o'clock before getting ready for another night on surveillance. If Ben comes over now, he will stay for dinner, and God knows how long afterwards. I don't want to tell him I'm doing surveillance every night. He will know it has to do with Janine's case, will get all twitchy about my safety, and will interfere.

If he is going to be here and might stay for dinner, I had better check what I have in the fridge for us to eat. A rummage in the fridge produced a couple of steaks. Right, dinner will be barbequed steaks and salad. After that, I will have to become very tired and suggest an early night. Who knows? He might even take the hint and go home.

Almost on the dot, 30 minutes later, Ben arrived. After demanding coffee on his way through to my office, he was in position and ready to view the footage as soon as I brought his coffee.

"Now, from where do you want to start the recordings?" he asked between sips. "Have you indexed the recording so you can find the exact place again?"

While I had indexed where the motorbike first appeared on the recording, I wouldn't let him start watching it from there. Before he arrived, I had rewound the recording to the start of the segment from the camera near the double gates. He could watch it from there and make his own notes of the time stamps as the tape progressed.

As it neared the point where the motorbike first appeared, I slowed the playback speed to make it easier to identify everything that happened. Ben shot me an irritated look as the recording began inching forward. I ignored it and focused on the screen.

"There… there it is," he yelped at his first glimpse of the bike as it roared up to the gate and the rider dismounted. "What's he…? Oh, he's picking the padlock. Hmm… looks like he might have done that once or twice before." I sat silent as the recording continued, but Ben was impatient.

"Bugger! Once he was in the park, we lost him. Does the camera pick him up again? We need to see what he does, where he goes."

"Oh, do shut up and just watch the recording."

Soon the bike flitted across the corner of the image again, and a bit later, we glimpsed it elsewhere on the screen. The bike's next appearance took us to the end of that part of this segment I had watched previously. I paused it while I explained that to Ben.

"So, Ben, I don't know whether we see the bike again or not while it's in the park, but it has to leave by that same gate and, therefore, should appear again at some stage. Because we haven't seen anything to suggest otherwise, to me, it looks as though the bloke is indulging in a spot of joyriding. Although, why he would go to the trouble of picking the lock for nothing more than a joyride in the park is beyond me."

"Yes, that might hold true if he broke into the park just to go joyriding, but there is another reason he might have been dashing about through the park at that time of that evening. He might have been searching for his target. Think about it.

He might have known about Janine's habit of a Friday evening bike ride through the park. Maybe he didn't have a plan before he arrived and came up with something on the spur of the moment."

"You're not suggesting what happened to Janine was an accident?"

"No, I think it was intentional. In fact, I wonder if it wasn't always intended to harm Janine that night. He just hadn't worked out all the details of how to do it."

I needed to think about Ben's reasoning, but maybe further along in the recording, there might be something to support his thinking – or discredit it. I pressed PLAY, and images crept across the screen. The footage kept rolling by, but we saw nothing of interest for a while. I was becoming restless. How much of the night had elapsed by then? I checked the camera's time stamp that ran along a ribbon below the images. Hell, I thought, that's almost the exact time Janine claims the incident happened. Then I realised I must have thought it aloud.

"Then, slow it down further if you can," Ben said. "Let's see if the camera picked up anything, no matter how insignificant." I complied, but the video continued to sneak along without any sign of the bike or Janine. Then, in the top corner of the next frame, a blurred partial image of a motorbike appeared.

"There at the top… it's the bike coming back," I shouted.

"Okay, okay… Freeze it so we can have a look at it." Ben demanded. I ignored him and inched the next frame onto the screen.

"Yep, that's the bike we saw earlier," I confirmed, "and it looks as though it's coming back to the gates. Might be a case of 'mission accomplished, time to go home'," I suggested.

"Keep it rolling frame by frame until it disappears through that gate again," Ben said, but I was ahead of him and kept it inching forward. At last, a clear image of the bike occupied the centre of the screen.

"Hang about," I yelled as I hit PAUSE. "Now, how do I do this?" I muttered as I fiddled with buttons on the keyboard. "Ah, yeah, that's better."

After working out how to do a screen-capture, I enlarged and cropped the image to retain just the centre portion of it. The motorbike now occupied the whole screen.

"Look! Look at the fairing! See, it has been damaged." I was barely able to speak. My pulse was racing, and I think I was hyperventilating. "I didn't notice any damaged fairings when the bike entered the park through that gate."

"Hmm… can you print that? Maybe make a few prints while you're at it? Can you read the plate on it?"

I tried a few things without success. "Beyond my capabilities, I'm afraid. Your Tech team might be able to do something with it." I saved a copy of the image before returning to the remainder of the footage.

The images continued to inch forward as we watched the motorbike exit the park through the gates left open after its arrival. Again the rider dropped the bike onto its side stand once it was outside the gates. We watched the rider close the gates and replace the padlock. I wound back a couple of frames to the clear shot of the rear of the bike after the rider put it on the side stand. Another screen-capture and the image was saved along with the previous one.

"What are you doing?" Ben sounded exasperated.

"Just after the rider dismounts, there's a good image of the rear of the bike. The Tech boys should be able to get you the registration number off the rear plate. I've saved the image to make it easier for them."

"Humph… good thinking." I let the recording ease on to where the rider replaced the padlock.

"Oh, yes, I thought he did that. Let's see what we can do with that image," I murmured.

"Okay. What the…. What are you doing now?" Ben demanded.

"See… the bloke lifts his visor to be able to see more clearly what he is doing." I knew it was a long shot, but a few seconds later, after another screenshot and more enlarging and cropping, an image of the rider filled the screen.

"Is it, or isn't it?" I murmured, more to myself than Ben.

"How would I know? I don't know what you are doing, or even what the question is about." I ignored him and reached for my case file.

Turning to the plastic sleeve in the back of the file, I extracted the photo it contained. It wouldn't be easy but, maybe if I just concentrated on the eyes, it might work. But Ben had become irritated, and I knew I needed to rectify that situation.

"Ben, I'm trying to compare the photo I have of Blake Carter with the bike rider. While we can see a fair bit of his face in that image of him with the visor up, the protective padding in the helmet squishes his face out of shape. Basically, that just leaves us the eyes to compare. What do you think? Are they the same eyes?"

"Dunno; I can't tell. Do you think they are?" Ben asked as he held up the photo beside the image on the screen.

"Hard to know, and I can't be sure. But I'm inclined to think they might be the same." While that was what I thought, I might have been talking myself into seeing something that wasn't there.

We agreed to leave it for another time and to return to the footage and continue the segment recorded around the double gates. When the recording resumed, we saw the rider flip the padlock, now back in place, to check it was locked properly. Then he dropped his visor, swung his leg over his bike and rode off the screen.

"Well, we've enough evidence to confirm at least part of Janine's story, and possibly a bit of footage to suggest the rest of it also might be true," Ben mused as he checked the notes he had made as we watched the recording.

It was after five o'clock by the time we finished with the footage. I put copies of the enlarged and cropped images on a stick for Ben to give to his Tech boys to play with. He confirmed that the footage we'd been looking at was mine to keep. He had the other 'official' copy.

Although it was still too early to talk about dinner, I wondered how I might work up to suggesting we eat early tonight. As we finished up in my office, Ben proposed we adjourn to my back deck to unwind for a while. Neither of us felt like alcohol. I didn't because I would be working all night and would struggle to stay awake after virtually no sleep last night or today. We took iced teas with us instead. I thought we might sit in silence with our own thoughts for a while. I was wrong.

"So, how is your Janine Thomlinson case going?" Ben asked almost as soon as we sat down. "What did she tell you about the news we gave her about her stalker?"

"Argh, I don't know…. I couldn't give her any details other than to confirm she was followed home from work, and I had called the police when I saw him parked out front and taking photos. I thought it would unsettle her, but it didn't. She hardly batted an eyelid.

Something is going on with Janine, Ben. The woman who came to my office this morning was a different person from the one I knew as my client."

"What…? A different person claiming to be Janine came to see you?" He had swivelled around in his chair to face me, a concerned look blanketing his face.

"No, of course not. I mean, Janine was behaving differently. This morning, she was more like the woman I expected her to be… not quite, but definitely a lot more like her."

"And you put this down to….?"

"Dunno, but I'm going to find out."

My concerns about how to orchestrate an early night disappeared with the sound of Ben's phone. He checked the caller ID before wandering inside to answer it. Such a call usually summoned him to work. This evening was no different. He looked grim when he returned to the back deck at the end of his call.

"Sorry, I won't be joining you for dinner tonight. In fact, I suspect I will be having a very late dinner – if at all. They've found a body. The Millhaven natives are ensuring all my officers are kept busy."

"Anyone we know or might find interesting?" I asked, more as a polite response than for the answer I might receive.

"When we find out who he is, I'll let you know whether you should be interested or not."

A few moments later, I watched his taillights disappear down my driveway.

"Now for some sleep," I announced as I went back inside.

Chapter 17

The thunder and lightning woke me before my alarm, set for ten o'clock, had a chance to earn its keep. The dark clouds hovering on the horizon earlier became a full-blown storm and rolled over town while I'd been asleep. A strong wind accompanied it. I heard trees being blown about as I lay there in the dark, willing myself to get up and get moving... and praying the storm had run out of rain.

What was that? I thought I'd heard a noise, possibly on the back deck. I shot out of bed and retrieved my Glock from the floor safe in my wardrobe, and then stood still, listening, straining my ears for any stray sound. My breathing began returning to normal. The only sound was the wind – and the thunder. Perhaps the wind had blown one of the chairs about on the deck.

Hearing no further unexplained noises, I moved through the house, switching on lights as I prepared for another long night of surveillance. A quick shower to wake me up, a light snack of avocado on toast, and I was checking my bag ready to go. My gut suggested I should take the Glock with me tonight. I hesitated. I didn't normally take it with me, and I hadn't for the last two nights. Why would tonight be different? I dropped the weapon into my bag anyway before piling in the provisions I deemed necessary to sustain me until the sun came up.

On the dot of eleven o'clock, I was on my way to start surveillance of the Thomlinson Estate. Along with its suggestion to take my Glock tonight, my gut also suggested a change of vehicles might be prudent. So, I was in my big, boxy, dark blue wagon. Until I was settled in my surveillance place, only one thing occupied my mind: why was I so twitchy tonight? What had put all my senses on high alert? I remained none the wiser as I wriggled about to make myself as comfortable as possible on the hard ground.

It looked being another long, boring night of nothing crime-wise happening. Although the storm had abated, the wind hadn't dropped much, and the clouds remained dark and threatening. At about two o'clock, a few big raindrops splashed down around me. I swore under my breath. The last thing I wanted was to be soaked, especially with the wind still howling around me. Perhaps I should go back to my car to fetch a poncho. Maybe I'll wait a few moments to see if it is really going to rain or if it's just teasing me. After another few minutes of no further raindrops, I decided a poncho wasn't necessary.

Lost in my own thoughts, I was jarred back to reality when the front door of the Thomlinson house opened a fraction. I sat forward in anticipation. Nothing more happened. The door didn't open further, and no one came out. I dragged out my camera and set it up in readiness to record whatever happened. But scrabbling around in my bag for my camera reminded me I had muesli bars in there too. Whatever was going to happen at the house isn't happening, so I might as well sit here and chew a bar while I keep watch.

A sound behind me made me swivel around to look over my shoulder to where I thought it originated. Was I imagining it, or was it just the wind blowing leaves about? The sound had been indistinct, almost lost in the howl of the wind, but I knew I'd heard something... The sound of a footfall on twigs. Forget the muesli bar, the little voice in my head told me. Investigate that sound, it insisted. It was right. I needed to be sure.

While I waited, listening for another sound to verify its location, I kept my eyes and camera on the front doors of the Thomlinson house. A figure eventually emerged and stood, hands on hips, on the top step.

Yep, he's definitely waiting for something. That was not a man out for a stroll... and he wasn't last night either. If that is Stan, he is up to no good. He is not coming outside to benefit his health or for the night air to help keep him awake. He is up to something, waiting for something – or someone. But why wait outside? Surely he needs to be in the control centre to open the gates or whatever is required. What can he do outside? While I internally debated the man's actions and scrabbled around in my bag for a muesli bar, my camera kept itself busy taking continuous shots of the front of the house.

Then the sound came again, closer this time, and I knew it was something or someone moving about. Damn the thunder. Maybe it had been there moving about the whole time, but I could only hear it between claps of thunder. Time to investigate, I told myself. Forget the muesli bar, the voice in my head demanded again. This time I agreed. There was something more important than food right now.

I felt the cold steel of my Glock and slipped my hand around it, before slipping my spare hand into the bag as well to work the slider. The sound came again. Closer now – very close. I spun around on my backside to face the direction of the sound. A bolt of lightning lit up the patch of bushes ahead. It lit up something else as well.

It illuminated a semi-crouched figure with one arm extended above his head. I sprang up, knocking over my tripod and camera. The lightning had also glinted off something shiny in the figure's raised hand. There was no room in the tiny clearing I used as my vantage point, but springing up, I managed a couple of paces to one side and a little further away from the knife-wielding figure. I could almost smell him. He was too close to allow any clever evasive moves.

Sensing I was cornered, he rushed at me, raising the knife even higher as he came –instinct kicked in. I raised the Glock and fired – twice. I heard a grunt as the first shot hit its target. The second shot was an automatic reaction. I didn't know whether it was necessary or not, but I wasn't hanging about to find out. My training dictated loosing-off three shots. Tonight, two would suffice. The figure was crashing its way through the bushes as it escaped. I maintained my position and remained ready… just in case.

About a minute later, a vehicle in fairly close proximity came to life and roared off. I remained still and waited probably another minute before feeling safe to make a move. With the Glock still in my hand, I gathered up my stuff. As I stuffed the camera into my oversized tote bag, I hoped it hadn't suffered too much damage from being knocked over. I didn't waste time checking. Then, with my bag over my shoulder and the Glock in my hand, I jogged to my car. After engaging the safety on the weapon, everything went onto the front passenger seat.

Moments later, I was roaring back towards the city. I told Siri to call Ben's number.

"What…?" he barked by way of a greeting. "Do you know what time it is? Oh, let me guess. You're in trouble. Where are you, and what have you done?"

"Good evening to you too. I've just turned onto your street … Be with you in a few seconds."

I ended the call as Ben's place loomed up ahead. I slowed and eased onto his driveway before killing the engine and sitting in the darkness to drag in a few deep breaths. The porch light came on and had me scurrying for the front door.

Millhaven's top cop, tousled-haired and wearing nothing but a pair of hastily pulled on shorts, was not pleased to see me.

Many years ago, Ben and I became more than good friends and were contemplating maybe taking the next 'big step' before life got in the way. Our careers took us to different parts of the state. In the years before we met up again in Millhaven, I had been married and widowed, and Ben was busy climbing the rankings ladder. Suffice to say, along the way, I had become familiar with Ben's sleep attire. Tonight, he pulled on trousers….

"Right, of course, I didn't want a good night's sleep. So, why don't you tell me what sort of jam you managed to get yourself into tonight."

"I've just shot somebody." I watched a stunned look spread over his face and endured the few moments of stony silence that followed.

Then I was being led over to, and pushed down onto a lounge chair. Ben dragged another chair over to sit in front of me. His voice was quiet and calm.

"Okay; you shot someone. Is that someone dead?"

"No," I said, shaking my head. "Whoever it was got away. I fired twice. I think the first shot found its mark, but I don't know about the second one."

"Good; at least I don't have to retrieve a body and explain how it came to be dead. You had better tell me the whole story – like where it happened, when, and why."

"My camera… I need my camera. I'll fetch it from my car before I tell you about tonight."

He wasn't having any of it and insisted on fetching my bag. Dumping it on the coffee table beside me, he demanded, "What the hell do you carry around in this thing? It weighs a tonne. Ah hah, and I suppose your Glock is in there too."

The Glock was of no interest to me at that moment, but I nodded my agreement as I rummaged in my bag for my camera. Ben was into one of his 'reading me the riot act' performances about surveillance alone after dark and not telling anyone beforehand where I was going and for how long. As he regurgitated stuff I'd heard dozens of times before, I checked my camera. It looked undamaged by its ordeal. A tiny flake of plastic was missing from an area of the case, but I decided it was superficial and of no consequence.

"Are you paying attention?" Ben demanded. "Have you listened to anything I've said?"

"Not really; I wanted to make sure tonight's photos were all right. Okay… now, if you stop yapping for a few minutes, I have something to show you. It might help explain where I was and what I was doing."

I had wound back to the previous night's images and gave him a running commentary as he flicked through them and continued viewing through to the end of tonight's shots. Instead of commenting as I expected, he started going back through the photos again in reverse order, image by image. No commentary was provided this time. I waited in silence until he finished. After handing the camera back to me, he appeared done with it, but he still didn't speak for a moment. The pensive look on his face told me more was coming.

"Anything happen to give you any clues about what he was waiting for?" he asked almost absentmindedly. "What about those headlights last night? Did you get any details of the vehicle?"

"Ben, can we focus for a moment? I'm here now because I shot a man. A man who was about to stab me. I don't know whether that person had anything to do with the headlights I saw last night, or why he wanted to stab me… that is, other than because I was watching the Thomlinson Estate."

"That has to be what it was about, but the big question is, what was the security guard waiting for?"

"You agree then? The guard was waiting for something or someone?"

"Oh, yeah, he was out there waiting for something, and whatever it was didn't arrive on the first night. So, tonight, he was waiting outside again. Do you think you were sprung? Someone might have discovered what was happening or saw you hiding in the bushes?"

"I don't see how. Last night, there wasn't even any traffic around when I drove out to the estate, and I'm sure I wasn't followed. For a while, I did wonder if I'd picked up a tail tonight. One car did travel out that way, but it turned off long before the estate. I wasn't followed the rest of the way to where I left my car."

"Any other incidents happen lately? Anything out of the ordinary, or that might seem suspicious now, although not at the time?"

"No… No-o, I wouldn't say suspicious. A vehicle ran me off the road the day before yesterday. Where it happened, there was plenty of room to take evasive action. I veered off the road onto a clearing alongside it, and no damage was done. I don't know if it was deliberate or not, but I didn't think so at the time. I put it down to a careless young driver fiddling with his phone or the car's sound system and not paying attention to the road."

"Nothing else? How come you had your weapon with you tonight?"

"Pure coincidence... I suspect someone has been hanging around my place at night. My neighbour's dog carried on a treat a few nights and probably scared off whoever was hanging about. Yesterday, the dog went into the kennels for a week. Then, last night, I thought I heard a noise on my back deck. I wasn't sure because of the storm. I checked and found nothing and no one. I had my Glock when I checked, and then, almost as an afterthought, I threw it in my bag to take with me.

Look, this is all very well, but shouldn't we be doing something about the bloke I shot?"

"You said he wasn't dead. We don't have a body to worry about. If, as you think, he's wounded, he's likely to seek medical attention. Gunshot wounds are reported immediately medical treatment is sought. We'll know about it in due course. Why make a needless fuss now?"

This bloke I'm talking to looks like Ben Richards, Millhaven's top cop, but he certainly doesn't sound like him. On any other occasion, he would be ranting and roaring and running around trying to discover every possible detail about the incident. For a moment, I wondered if he knew something I didn't, but dismissed the notion. After all, what was there to know? His strange behaviour continued.

"It's a bit early, but we might as well have breakfast now. With any luck, we might be busy for the rest of the day."

Breakfast! Humour him, the little voice in my head urged. "Yes. Why not? Breakfast sounds good – especially as I only had a snack last night."

My plan was to play along and hope he might tell me what was going on. But breakfast happened without further enlightenment. Immediately afterwards, Ben appeared to go about his normal routine – showered and dressed for work – while I sat around wondering what I was supposed to do. By the time he reappeared, dressed and ready to leave, I'd had enough of playing his game.

"Right then, I'm going home for a shower and a sleep while you go to work. Talk to you tonight, if not before," I said as I picked up my bag and headed for the door.

"Where do you think you're going? We have a serious crime to sort out – more than one crime now. Do you still keep a change of clothes in the car?" I nodded. "Okay… shower and change here. Then we have a crime scene to inspect. Which security guard is on duty at the Thomlinson Estate this morning?"

"Stan should be on from midnight to midday. Brett will likely arrive at about 11.30AM for a debrief before they change over."

"We need to talk to them both, but I'm not sure in what order. Never mind, we'll play it by ear and see where it takes us."

At last, normalcy returned, but I couldn't help wondering what Ben's game had been when I first arrived. It was out of keeping for him to be unmoved by the fact that I'd shot someone. When in doubt, just play along. You never know where it might take you, I told myself.

When we were ready to leave, he insisted we take his vehicle and leave mine in his garage. As we drove off, he said, "I need to call at the precinct first. It will only take a minute, and then you can show me where the shooting happened."

It was only a brief stop at the precinct before I directed him to where I had parked my car last night. Ben parked in the same place, and I led him to my surveillance point. As we were about to push our way through the thin line of bushes that hid my spot, Ben stopped.

"Hang on a minute. What's this? It looks like blood. Was it here last night?"

"How would I know? It was dark when I made a hasty escape. It could have been there, but I didn't see it. The bloke I shot probably spilled it as he made his getaway."

"Any idea where his vehicle was?"

"No, but it sounded close by when he drove off after being shot. The sound of the vehicle I heard leaving came from somewhere in that direction. Is there a particular reason for the question?"

"Look at the blood trail." Ben strode about three metres in the direction I suggested the victim's car might have been parked. "See, the trail seems to end here. Unless his vehicle was parked about here, how come he suddenly stopped bleeding?"

"Good point, Ben, but I don't see any evidence of a vehicle having parked here, and I don't see how it could have been. Various devices block vehicular access on three sides of this narrow strip of parkland. A section of the Thomlinson Estate's security fence runs along the fourth side of the park." I could see Ben wasn't interested in anything I said, so I tried again to make my point. "All I'm saying is that, wherever the victim parked his car, it had to be outside this area of parkland. If we examine the area thoroughly, we might find something useful." He seemed sceptical but didn't argue.

Ben didn't move. His phone had silently demanded his attention. He never has it set on silent vibrate. Why would he have it set that way today? Approaching voices caught my attention. Three figures in forensics scene-of-crime outfits marched across the park in our direction. Despite the hooded white overalls, mask and bootees, it was easy to identify Emily. She was speaking on her phone as she led the trio to us. All three carried equipment, but one had an interesting long case of some sort. I gave Ben a questioning look.

Ignoring me, he told Emily, "If you start here and follow the trail back that way, it will take you to the site of the incident."

Moments later, the three white-clad forensics team members were on-the-job, and Ben resumed the search for where the victim had parked. I decided it might be an opportune time to run a few things past him.

"Ben, what did you make of those images I captured outside the Thomlinson's front door? Do you think the bloke was Stan, the other security guard?"

"Whether it was Stan or not, I can't say. I haven't met Stan, but I'm sure the bloke in the images was the security guard on duty on both those nights. As for his actions, I think it is pretty clear he was waiting for something. The night before last, that 'something' almost happened. Those headlights had something to do with it. But something aborted whatever was supposed to happen. It scared off the vehicle.

I can't help thinking you might have been 'made', that someone found out where you were and what you were doing. Then, last night, the guard waited for whatever was supposed to happen the night before – but again, it didn't."

"But, last night, no vehicle came near the gates; no headlights were seen."

"No, but someone knew where to find you and intended you shouldn't be a continuing problem. Put everything else aside for the moment. Concentrate on how and when your surveillance might have been discovered. Think about every vehicle you saw, everything you noticed – no matter how innocuous it seemed at the time. Do you understand what I need you to do?"

Of course, I knew what Ben wanted me to do, and I was way ahead of him. Ever since we left his house, I had gone over in my mind every moment of my two nights of surveillance. Nothing jumped out at me. There had been only one car this morning, and it hadn't followed me as far as the Thomlinson Estate. I had seen no one and no other vehicles. The only person I saw was the guard patiently waiting on the top step outside the front door.

"What caused the change of plan on the first night? Why did the vehicle drive off?"

"What…?" Ben demanded. "I didn't hear what you said.

"Eh?... Oh, sorry; I must have been thinking aloud. I was thinking about what caused the driver to abort whatever was planned for that first night."

Further discussion was curtailed when one of the forensic team shouted something.

"They've found it," Ben announced before jogging back to where the forensic team was working.

"Found what…?" I asked as I tried to keep pace with him.

My short legs couldn't match his long strides, and I soon lagged behind. When I reached them, all four of them were standing near the place where the blood trail began. Ben was clicking off photos with his phone. One of the forensic team was using a camera with an impressive-looking lens to capture images of something in the same area.

Chapter 18

"Who found what?" I demanded as I reached the others. "And should I be concerned about it?"

Emily held up an evidence bag. "We found the knife," she announced, waving the bag at me.

A long, thin-bladed knife resembling a stiletto lay in the bottom of the oversized evidence bag. No doubt it must be the knife my unwelcome visitor threatened me with last night, but I had trouble accepting it. Somehow, that knife seemed bigger, more menacing than the one in the evidence bag. Perhaps they didn't find the 'right' knife.

"Are you sure it's the right knife? Somehow, it doesn't fit with what I remember seeing. It was only for a second in a flash of lightning, but the knife I saw seemed bigger than that one." I heard Ben chuckle.

"Right… I understand your scepticism. People probably chuck knives around in these bushes on a regular basis. Maybe the team should run the metal detector over the rest of the park – just in case this isn't the right one."

"Okay; apologies… I know it was a stupid question, but I was surprised you could be so sure this was the knife."

"You might remember I received a phone call as I was going for a shower this morning. A bloke with a gunshot wound had presented at the hospital. The doctor on duty in A&E called the police – as they are supposed to do – and the duty officer called me. Before you think up more arguments, the clincher was the other bit of information the doctor provided. His patient with the gunshot wound had a spring-loaded knife sheath strapped to his right forearm.

We knew we were looking for a stiletto-type knife that fitted that sheath, and this looks like it." He grinned at me. "Of course, we can't be sure until we test it, but I'm confident the wounded man's fingerprints will be on it, and the knife will perfectly fit the sheath he was wearing."

While Ben sorted me out, the forensic team had continued combing the area for evidence but were now packing up their gear.

"We're done here," Emily called to Ben. "We'll check for any sign of car tracks on our way out, but I don't hold much hope of finding anything useful."

"Happy now?" Ben asked as we watched Emily and her team working their way out of the park.

"Hmm… I suppose so. Do we know who the bloke is?" I asked. "I suppose it's too much to hope he is Blake Carter. So, what do we do now? Is there anything more we might do here before we get on with the rest of our day?"

"There is something we need to do. We need to check every nook and cranny of here and the surrounding area."

"You have the knife. What else are we supposed to look for?"

"I don't know… but we will know when we find it. Just search around the trees, in the bushes, everywhere, for anything that looks out of place or shouldn't be here."

"Oh good, that should be easy then," I quipped, with a heavy dose of sarcasm for good measure.

After marching back to the spot where I had sat for several hours over the last couple of nights, I used my hand to flail the bushes that had shielded me from view from the house. No surprises; nothing erupted from the foliage to greet me. Best I stop sulking and put more serious effort into finding whatever I'm looking for, I told myself. I started working outwards in concentric circles from where I had sat.

The exercise yielded no results. After a few minutes, I was fast losing interest – and belief – in what we were doing. I was just about to announce I had done as much as I intended and was going home when I heard Ben grunt.

"What? What's happened?" I demanded as I rushed to him. But I was stopped dead in my tracks by what I saw.

He held a finger to his lips in the universal warning not to speak. Picking my way as silently as possible to stand beside him, I raised my eyebrows in unspoken question. Ben stood at the base of what was left of a big old dead tree. Without a word, he pointed up the trunk to a hole. It was the sort of hole in a dead tree that a possum or parrot might call home. Then, dragging me by the arm around to the side of the trunk, he again directed me to look up.

Despite my best effort not to, I gasped. From my new position, I could see the sun glinting off something shiny in that hole in the trunk. Stunned by what I saw, I stood there staring upward as Ben snapped several photos with his phone. Then he moved closer to whisper in my ear.

"Without making too much fuss, leave here and race after Emily and her staff. Bring them, and that chainsaw they carry around with them, back here as quickly as possible."

'As quickly as possible' took about ten minutes for everyone to be in place and with the chainsaw at the ready. Ben and I moved back a safe distance as Emily's hefty staff member went to work with the saw. He was no stranger to a chainsaw and soon had a scarf cut in the trunk at a point about a metre below the hole. Ben's instructions were not to fell the tree at this time, but to come back after lunch and drop the top part of the trunk then. He would arrange for someone from his Tech team to return with them to make sure it was safe to cut through the trunk without the risk of being electrocuted or something similar.

While the rest of us stood watching the chainsaw in action, Ben had moved away and was working his phone. Then, with nothing more to be done with the tree until after lunch, we all picked up our gear and headed for our vehicles. Ben called me back.

"I've arranged for a couple of officers to guard the tree until we return, but I'm not leaving until they are in position. If you are in a hurry to leave, maybe you can ride back to town with Emily and her blokes."

"After we finished here, I thought we were going to talk to Stan, the security guard. I was hoping to tag along for that."

"Change of plan; I'll wait until the change of shift to talk to Brett instead. But, as soon as my officers are in position, I'll return to my office until after lunch." I decided to try cadging a ride back to town with Emily and jogged off across the park to catch up to her.

As she dropped me off across the street from my building, she leaned close and murmured, "I'll let you know if we find anything interesting." She drove away, and I waited for a long line of traffic to pass before crossing the street to my office. As I watched the cars stream past, Janine called me.

"Sonny, have I called at a bad time?"

"No. At the moment, I'm standing on the pavement waiting to cross the street to my office." I would have to be deaf not to hear the tension in her voice. "Has something happened?"

"Uhmm… yeah, I think so. Is it possible for me to see you sometime today?"

"Come to my office as soon as you can get away. I promise I will be there by the time you arrive."

That gave some added impetus to my efforts to cross the street, and a car holding up traffic while making a hash of trying to reverse into a parking spot a little further along from me was the break I needed. Back in my office, my priority was to fill the coffee machine. By the sound of Janine, she would be in need of a coffee, and I certainly was due another one.

Then I booted up my computer so I at least looked as though I was still in business. Janine arrived about five minutes later… and needed a coffee. Thank you, God, I thought as I returned to my kitchenette. I didn't think I could survive a long session with Janine without more caffeine to keep me awake and functioning.

We both indulged in a few sips of the steaming brew before I judged it appropriate to start asking questions.

"Janine, your call concerned me. I heard the tension in your voice, and now I can see how uptight you are. Tell me what has happened." She looked uncertain and didn't answer straight away, so I encouraged her. "Has your husband returned, or have you heard from him, or something about him?"

"Eh? Oh, no, he hasn't come back, and I'm not sure I want him to anymore. But something else's happened, and it scares me. The last time we spoke, I mentioned we were doing a financial audit as you had suggested, and had already identified anomalies. As you probably appreciate, my company has a number of people working in its financial department.

A key member, although not the chief financial officer, was undertaking the audit. That is his job, overseeing all the processes and procedures. He was the only person, other than myself, who knew about the audit – or so I thought."

"Good move; it's best not to advertise such operations. Has he uncovered something more disturbing than the anomalies you mentioned previously? And what do you mean by *or so you thought*?"

"I don't know… And I fear I'm never going to know. Griffin appears to have disappeared without a word to anyone beforehand – even to me."

"This is a serious situation if your assumption is correct. It would be helpful if you outlined what you know of Griffin's activities leading up to his possible disappearance."

"There's only so much I can tell you. The last time we spoke was just after I told you about the audit and the anomalies he had identified. He called me at home that night to tell me he had found something serious and wanted a meeting first thing next morning. He suggested we didn't meet in his office. He would come to mine instead. I agreed and expected him at nine o'clock.

When he didn't arrive on time, I wasn't too concerned. Things come up unexpectedly. He was busy. I was busy and didn't notice time slipping by until it was after ten o'clock, and there was still no sign of him. I called his personal phone. When he didn't answer, I called his office number, with the same result. His assistant – well, she is more of a secretary – is on leave. So, as almost a last resort, I called the main financial department number and spoke to the receptionist. She told me Griffin hadn't come in, and she didn't think anyone knew when he would be back."

"Do you have his home address, and does he have a landline at home?"

"Off the top of my head, I don't know that information, but it should be on his personnel file. If you need the information now, I could ask my secretary to look it up."

"Please do that. We need to be sure he is okay before we go any further."

While trying to look engrossed in the documents in Janine's file, I kept my ears tuned to the conversation happening on the other side of my desk. I heard Janine give her secretary an overview of what she was to do. Then, after a brief pause, Janine gave her secretary some sort of code that I assumed was Janine's personal code to access staff personnel records. I pushed a notebook and pen across the desk for her to record the details she was given. I stayed tuned to the one-sided conversation on the other side of my desk.

"Okay, so now you're in, search for Griffin Davidson's file … Good, now, what's his residential address? … Does it have a landline number for that address? … How does it look wrong? … Okay, don't worry about it. Thanks, that's all for now, so you can log out now. Uhmm, I don't know, but I might be a while longer. Is there anything urgent requiring my attention?...Okay, good. If anything does come up, call me."

Her call ended, Janine slid my notebook and pen back across the desk. "That's his address and landline number, but my secretary thinks the number doesn't look right. She doesn't know why she thinks that's the case, but says it just doesn't look right to her."

"Only one way to find out. Let's try it and see what happens." A mechanical voice told me I had dialled an incorrect or incomplete number and I should hang up and try again. "Top marks to your secretary for her intuition," I quipped as I ended the call. "Janine, what do you know about Griffin Davidson, apart from what's just come out of his personnel file?"

"Nothing much… what sort of information are you wanting?"

"How long has he been with you? How old is he? What does he do outside of office hours? Is he married? What was he doing before you employed him? You know, any of that sort of personal information might be helpful. For instance, if he belongs to any clubs or organisations, they might be able to tell us more about him or what went on in his life."

"Right… well, he started with me about three years ago and came highly recommended. Prior to that, he held a couple of high profile positions, the last being a forensic auditor working with the Victorian Police Service. He is 49… ah, no, he turned 50 about three weeks ago. They had a cake and drinks in the office after work to celebrate it. I know his CV says he is single, and employers are not allowed to ask for more information than is required to be sure his salary is taxed at the right rate.

He seems married to his work. I doubt he has a life away from the office, and I doubt any of the Finance Department would know about his private life. In the workplace, he is *the invisible man*, and that's the way it is supposed to be for that position. You can't have someone who audits everything that happens in the department becoming too friendly with the people he is auditing."

"In that case, how did the others in that department know it was his birthday? If he is such a private person, he wouldn't have announced it." She only shrugged, but I could see her mind was working flat out on the question.

"I'm sorry, but I don't pry into my staff's private lives. Maybe I should take more notice in future. Do you think something has happened to Griffin? I mean, something bad?" She attempted to joke about it. "I'll be developing a reputation if this keeps up. Losing a husband is careless, but losing someone else as well suggests something more sinister."

The clock on my wall told me Ben would soon be wanting to talk to Brett once he came on duty at midday. I moved to wind-up the meeting with Janine before remembering something I wanted to ask her.

"Janine, there is something I wanted to ask you. It's not about Blake or Griffin. It's about you.

Have you changed anything in your normal routine in the last few weeks?" The puzzled look on her face told me to be more precise. "I mean, have you changed anything, like your brand of coffee, your toothpaste or shampoo, or even your laundry detergent?"

"No… Oh, hang on a minute. Toothpaste… yes, I've changed the toothpaste I was using. I developed a sensitive tooth, one of those that reacts to hot and cold stuff. So, I bought a tube of toothpaste for sensitive teeth and have been using that for about a week. My tooth is okay now, so I'm about to revert to my usual brand. That special stuff is so expensive. I'll put what's left in a drawer until the next time I need it.

Sonny, I'm sorry, but I don't understand your interest in my toothpaste. Are you trying to tell me something about my teeth?"

"There's nothing wrong with your teeth, but please keep using that toothpaste for sensitive teeth for a bit longer. I assume you were part of the way through a tube of your usual brand before your tooth played up?" She nodded but still looked puzzled. "Do you keep a spare tube of your usual brand in the cupboard so you're not left short when your current tube runs out?" More nodding. "Good. Please collect the partially used tube of your usual toothpaste and the spare tube and drop them into me as soon as possible. In the meantime, keep using the sensitive toothpaste until I tell you otherwise. Can you do that?"

"If it's important, I can fetch them now. My unit on Richmond Street is only a couple of blocks away. But what's so important about my toothpaste?"

"I don't know yet if there is anything important about it, but I want to be sure."

Though still confused, she left and returned about ten minutes later with the tubes of toothpaste. For a moment, she looked as though she would settle in again. Short of being rude, I wasn't sure how to see her on her way before Ben called to say he was leaving for the estate, and I needed to be ready to go with him. Janine's phone solved the dilemma. Her secretary called about something requiring Janine's presence at work. After apologising, she made a hasty departure. I breathed a sigh of relief and wondered whether I had time to duck downstairs to find something for lunch before Ben called.

It wasn't to be, but it wasn't a problem. Ben called while I was still tossing up whether to go in search of food or go without.

"Are you coming to the Thomlinson Estate with me?" Another inane question… Of course, I was going with him. "Right; pick up something for lunch for both of us, and I'll collect you from your carpark in about fifteen or twenty minutes."

Although curious about when we would have time to eat the chicken and salad rolls I bought, I was waiting in the carpark behind my building when he arrived about fifteen minutes later. As I scrambled into the passenger's seat, I waved the bag containing our lunch at him.

"When and where were you planning to eat these?" I asked. I felt peckish and hoped his plan involved eating lunch in the next few minutes.

"Hmm… depends on how long we are tied up with Brett, but it won't be until after we leave Thomlinson Estate. How's your day been since this morning? Anything exciting happening in your world?"

"Funny you should ask… I think we might have a problem. I mean, *another* problem." His look didn't encourage me to share my latest information, but share I must, so I plunged into the story of Griffin Davidson's disappearance.

"Janine Thomlinson has become more than careless. Losing people is becoming a habit for her, first her husband, then her financial guru. What's next?"

"I'd prefer it wasn't her life." My remark had a sobering effect. Any trace of sarcasm disappeared, and his tone became all 'business' again.

"So, at this stage, we don't know if this Griffin What's-His-Name has disappeared or he simply decided to take a day off work. He could be lolling by the pool, in bed with a cold – or a wild woman…."

"…Or dead, or lying seriously injured somewhere."

"Right, but let's leave this Griffin bloke until after we speak to Brett. Anyway, who names their kid Griffin?

"The Welsh…? Just as a matter of interest, what is it we are keen to speak to Brett about?"

"Until we found that tree this morning, I thought we were going to ask him about Stan and the other security guard who has been off on sick leave for some time. Now, I think we have much more to ask Brett about, like who receives images from that camera in the tree in the park. I doubt it is part of the Thomlinson Estate security system and, therefore, its feed won't be to the control centre monitors."

"No; I imagine it has a direct feed to a mobile phone somewhere, or a laptop or tablet. That begs the question: whose device and where?"

"In that travelling trunk thing you insist on calling 'your bag', do you have those images you took of Stan waiting on the front doorstep for something?"

"Yes. I downloaded copies to my computer, but the images are still on the camera, and the camera is in my bag. Do you plan to show them to Brett? Is that wise? Might it place him in a difficult – dangerous – position?"

"Brett might be working as a security guard while on special training release, but he is still a copper, and I have the right to utilise him in my investigation. He is a bright lad and keen to get ahead in the Service. I think you'll find he is more than willing to become involved."

As we turned onto the road running past the Estate, Ben called Brett. Miraculously, the wrought iron gates swung open, and we drove through them. Then Ben made a second call before climbing out of the vehicle. He explained the call at about the same time as I heard a chainsaw somewhere come to life.

"That tree in the park, the one with the camera, is about to come down. I decided to wait until after Stan went home after his shift."

"The camera must get power from somewhere. Is the bloke on the chainsaw going to be safe cutting through that tree trunk?"

"Yep, it's disconnected and safe for the surgery to go ahead."

We were met at the front door and shown inside. After securing the door behind us, Brett led us to the control centre. I saw Ben pull out his phone and fiddle with it. His ringtone tune started playing. He increased it to full volume as he leaned in closer to speak to Brett. Thanks to the racket from Ben's phone, I had to strain to pick up any of what he said to Brett.

Ben told me later that he had asked if the control room was monitored and if anyone was likely to record or listen to their discussions. I had seen Brett shake his head in response to Ben's questions. But then I saw doubt creep across his features. He looked apologetic. I moved closer to hear his comment.

"Sir, I can't confirm that. While I don't think so, I don't know." Ben nodded and silenced his phone.

With conversation no longer blanketed by his phone, Ben employed almost comic mime to pose his next question: what about the rooms upstairs? Brett shrugged and shook his head. Ben took out his notebook and scribbled a message before shoving it in front of Brett, who nodded and gestured for us to follow him.

Chapter 19

We were crammed into the minuscule handbasin area of an upstairs bathroom. Brett again looked apologetic – and embarrassed.

"Sorry about this, Sir, but this toilet area is the only place I'm reasonably sure isn't monitored or bugged. Actually, I'm pleased you're here, Sir. I was going to try to see you tomorrow morning but was concerned about wasting your time."

Ben assured him he would not be wasting anyone's time if he wanted to discuss a case under investigation. Brett considered that before launching into what he wanted to tell us.

"There's another ghost on the tapes. It probably was done by the same person who interfered with the recording the last time. Whoever it was still don't know how to do it properly."

"Was this on last night's tape?" Ben asked while keeping his eyes on me.

"Not last night; no, it was the tape from the night before. I had decided I would check every day's tape for anomalies. I wasn't looking for anything in particular, just checking there was nothing out of the ordinary on them."

"Good move," Ben said. "And this anomaly – this ghost – you found, at what time of the night did it appear?"

Brett gave him the approximate time of the morning the anomaly appeared on the tape. Ben turned and gave me a hard, meaningful look. No words were needed. I had already hauled up my bag and dumped it beside the handbasin. Moments later, I opened the gallery of images on my camera and located the shots from the night before last. The images spooled past until I stopped it at the point when Stan, or whoever it was, came out onto the top step.

Moving over to stand close to Brett, I held the camera up in front of him so he could see each image as I slowly advanced the camera roll.

"I think you might find the next few images interesting, Brett," I told him as he peered at the figure standing outside the front door. I drew his attention to the time and date stamp. "Do you recognise that person? At that time of the morning, and given your current roster, the guard on duty should have been Stan. But, as neither Ben nor I have met Stan, we don't know what he looks like."

"Ye-e-s, it might be Stan."

"What do you mean by 'might be'?" Ben demanded. Is it or isn't it Stan?"

"Well, yes, it does look like Stan, but I would need to see the image on a bigger screen before I would swear to it."

"Okay… Let's rethink the question," Ben suggested. "If it is not Stan in that image, who else could it be? Was anyone else supposed to be on duty that night? Someone else wearing a security guard's uniform?"

"Perhaps if I advance the images, there might be a clearer shot of the figure that would allow a more positive identification," I suggested. Brett shrugged without appearing too negative about my suggestion.

The images spooled by… a figure on the top step … a figure going down the stairs … a figure standing on the path at the bottom of the stairs … a figure pacing up and back along a length of the path. At that point, I stopped the spooling.

"Any good, Brett?" I asked. "Did any of those shots help with a positive identification?"

"Would I swear to it in court? No. But, yes, it probably is Stan. I don't understand what he is doing. He is not supposed to be outside for any reason, and … well … it looks as though he is waiting for something. Given different circumstances, you might think he was waiting for someone to collect him, or maybe the milkman with today's delivery, or even a teenage son's late return after a night out."

So, you think it looks as though he is waiting for something?" Ben checked. Brett nodded. "Is it possible he was waiting for something to do with this place? Delivery of a parcel perhaps, or maybe he forgot his crib, and his wife was bringing him a meal… anything at all?"

"None of that washes with me," Brett replied. "We are not allowed to go outside while on shift. That's it, no exceptions… and that includes starving because you forgot your lunch box. Are there more images? Did whatever he was waiting for show up?"

"Almost… maybe…." I answered. "Have a look at the next few images and tell me what you think."

Moving the images forward for him frame-by-frame, I paused briefly on each one to allow him to examine it before moving on to the next one. They were the images of the headlights at the gates, and there weren't many of them. After allowing him to examine the last photos, I lowered the camera.

"Is that it? What happened after that? Did the vehicle come onto the estate, or did Stan go to deal with it in some way?"

"So, that is Stan?" Ben queried.

"Yeah, that's Stan … and that's who I relieved when I came on duty at midday. Why do the images stop at that point? What happened after that could be important to your investigation."

"There are no further images because nothing happened to record." I brought up the last of the images again to show him. "See… in this shot, the headlights have started to swing away from the gates. The vehicle just turned around a drove off. It wasn't possible to see, or even hear it clearly, from where these photos were taken."

Brett had trouble comprehending what he had seen and, after a moment, wanted to know more to help understand it. "So these images were from the night before last…," he murmured more to himself than me as he checked the time and date of the image on the screen, "but then last night was a repeat performance. Have I got that right?"

"Not quite," I told him. "Last night, Stan came out onto the top step again and paced about as though he was waiting for something. But nothing happened last night – no headlights, nothing."

Ben, who had been silent while Brett examined the images, elected to join the conversation again.

"You said you discovered a ghost on the recording from the night before last," Brett nodded his confirmation, and Ben continued. "Did anything similar appear on last night's tapes?" Brett looked sheepish and hesitated a moment before replying.

"Argh, I haven't checked last night's recordings yet. I was about to do that when you called to say you were on your way here. I could check them now while you watch if you like." Ben did 'like,' and we all traipsed back to the control centre, where Brett did something technical to load last night's recordings onto a stand-alone machine on another bench. He played the recording at a slower than normal speed for some time before slowing it down even further.

"Yeah, there… see that blur? That's the same as on the recording from the previous night, and it is at almost the same time as the previous night too."

While the recording was paused with the ghostly image filling the screen, I checked my shots of Stan pacing the top step last night. The time on my photos matched the time when Brett's ghost appeared on the recording. I showed Ben the correlation.

"Sonny, your camera continued taking shots until you knocked it over. Was Stan still outside on the last of your images?" I ran my images through to the end and studied the final shot of the house before replying.

"No, I don't think so. Look, I'll show you what happens." I rewound a few images before moving them forward again, frame-by-frame. "See, here he is waiting for something. Then he appears to be alerted by something he hears or sees. Whatever happened made him stand still for a moment before turning and rushing back inside. My last shot before the camera fell over is of the front door starting to close behind him."

Until he spoke, I hadn't been aware of Brett peering over my other shoulder as I ran the images through for Ben.

"Hold it there for a moment, please," Brett said as he rushed back to his recording from last night. "What was the time of that last shot you took?" I read out the time shown on the image. "Okay, a couple of minutes for him to rush back here to the control centre and carefully reset the recording and… that's about the time of the first image after the ghost."

"So, it looks as though Stan is playing games with the recordings from at least one of the estate's cameras," Ben said. "Do we know which camera's recording is being tampered with, and was it the same camera on both nights?"

Brett confirmed it was the same camera. The one monitoring the area from the front door to the gates.

"And I don't suppose you know of any reasonable explanation for why he might be playing silly buggers with the recordings?" Ben added. Brett looked embarrassed and simply shook his head. A thought rattling around in the back of my mind for a couple of days finally came to the fore.

"If I remember correctly, earlier, you mentioned a third security guard who is off on sickness leave. As a result, you and Stan are doing twelve-hour shifts to cover his absence. Is there any word on when that third guard might return?"

"Not yet; I queried our boss about it yesterday. It seems the chap's medical certificate is still good for another week. Who knows what happens after that? Anyway, it looks as though Stan and I will be doing long shifts for a while longer yet.

Actually, I was hoping he might be back by the end of this week. I would like him to be back soon in case the other security firm I applied to wants me to start with them for the rest of my time on release-from-duties training. This place is okay, but it doesn't give you much insight into the life of a security guard. Nothing ever happens here, and it's a bit monotonous and boring. If I'm to learn about what goes on in the security industry, I need to experience it."

"You might have to amend that statement," Ben suggested. "You've had a bit of a taste of what can happen, and there is still plenty more going on that we need to uncover. I would prefer you remained here for at least a bit longer. We need someone on the inside to help sort out this case.

But I can understand how you would want to accept a different position if one is offered. I can't insist you remain here, but I would prefer it. Ultimately, what you do is your decision."

"Thanks, Sir. I do now appreciate how this job might become a lot more interesting – and I haven't been offered another position yet."

Ben appeared deep in thought for a moment before cocking his head to one side and nodding a couple of times. I recognised the signs and knew he was about to throw in something from left field. He gave Brett a hard look before airing his thoughts.

"Have you noticed anything different? In this control centre, I mean?" Anything at all, even a new piece of equipment, maybe?"

"No-o, but I'm not sure how anything new or different might have been installed. Perhaps, if I knew what you had in mind, I might at least be able to look for it."

"True… but the problem is, I'm not sure what it might look like. We've come across a camera over there in the park. I don't know where it feeds to, but I suspect it was meant to cover an area outside the fence and some portion of this estate's grounds. Now, that camera might be part of the estate's security system, and its recordings could feed into this control room… but I don't think so. Are you aware of any cameras outside the estate's perimeter?"

"Outside…? No, and I don't know that such a thing would be legal anyway. As you can see, there are plenty of monitors in here. But, unless you were familiar with the layout of the house and its surroundings, you wouldn't know from which camera any of the images were coming."

"Damn, that doesn't help much. I suppose I'll have to park that idea for the moment." Ben scribbled a note in his notebook, no doubt to remind him to revisit the idea in the future.

"But, there is a way to find out a bit more about the camera feeds," Brett added almost as an afterthought. "Not long after I started working here, I had trouble with one of the cameras one night and decided to try a bit of personal troubleshooting. It wasn't what I was looking for at the time, but I came across a file relating to the cameras. As it wasn't what I needed, I didn't look at it too closely, so I'm not sure exactly what details it contains.

If you like, I could try to find the file again, but I can't guarantee it will be much use to you."

Of course, Ben wanted the file found, and about five minutes later, Brett let out a yelp.

"Yep… this is it. This is the file I was looking for. Oh, it might be more useful than I thought." Brett moved the file across to a separate big screen so we could see it. Ben moved across to stand beside Brett to look at the screen. Between them, they almost blocked the view. I was reduced to trying to look over their shoulders to see anything on the monitor.

It took me a while to work out what I was looking at, and my first impression was that it wasn't helpful. Ben seemed to have the same problem and asked Brett to explain it. Brett took a while to respond.

"This is a section of the system's main program. It lists all the cameras and gives a rough indication of the area covered by each one." He used the camera covering the area outside the front door as an example before explaining what was on the screen. "Okay. Then this next piece of information against each camera tells us which monitor its images feed to here in the control centre." Again, he used the camera covering the front door area to show us how its images were fed to the third monitor in the row along the far wall.

"Right…" Ben said as he checked the cameras against the monitors. "Hang on, that can't be right," he exclaimed. "There are more cameras listed here than there are monitors over there. How does that come about?"

"What?" Brett hissed and returned to the list of cameras. "You're right. There's an extra camera listed on the program, but its information is incomplete. See… It doesn't say what area it covers or to which monitor it feeds images." Ben and I craned our necks in closer for a better view. While I could see what Brett had explained, I still wasn't sure what it told us. Before I could question Brett further, he had the cursor on the move again.

He slid the cursor further down the list of cameras to bring up the last part of the list that had been hidden. "Jesus! There's another one. See this one at the end of the list… its entry doesn't tell us any more than that it exists somewhere. I'm sorry, Sir, but I don't know anything about those two cameras or why they are listed."

Silence filled the control room for a heartbeat or two as we considered Brett's comments, but my mind was running at full tilt in its own chosen direction. I broke the silence with a question – and earned myself a scowl from Ben.

"Brett, could that camera we found out there in the park be one of the two apparent 'rogue' cameras on that list? I know there's precious little information to go by, but could it be one of those two?" Brett shrugged, but I continued. "An alternative explanation just occurred to me, but you probably won't be able to answer that either."

"You're right. I probably won't be much help, but tell me what you're thinking."

"What if the original security system plan included two extra cameras, but they were never installed for whatever reason? Perhaps provision for them was left on the system in case, at some time in the future, the security coverage of the estate needed to be expanded."

"Either of those explanations is a possibility, I suppose," Brett admitted, but didn't seem reassured.

"I'm more inclined to lean towards your first possibility: two rogue cameras somewhere," Ben stated. Brett nodded as if to signify it was his preferred option as well.

The two men went into a huddle to discuss the situation in 'police speak', which I found mostly unintelligible. Besides, my mind was off and running in a direction that didn't appear to bear any relation to the two men's topic. At last, my mind sorted itself out sufficiently for me to realise I hadn't yet asked Brett about something that puzzled me.

"Gentlemen, while I acknowledge your discussions are important and of the highest order, I do have a question regarding something bothering me since about two nights ago. Brett, out where we found the hidden camera, there appear to be two fence lines with a narrow corridor of almost bare earth between them. Do you know what that is all about?"

"Yeah, sort of… It only came up in conversation once, so I don't know much about it or how accurate my information is. As I understand it, when the original security system was installed, the fence between the park and the estate was a constant source of alarms. That was in the early days before the system was upgraded to include the cameras and other bits and pieces.

There had been a couple of years of drought. The park was almost bare of grass, while the estate remained lush and green thanks to irrigation. The wallabies inhabiting the park were hungry and attacked the perimeter fence, trying to access the grass on this side. Somebody's solution to the problem was erecting a second fence outside the main fence, with a gap left between the two fences. That second fence is an electric fence, but different from the ones you see around stock paddocks.

It looks like an ordinary security fence, but it is electrified. And the area between to two fences has been kept clear of all vegetation ever since to deter the wildlife. All I can say is, it seems to work."

"Sonny, is this likely to be relevant in any way to the problem at hand?" Ben growled. He was not happy I had moved the conversation away from the cameras – but I hadn't, not really.

"Perhaps, but I'm not sure. Ever since we found that camera in the dead tree out there, I've wondered about its power source. If it relied on batteries, someone routinely would need to change the batteries. It doesn't seem like an effective way of doing things, but we didn't find any solar panels that might be powering the camera."

"Are you suggesting the camera might be tapping into the electric fence's power somehow?" Brett asked.

"Well, yes, I did wonder if that might be a possibility, but I admit I don't know enough about such things to judge its likelihood."

Ben pulled his phone out. A number was dialling as he walked out of the control centre to make the call. After a short conversation, he returned a couple of minutes later.

"We should go. Oh, before we do, I have one last question for you, Brett. Does the name Griffin Davidson mean anything to you? Ring any bells at all?"

"Can't say I've ever come across it before. Is there a reason I might know the name?"

"Probably not, but I thought there might have been a possibility he visited here at some time."

"Not that I'm aware of. But, if he accompanied Miss Thomlinson or Mr Carter to the estate, the guard on duty wouldn't be told his name. He would probably appear nameless in the logbook and simply referred to as 'and guest'. Is there something about him I should know in case he does appear?"

"You shouldn't worry about it. He's disappeared… apparently."

"Along with Miss Thomlinson's husband…?" Brett asked, cocking his head to one side.

"Yeah, I know. Becoming careless, isn't she? At this rate, maybe we should be worrying about who is next to disappear." Ben replied.

"Ah, well, I think I can answer that: ME. I think that was the intention last night – that I should disappear too," I said

"But not quite the same, I don't think. The other two disappeared without a trace – so far. If they had succeeded last night, it would have been messy and quite a different situation."

Somehow, Ben's comment didn't make me feel any happier. I'm beginning to think this mob —whoever they are – has never heard of the sanctity of life. Perhaps my Glock will be a constant companion for the next little while. But there was little time to dwell on any of that. Ben was on the move. We were leaving the estate, and he appeared to be in a hurry.

As we strode across to Ben's car after Brett let us out, I dared to ask my question.

"Ben, I appreciate you are in a hurry, but where are we going?"

"We're going to have a chat with the Tech boys who are dealing with that rogue camera."

"Hell! Are they aware it could be dangerous if it's fed with electricity from that fence?"

"Yep, they were well aware of that before I called to warn them about it. So, instead of just hacking the tree down, as was the original plan, they removed the camera without damaging its connection to its power supply. I'm hoping that when we talk to them, they'll know more about its operation."

"Should we assume a similar situation applies to that second rogue camera we saw on the list and that it is also located somewhere outside the estate's perimeter fence?"

"It's possible, but we won't waste time looking for it. I'll schedule some of the Tech team and another couple of officers to comb the area. I feel that another camera might be focused on an area that captures anyone or anything approaching those wrought iron gates.

We will leave others to deal with that while we check out our missing Mr Davidson."

I stayed quietly in the background while Ben discussed the camera they had retrieved with the Tech team, and he alerted them to the possibility of a second camera somewhere close by. Then we were on our way to the address Janine gave me for Griff Davidson.

Chapter 20

Surprise, surprise; no one answered the door at Griff Davidson's apartment. I had hoped a cleaning lady or a housekeeper would be there, but I never expected Mr Davidson to be. I didn't believe he was ill or simply skiving off for a few days of R&R.

Ben played something resembling a Wagner classic on the doorbell without any more success than the first time he tried it. Then, just for good measure, he thumped on the door several times.

"Oi, you… what the hell do you think you're doing?" an irate woman from another apartment demanded. "The residents of this building are entitled to peace and quiet. We don't appreciate people who come here carrying on like hooligans. Leave before I call the police."

"It's your lucky day. They're already here. I am the police," Ben, in civvies instead of uniform today, growled and waved his badge at her. The woman inched back towards her still open door.

"Wait there, please. You might be able to help with our inquiry. We are keen to talk to your neighbour."

"Good luck with that; I don't think he's home. He might have gone away for a few days."

"Why do you think that? Did he say something to suggest he was going away?"

"Say something…! He never speaks to anyone in this building. He probably thinks he's too good for the likes of us. But I think he's away. His phone's been ringing on and off since yesterday. You'd think it would be flat by now. There's nothing more I can tell you. He keeps to himself, doesn't talk to anyone, and seems to lead a pretty solitary life."

Ben asked about Davidson's car. The woman told him its colour and where to find it in the building's basement car park.

As soon as Ben thanked her for her help, the woman scuttled back into her apartment and slammed the door. He tried the doorbell of apartment 9 again and received the same response as earlier.

"I'll go down to see if his car is still here." Then with his tongue firmly planted in his cheek, Ben added, "Then I'll come back to see if he was kind enough to leave his door unlocked."

To anyone else, it might have sounded like a strange comment. But, to me, it sounded like an invitation to scratch around in my bag for my set of 'special tools'. So I did. After a few moments of deft manoeuvring of said tools, Griff Davidson's door was indeed unlocked when Ben returned.

"The right coloured car is in the correct parking bay to be Mr Davidson's, but I've asked the precinct to run a registration check to be sure. Now, let's have a look at this door… Oh, how kind. He's left it unlocked for us."

Pushing the door wide open, Ben took a couple of strides inside, announcing as he did so that the police were about to enter. No response to his announcement, so he continued into the apartment while announcing several more times that it was the police who were roaming around in there. I followed him in and didn't have to go too far inside to know something unpleasant happened here. Evidence of a major brawl was everywhere through the open plan living area and along to the bedroom. But the bedroom presented a more alarming picture.

It was obvious this was where the trouble had begun, and the blood on the bedclothes told its own story. I had barely entered the bedroom when Ben stopped me.

"Don't come any further, and don't touch anything. Pick your way carefully to the door and wait outside. I need detectives and the forensic team here immediately. It's best we don't mess up the evidence by traipsing around any more than we already have. As I made my way out of the apartment, I heard Ben on the phone organising for various officers to work the potential crime scene.

My instructions to wait for him to join me had given me a chance to think about what evidence might be available to us apart from whatever was found in the apartment. I shared my thoughts.

"Whoever is responsible for the chaos inside is probably also responsible for the resident's disappearance. They would have needed a vehicle to cart him away, regardless of whether he was dead or alive at that point, and they would have needed it to be somewhere close and inconspicuous. Are there any spare parking bays downstairs?"

"Some bays are empty, but that's likely because the owners have taken their vehicles to work. All bays look as though they're in current use. Before you ask, yes, I did check for CCTV cameras. One on the front of the building monitors the building's driveway and that small parking area out front."

"Hmm… Might give us something useful if we knew where to locate the recordings," I murmured. "Do you think your new friend, the vocal neighbour, might know where to find those recordings?"

"I was hoping not to go another round with her but, now I have established my credentials, maybe she'll be a little more friendly this time." Ben turned on his heel and marched up to the neighbour's door. She opened the door almost the moment he rang the bell.

While Ben had a brief conversation with the neighbour, I remained outside Davidson's door. I guessed we were about to leave the apartment, as there was nothing more we could do there, but I was concerned about leaving it unlocked. As soon as Ben wandered back to me, I aired my concerns.

"The place being unlocked is not a problem. My officers will be here in a few moments, and they will spend quite some time going over the place. They'll lock the doors from the inside when they leave and stick crime scene tape across the entrance. As soon as they arrive and they make a start, we will hunt down the footage from that CCTV camera out front."

Instead of waiting in the hallway outside the apartment, we went down to street level to wait for the officers. As Ben predicted, they arrived within minutes. Not wanting to intrude, when they came, I wandered away and found myself in the basement carpark. Working on an assumption the numbers on each parking bay reflected the numbers of the apartment to which they were allocated, it wasn't difficult to locate Griff Davidson's vehicle.

Although I walked all around and peered inside, I found nothing noteworthy about the vehicle. Ben was still talking to the officers, so I spent the next minute or so exploring the car parking area. As I was about to walk back outside, something made me stop and look up. I caught my breath. After a hard look at the object, I rushed out. Ben had finished with his officers, and they were on their way upstairs. Ignoring any proper protocol, I called out.

"Ben, come here, please. There is something you should see." I waited at the entrance to the carpark for him to join me.

He did not look pleased, but I ignored it. I pointed upwards at the small round object high above the entrance doorway, almost unnoticeable amongst the cable tray and pipework decorating the underside of the floor above us.

"Oh, another camera… Now that could be useful. It looks as though it monitors all the carpark, including the area with the stairs and the lift for accessing the upper floors.

Even if all the parking bays were occupied, and our unwelcome visitors only nosed their vehicle partially into this area, the camera should have captured whatever they did. That lift allowed them to bring their victim, relatively unseen, from his apartment to their waiting transport down here."

"So, where do we obtain the footage from those two cameras?" I asked as we walked to his car.

"Dunno… all we can do is ask the mob who manage the building about their security firm and where we might access those tapes."

My phone interrupted further conversation. It was my Tasmanian colleague, James Rothwell. I didn't want to talk to him with Ben around. Citing being out of my office, I suggested I call him back in about half an hour. Ben doubted we would obtain copies of the recordings we wanted today and suggested he drop me back at his place to collect my car. About fifteen minutes later, I drove into the parking area behind my building. After visiting the bakery, I was upstairs in my office a few minutes later.

Coffee and cake were a priority before returning James Rothwell's call. He sounded excited. My anticipation level ratcheted up a couple of notches.

"While I still don't know the whole story, I think I am hot on the trail of your man – and I no longer feel inclined to call him Blake Carter. I've discovered his real name is Roy Gilham, and what a chequered life he has led, not all of it of his own making, though. After a rough start, his life doesn't appear to improve much."

"…Until he landed on his feet here as Blake Carter," I added with a heavy dose of sarcasm.

Nothing more came out of our conversation. One of his clients dropped in unexpectedly, and he had an appointment at the top of the next hour. We left it for him to call me again in the next day or so when he was free and had more to share with me.

With nothing else needing attention, I returned to the recordings from the park on the night Janine was attacked. Without a particular purpose in mind, I skipped through to the first sighting of the motorbike at the park's double gates before advancing the recording frame-by-frame and pausing it at each subsequent appearance of the bike.

Nothing new was found in the images. I was in danger of crashing face-first onto my desk. A combination of lack of sleep and nothing new on the recordings had me struggling to keep my eyes open. This is ridiculous, I told myself. I'm not achieving anything, so why don't I just go home? A nap is the most appealing thing I can think of right now. That was until my phone intruded.

"Sonny, are you free, and will you be in your office for a bit longer?" Emily asked.

"Well, I was going to go home, but I'm happy to stay here."

"No. Go home. That might be even better. I'll see you there in about half an hour."

So much for the nap I was longing for, I grumbled to my empty office as I gathered up everything to take home with me and made my way down to my car. My departure missed the afternoon peak traffic and gave me a clear run all the way home.

Emily arrived about ten minutes after I had washed my face with cold water to wake myself up a bit. I was intrigued. Why was she so keen to see me right now? It meant she left work earlier than usual. And why did she think discussing whatever it was at home was better than in my city office? It didn't take long to find out.

"I have the results of the tests on those tubes of toothpaste you gave me. You did the right thing by telling her to keep using the new tube of sensitive paste. All the tubes you gave me have been contaminated." She mentioned the drug by its scientific name, which meant nothing to me until she described its likely effects.

"Christ, that's exactly what was happening. Janine wasn't with-it at all. She was vague and indecisive, halfway to 'zombie land' almost. If she had used this toothpaste, say, twice a day for a few weeks, would it have an increased cumulative effect? And, if she stopped using it, how long before the effect might start to wear off?"

"That depends on a number of things, including the person's physiology. But, to answer your questions, yes, significant usage would result in a somewhat more profound effect – but only up to a certain point. The dosage received with the use you suggested is not significant. It would have taken usage over an extended period to produce a gradual change in the victim.

On the other hand, once the regular dosage stopped, the effects would start to wear off noticeably after two or three days."

"Okay. So how were the tubes of toothpaste being doctored? How could the contents be contaminated without any visible sign on the outside of the tube?"

"As soon as I flipped the cap on the unused tube, a quick look told me how. I suspect a hypodermic fitted with a very long, quite thick needle was used. The needle was inserted in the centre of the top of the paste and pushed through to almost the bottom of the tube. Then as the needle was slowly withdrawn, the chemical was released into the paste for the entire tube length. Once the cap was closed and the tube returned to its box, there would have been no obvious evidence of tampering."

"Clever… But, if the chemical was injected down the centre of the contents of the tube, wouldn't that result in uneven doses? Wouldn't it sometimes result in a heavy dose and almost no dose on other occasions if there was no way of mixing the stuff through the contents?"

"No. I carried out a trial on a separate small tube of toothpaste I bought on my way to work. It appears the chemical mixes readily of its own accord with toothpaste, and the action of squeezing some out of the tube enhances the mixing process. It results in a fairly consistent contamination throughout the tube's contents.

You know what it's like when you start a new tube of toothpaste. You grab a box, tip out the tube, and open the cap, manhandling the tube a bit as you go. Then you squeeze an amount onto your brush. You don't pay any attention to what the toothpaste looks like once you pop open the cap. It's a simple and effective way of achieving a specific outcome."

"It explains a lot and tells me even more about the state of Janine's marriage. She might still be besotted with Blake Carter, but I think he has long been implementing a plan to provide him with a sound future... and not necessarily one including Janine."

Emily was going to stay for dinner. As I hadn't heard whether Ben would be joining us or not, it seemed wise to organise something for three. I had a pasta sauce simmering when Ben called. If it were okay for us to eat early, he would join me at 6.30 for dinner. I told him an early dinner was fine and not to bring anything as I was cooking.

Instinct told me to scrap surveillance on the Thomlinson Estate tonight. While I still needed to know what was happening out there, I needed a new strategy. To develop one, I needed to know what else Ben's team had discovered in the area surrounding the estate and what else Ben had discovered about Stan, the security guard doing twelve-hour shifts with Brett. Ben might have something to share tonight, but regardless, I will be staying home tonight.

Ben arrived, and the three of us spent a brief period together on my back deck before I left Emily explaining Janine Thomlinson's toothpaste tests to Ben while I finished the pasta for dinner. Ben seemed a little distracted since his arrival, and it came as no surprise when he announced at dinner that he would not be staying long tonight.

Emily took advantage of his announcement and said she also wouldn't mind an early night. Her forensic labs had been working around the clock, and she was beginning to feel exhausted. I suffered pangs of guilt about creating extra work when I gave her Janine's toothpaste to test. It was only a few minutes before eight o'clock when Emily took her leave, and Ben was also on his feet and making noises about going home.

As I walked him to his car, he stopped abruptly and fished around in his pocket before handing me a memory stick.

"Almost forgot about this," he said, slapping it in my hand. "A copy of the recordings from the security cameras at Griff Davidson's building was delivered late this afternoon. The Tech team worked their magic on it and made two copies for me. I haven't had a chance to look at any of it yet, but I thought you might be keen to make a start tonight.

Suddenly I didn't feel half as tired as I thought I was earlier this evening. Nevertheless, I didn't promise to do anything with it tonight. That was a lie. I knew the moment he left, I would be straight into my office.

With the biggest mug I owned full of strong black coffee beside me, I booted up my computer and drummed my fingers impatiently on the desk while I waited to insert the memory stick.

The first recording was from the camera mounted on the outside of the building to capture activity on the driveway and the small parking area out front. With no idea when Griff Davidson disappeared, Ben had asked for a copy of about three days' worth of footage. Without wasting time, I launched the recording and sat back to sip my coffee while I watched.

"This is not good," I told my empty office. "If there isn't some action soon, this coffee won't be enough to keep me awake." Not much activity had been recorded out front of Grif's building.

One by one, in fairly quick succession, a number of vehicles exited the carpark under the building and appeared onto the driveway. The time stamp on the images suggested they were residents off to work in the morning. I stopped the recording and checked each car as it appeared. Davidson was not among those heading off to work that morning. At least, his car wasn't among those leaving the building at that time. There followed a long period of nothing happening. The tape recorded a place completely devoid of activity. Images rolled across the screen, but nobody came, and nobody left.

Then, as I struggled with leaden eyelids, a vehicle shot out from under the building. "What the…?" I squawked as I reached for the stop button.

After blinking several times to ensure my eyes were working and focused, I rewound the recording before advancing it frame-by-frame. "So Griff Davidson is going to work today," I told my office. "Pity about his poor timekeeping. I doubt he'll be docked for his late arrival." I studied the grainy image of the driver. I wanted to shout, *so that's what he looks like*, but I couldn't. All I could glean from the pictures was that the driver probably was a man.

I sullied the pristine blank page of my notepad with my first entry about the recording. It was a scribbled note of the event and the day and time it occurred, as well as how far into the tape it was when Davidson's car appeared. Now, I wasn't feeling quite so sleepy anymore, but a shower might make me a little more alert.

Still towelling my hair dry after my shower, I was halfway through the kitchen on my way to my office. Suddenly I froze. Not game to move and barely breathing, I strained my ears. There it was again. But, this time, the strange noise differed from the one I'd heard a few moments before. If only Rusty were home tonight! I'll never again be annoyed at his barking.

At last, the little voice in my head made itself heard, and my feet began moving in accordance with its instructions. On tiptoes, I raced to my office and ferreted my Glock out from the bottom of my bag before turning off the lights in my office. As I stood there in the darkness and with every fibre of my being attuned for strange noises, I became aware of something else. I realised I was wearing only a bathrobe and felt very vulnerable.

What to do…? Should I continue my vigil from my darkened office, or should I sneak to my bedroom to dress more appropriately? The prospect of maybe having to deal with a dangerous situation while wearing nothing more than a bathrobe did not thrill me.

Right, the problem then is how to get to my bedroom without drawing attention to myself. Not easy, given every light in the living area between my office and the bedroom was switched on. Nevertheless, it had to be done. I allowed myself a few moments to work out the quickest and safest route without being detected. I inched towards the office doorway in preparation for a full-on dash to the bedroom.

Another noise stopped me in my tracks. This one was closer, perhaps on the back deck. Instinctively I eased away from the door and further back into my office. My leg bumped something soft and alien. It didn't move. With my pulse playing jungle drums on my ribs, I sprang away from it. Cold sweat moistened my top lip. Then I remembered.

That soft thing was a bag I'd thrown onto one of the chairs a couple of days ago. Oh, *that* bag! Of course… Relieved, I relaxed. It contained my gym clothes. The bag of clothes had been left in the car for a few days before I remembered it and brought it inside to wash them. They weren't clean and didn't smell so great, but they would do for now.

With the bag's contents spread out on the desk, I put the Glock down within easy reach to free up both hands. Then, in something approaching record-breaking speed, the bathrobe was tossed aside and replaced by underclothes, leggings, and a baggy T-shirt. With one less thing to worry about, I could now focus on that last sound I heard – definitely on the back deck and close to the kitchen door.

From just inside the doorway of my darkened office, I had a clear view of anyone entering the kitchen from the deck. Turning my head slightly, I could see along the hallway.

Feeling more focused now I was clothed and in position with Glock in hand, I waited for whatever made those noises to make its next move.

Chapter 21

Nothing happened, so I waited a bit longer. This is ridiculous, I told myself. The intruder was probably still on the back deck. So, why hasn't he made his move? What's he waiting for? There is no point standing around wondering what might happen next. After a few moments of thought and a couple of deep breaths, it was time for action.

First step: switch on the security cameras. I waited a few moments to be sure they were recording before making my next move. Then I dug my keys out of my bag and unlocked one of my office windows and its security screen. It was time to make my big move. With my keys tucked in my bra and Glock snugly tucked in my waistband at the small of my back, I eased myself out of the window and dropped the two metres to the ground without a sound.

The next step of my plan of attack was a bit sketchy but simple. I needed to move around to where I could see the intruder on the back deck without being seen while I was about it. Standing there in the dark, I allowed myself a few moments before tiptoeing across to the corner of the house. Then began the delicate manoeuvre of picking my way along the side wall towards the back deck.

It was pitch dark along that side of the house. If only Rusty, my neighbour's dog, was at home instead of spending the week in the boarding kennels…. As I eased my way along past the kitchen, it was time to implement the next stage of the plan. The back deck leads off from the end of this short wall. Holding my breath and praying they wouldn't jangle, I slid my keys out of my bra. Not a sound from the keys… So far, so good. The next step was tricky.

The remote for the security alarm system was on the keyring clasped gently in my hand. I felt around gingerly for the remote and ran my finger softly over it to locate the correct button to press to arm the security system. For some time, I had toyed with the idea of combining the cameras and the intruder alarm systems into one linked system, but I always managed to find reasons not to do it. Now, I wished I had done so.

Although armed, the system needed movement to trigger an alarm. My visitor appeared content to remain motionless just outside my kitchen door. I needed him to move. Even a small sound that made him spin around to investigate it would do. Any movement would trigger the lights and the alarm. The lights would allow the cameras to take clearer images of the bloke.

A sound… yeah, that's what I need. Nothing too obvious, though. It needs to be suspicious. Something heard, but indistinct, was required. I eyed off my rosemary hedge running along the fence. Would rustling those bushes be enough to arouse his curiosity? Only one way to find out. I reached out and, applying some force, ran my hand through the rosemary, before dashing back to the shadows alongside the house. A startled bird, probably the resident willy wagtail, flew out of the bushes with a screech as the air filled with the rosemary's perfume.

Startled, my intruder dropped into a crouch as he spun around to face the sound. The alarm sounded deafening in the still night. The deck and surrounding area lit up as the lights allowed the cameras to do their best work. I inched forward to the edge of the shadows. I was standing beside the start of the deck's railing. Taking a deep breath to steady myself, I peeped around to see what was happening on the deck.

My visitor appeared to have disappeared. He no longer stood outside the kitchen door. Had he scarpered down the back stairs without my noticing? That didn't seem possible. I would have heard him run the length of the deck to the stairs, but I didn't. There was a faint sound when the lights came on. Then the alarm started squawking. But I didn't hear any running. Somehow, he appeared to have vanished off the deck. I took another peep around the corner. No, still no sign of him.

Playing hide-and-seek like this achieved nothing. I was about to step out from the shadows when a thought slammed in from left field. What about another noise – a more definite noise – to see if it caused some action on the deck? I moved further back along the wall, away from the deck, before lumbering back to the edge of the shadows again. I hoped that stamping my feet hard and at a quick pace would sound like someone heavier than me running towards the deck.

At the edge of the shadows, I rushed forward a couple of paces further. There was a sound on the deck. A chair being shoved out of the way. I spun around to investigate. The next few moments were a blur.

Something large, solid and dark flew at me. I yelped as I hit the ground. I lay there dazed and with the air knocked out of my lungs. I knew I had to get up off my back. Rolling onto my side, I tried levering myself into a sitting position. My efforts were hampered by my right arm reaching around behind my back for the Glock I hoped was still in my waistband.

Later, I realised it all happened in a second. The intruder, vaulting over the railing, had landed on top of me and rolled off. As I struggled to get up off my back, he scrambled to his feet. His efforts were more successful than mine. He was a couple of metres away from me and had adopted a crouched position.

The deck lights glinted off the object he held in his raised hand. He came at me. Driven by the urgency of the moment, my hand closed around my weapon. I swayed to one side as I yanked the Glock free of my waistband, and I felt the sting cross my arm as he struck his first blow. I lashed out with my foot. My kick found its mark. Off balance, he stumbled backwards before losing his balance and falling to the ground. I knew I had only a couple of moments before he came at me again.

When his blade had found my arm, I was preoccupied with working the slider on the Glock. I knew he meant business.

Without taking my eyes off him, I scrambled to my feet. In that moment, it registered that he was considerably taller and sturdier than me. A strategic retreat might be wiser than an attack. I tried to run … but tripped and found myself on the ground again.

He had the upper hand. I was still on the ground.

He charged … I fired … his arm holding the knife flapped in mid-air … I fired again … but my assailant opted for a hasty retreat and was fleeing into the darkness. A grunt suggested my second shot might have found some part of the target.

At last, I was on my feet and in pursuit of the escaping intruder. He was surprisingly fast. Perhaps I was slow. By the time I reached the front corner of the house, there was no sign of him, just the sound of pounding feet coming from a long way down my driveway.

"Not worth chasing him," I muttered. He was too far ahead of me and probably had a vehicle waiting at the end of the driveway. As I took a couple of deep breaths to steady myself, I noticed the dark, shiny trail from the corner of the house across to and disappearing down the driveway. "So I'm not the only one oozing claret, eh? It looks like at least one of my shots hit some part of the target."

Then another grim reality occurred to me. What if his wounds were potentially fatal? I didn't need that hassle. Maybe, if he is found and treated soon enough….

My arm throbbed. I glanced at it and was surprised to see all the way to my fingertips was covered in blood. Further investigation revealed sizable areas of my shirt and leggings were much the same. And a small pool was forming next to my left foot.

"Don't just stand there. Move your arse," I snarled at myself. My arm required attention, and I had to call Ben.

With the Glock back in my waistband, I used my 'good' hand to fish my keys and the remotes out of my bra. I disarmed the alarm as I headed for the front door. When the squawking stopped, the resultant silence was wonderful. With the front door shoved wide open, I pulled up the hem of my shirt to use as a makeshift sling for my arm. I didn't need a sling, but I didn't want a trail of blood from the front door to the kitchen.

After raiding a kitchen drawer, I wrapped a clean handtowel around my bicep to help contain the bleeding while I called Ben. His tone confirmed he was not happy about again being woken at an uncivilised hour of the morning.

"And exactly what mess have you managed to get yourself into this time?" he growled by way of greeting. "And I suppose you now expect me to come and extricate you from it."

Suffice to say my response is best left unrecorded, but it was effective enough to have him out of bed and at my place about fifteen minutes later. Perhaps my final comment to him did the trick: *Leave your vehicle at the bottom of my driveway, or you will destroy evidence.* By the time he arrived, I had showered, had on clean clothes, and had a length of combo dressing strip wrapped around my arm.

The man-mountain that is Ben Richards never fails to amaze me by the speed at which he can move. Tonight was no exception. A vehicle turned onto my street and, moments later, Ben galloped up my driveway. He took one look at the bandage on my arm and demanded I go inside and sit down. That wasn't going to happen – not yet, anyway. The next few minutes were spent outlining the events of the night and showing Ben the intruder's trail of evidence.

"Blood? Where? What are you talking about?"

"I think I shot him… probably twice."

"Oh, shit… not again.…"

Then I left him outside calling his officers to action, while I went to my office to take a look at what really happened out there tonight.

It took about a minute to bring up the recorded footage from the security cameras. They picked up the action from where I made my way along the rosemary hedge on my way to the deck. Now I understood why I thought my visitor had left. As I armed the system, he had slid along the kitchen wall to stand in the corner close to the deck's railing. His position had him out of my line of sight when I peered around at the deck.

"Okay, now let's have a look at you, Sunshine," I murmured as I examined the recording frame-by-frame. It wasn't until he was startled and spun around, triggering the lights, that the images were of much use. Until then, all they showed in the darkness on the deck was an indistinct, even darker shape. Once the lights were on, I saw images of a solid-looking person dressed from head to toe in black. He wore a hoody, jeans, boots, and dark, close-fitting gloves, probably black. The recording didn't give me a clear image of his face. The hood being up over his head made sure of that. I was still poring over the images when Ben joined me in the office.

"Is that the footage of tonight's events? Anything useful?" he asked. I shook my head.

"Not so far, but something better might come up further along." I explained about the problem with the hoody.

"Should you be doing this now? I mean right now? Shouldn't you have your arm looked at first?"

"Eh? Oh yes, my arm… It doesn't need sutures, but it does need pulling together so it will heal better and without too much of a scar."

"Well, come on. Let's deal with that first."

Ben was right, of course. He found himself applying some of his first aid training as he helped pull together the edges of the long, shallow slash across my left bicep.

Once the wound was securely bandaged, he went outside to check on the teams of officers he had called to work the scene. I returned to the camera footage and, as I waited for the images to fill the screen, I glanced at the clock. It was almost three o'clock.

For the briefest of moments, I wondered whether I should continue or call it quits and go to bed for at least a couple of hours sleep before my inbuilt clock told me it was time to get up. Sleep lost out. Someone had come at me with a knife, full well intending to do me serious harm and probably something more final than that. There was no way I could sleep without knowing more about my intruder.

The first thing I needed to do was to download the camera footage into another file. One I could manipulate and enhance to help identify the bloke. I was playing with the downloaded file when Ben returned to my office.

"Found anything yet?"

I shook my head. That initiated a long debate about whether I should be asleep or fiddling about with the camera footage. Ben probably knew he was on the losing team from the outset but, after the discussion raged for a few minutes, he admitted defeat.

"Right; well, if we going to sit here until the sun comes up, put the images up on the big screen so I can see them too. Maybe between us, we'll pick up something useful."

He had a point about two pairs of eyes achieving more than just mine, but it wasn't how I wanted to do this. I needed to work through it on my own to get my head around the whole episode before discussing or sharing it with anyone else. My winning streak ended when Ben pulled a chair close to my desk and settled in with his feet up on another spare chair.

"Roll'em, Sonny, and let's see what the recordings tell us. If I'm going to be hanging about while my teams are outside, I might as well be doing something useful. Let's start from the beginning of the footage?" he suggested.

A heavy silence filled the room as the images rolled by in slow motion. When we reached the point where the intruder leapt over the railing and landed on top of me, Ben broke the silence. I had been watching him out of the corner of my eye. He had appeared deeply engrossed in something. Although his eyes had been glued to them, I suspected his mind wasn't on the images on the screen. Even so, I wasn't prepared for his next question.

"What happened after you heard the intruder running down the driveway?"

"What…? Are you asking what I did?"

"Yeah, that will do for a start. You came around to the front of the house and heard the bloke racing down the driveway. What happened next? Hang on, I'll rephrase that. What did you do next?"

I gave him a potted version of how I realised I couldn't catch up with the bloke because he was too far ahead, and opted to call Ben instead of chasing the intruder. Ben nodded, but I knew there was more to come. I had to wait only a couple of heartbeats to hear it.

"So, while you stood there assessing the situation and deciding what action to take next, what did you see? What did you hear?"

"It was dark… The security lights only lit up the first part of the driveway. Beyond that, the driveway was in darkness. I didn't see anything more before I unlocked the front door and went back inside."

"What did you hear?"

"Nothing…. Well, nothing other than the bloke running down the driveway."

"Okay, but once he reached the end of the driveway, you would no longer hear him running."

I gave a curt nod of agreement.

"So, after you no longer could hear him running, what did you hear? There might've been a small pause between running and something else. Think back. What did you hear?"

"Like I said, not a …." I left my reply unfinished. A shadowy recollection was trying to grab my attention. "Wait a minute. There was something. I heard something… A vehicle went along the street."

"Now we're getting somewhere. What did this vehicle sound like? A car, truck, motorbike… what did it sound like?"

"A motorbike… Yeah, a motorbike, and it travelled out of this street. I mean, it wasn't a motorbike entering the street. Aw hell, yes, of course… He had to have a vehicle of some sort waiting for him when he finished his business with me, and it probably was a motorbike." A grin lit up Ben's face as he scribbled something in his notebook.

Realising that a motorbike was the getaway vehicle brought the park incident to mind: a motorbike almost did for Janine that Friday night. Was it the same motorbike? My camera footage couldn't help with that, but maybe the images it did record might tell me something about the rider. I knew it was a tenuous line to follow. After all, we had no clear shots of the rider involved in the park incident. Still, I was going to try for a match, or at least some close resemblance.

After returning to the start of the footage, I inched the recording on to the first clear image of my unwelcome guest. My best chance was the shot of him when, startled by the security lights coming on, he spun around to see what was happening. I froze that image, and craned my neck and strained my eyes to make something of it. After a few moments, I accepted it wouldn't tell me anything without considerable enhancement.

"That's okay. We have the technology," I told the image on the screen as I opened another computer program. Then, with a copy of the frozen image loaded into the newly open computer program, I set about tweaking and enhancing it to the best of the program's capabilities.

"Ooh, yeah, now we're cooking," I crowed to the universe. "Gotcha," I hissed. "Now, where's that image from the park?"

"Is this a private conversation, or can anyone join in?" I looked up to see a grinning Ben standing in the doorway.

"No, it's not private, but you might be a bit premature. Go away for a while. I might have something for you later." He wasn't pleased by my suggestion, but threw his hands in the air and went back outside.

About fifteen minutes later, I went in search of Ben. He was engaged in conversation with one of the forensic team at the start of the driveway. Rather than interrupt, I waited on the doorstep until their discussions ended. As I stood there, another forensic-suited figure joined the conversation. Despite all the necessary gear, this one I could identify. Emily had come to take charge of her team. When the first person Ben had been speaking to moved away, I felt it safe to join the discussion.

"If I'm not interrupting anything too important, perhaps you might like to take a look at something in my office." I spoke directly to Ben before assuring Emily she was welcome to come too.

I led them into my office. With a grand gesture, I directed them to the two images, side-by-side, on my big screen… and was instantly aware that it made my arm throb.

Chapter 22

My two companions stood with their noses almost up against my big screen as they compared the two images. What's taking so long? The likeness is fairly obvious. Determined not to prompt them, I was almost at explosion point when Emily commented.

"Yep, I think there is a likeness between those two images." She stepped back from the screen, satisfied with her assessment.

Ben took a little longer. "Okay. There might be something about those images – something similar."

I grabbed a manilla folder. Then, standing almost up against the screen, I held the folder up to the screen to cover the lower half of the image of the face recorded on my deck earlier tonight.

"Aw yeah, the eyes are the same," Emily chirped. "Yep, I reckon it's probably the same person."

Grudgingly perhaps, Ben agreed but needed more convincing. "So, what are we saying? That the person responsible for the incident in the park and the bloke who interrupted your sleep tonight are one and the same person."

"That's exactly what I'm suggesting," I confirmed.

"Now we've agreed they could be images of the same person, where does that get us?" Emily asked. "Without an identification, we don't know anything about him other than he rides a motorbike and isn't too fond of females."

"You are right about needing an identification," Ben agreed. "We do have someone who might help with that: Janine. We show her the images and see what she says about them. See if this bloke could be a mate of her husband, or one of her disgruntled employees."

"No, we are not doing that – not yet anyway. Janine is traumatised already without being shown images that might in some way add to her trauma. Leave it with me for today. I have a couple of ideas. If they don't pay off, we move to Plan B tomorrow."

Emily's team were finishing up. She needed to talk to them before leaving with them. I hoped Ben too might need to check on his officers, but it seems he didn't feel any such need… And I knew the look. His face said he didn't buy my proposal, and I was in for a long argument about not showing Janine the images today. I was right, and after some debate, he agreed I could have today to try to identify the bloke in the images. But I had a few things to do before progressing with my plan.

Then Ben decided he would stay for breakfast. I hadn't mentioned breakfast but told myself two for breakfast was no more trouble than one. I did my best to expedite the event in record time so Ben would leave. With breakfast over and Ben gone, my priority was to call Janine.

At a civilised hour, I called her. It dialled for ages. The butterflies in my stomach had morphed into elephants by the time she answered. I tried for a laid-back conversation and emphasised I was just checking she was okay.

"Yes, I'm fine, unless you are going to tell me something different. Has something to concern me happened?"

"No, I'm just checking that you are okay and nothing untoward has happened. Every so often, I might call for a quick check."

She sounded grateful. I wondered whether she was as 'fine' as she claimed to be. I tried reassuring myself that it was natural for her to be on edge after all that had happened, but I'm a realist and didn't buy my sales pitch.

Janine dealt with, my next task was the most pressing one. At nine o'clock, I called Nick Spargo and arranged to meet him in his office at the university. Taking a thin file with me, I headed for the appointment.

My plan was simple. Don't waste Nick's time. Show him the images in my file and ask if he recognises my intruder. If he couldn't, ask where else I might try my luck with the photos. In the end, our meeting was as brief as I planned, and more successful than I hoped.

"Hell, yes, I recognise him. That's Blake Carter. Interesting images though… I don't suppose you might like to tell me about this photo shoot?"

"Not right now, but I will, just as soon as circumstances allow it."

There was nothing else to say. My suspicion about the identity of my unwelcome intruder was confirmed. In the university's visitors' carpark, while recording an update for my case file, I pondered what that meant.

"So Mr Carter remains alive and well and in Millhaven. That raises a couple of issues to pursue. Did he park a motorbike near the start of my driveway in readiness for a quick getaway? Was it the same motorbike that rammed Janine in the park, and was Carter the rider on that occasion? They were questions for Ben if I wanted answers, but now something else nagged me.

Regardless of the answers, Carter's continued presence in Millhaven meant he was staying somewhere, and if not in the town, then somewhere close by. That begged another question. Was someone helping him remain under the radar, and was that someone directly involved in recent incidents?"

As I drove off the campus, I reminded myself that having questions was fine, but finding answers was difficult. Some of those answers might require someone else to find them for me. While I sat at the lights, another question slammed in. Did Blake Carter own a motorbike? Ben might need to deal with that one – unless Janine knew. I doubted Janine did know, or she would have mentioned it. Without its registration number, it would be difficult even for Ben to find out who owned it. Maybe CCTV cameras on streets around my home captured something.

Was there anything else I needed to do before I shared with Ben what I had learnt this morning? I continued to ponder that question as I climbed the stairs to my office in the city heart. Perhaps caffeine, along with the sugar fix from the cakes I bought from the bakers, might generate inspiration about what to do next. I took my coffee and a custard tart to my desk so I could indulge as I checked my emails. That's not how it worked out.

Two sips of coffee later, and before I even started on the custard tart, a phone call scuttled any plans I had for the rest of the day... except for the need to contact Ben. A call from my Tasmanian colleague, James Rothwell, banished the custard tart from my priorities.

"Sonny, I know it's taken me some time, but I can now confirm my earlier information about the identity of Blake Carter. His birth name was Roy Gilham. I have not been able to find evidence of an official name change, but I have located a photo of him as a teenager. It's a good match with the image from his wedding. As that image of him is not a front-on shot, it's hard to be absolutely certain of a match," James warned.

"Your bloke had a chequered childhood. Abandoned as an infant, he was in an orphanage on and off over the next few years. Fostered out several times, he proved too difficult to manage and always was handed back after only a short stay. As far as foster parents were concerned, his teenage years proved no better, but placements with those families lasted longer than his earlier ones."

"James, I understand how difficult this investigation has been, and I feel guilty about involving you in it. Send me your account, and please feel free to opt-out anytime it suits you. I'll have no hard feelings about it."

"Hey, hang on, Sonny. I have yet to give you the whole story – as I know it. It appears young Roy – or Blake, if you prefer – made himself known to the local constabulary almost at the start of his teenage years. Because of his age, and a good deal of indulgence on the part of his victims, he escaped without a conviction or a custodial sentence. Local scuttlebutt has it that, at about age twenty, his luck was about to run out, so he pulled a disappearing act... before they found the bodies. Before you ask, yes, that is plural. It's rumoured to be more than one."

"According to my client, that's about when he legged it overseas. Have you discovered if he reappears in Tasmania at all after that?"

"Yep, a couple of times at least. But you have to understand this background stuff comes from 'shadier' contacts. Although, one did claim to know him well when they were growing up. Anyway, his story intrigued me. I decided to check if a passport had been issued for Roy Gilham or Blake Carter."

"And…? I almost don't want to know the answer."

"Oh, you do. This is where it gets really interesting. A passport was issued to Blake Carter around the time of his supposed first disappearance from Tasmania. The story had me hooked, so I did some digging into the Blake Carter who applied for a passport."

"Well, don't stop there. What's the story?"

"When about ten years old, Roy was fostered by the Carter family, whose son, Blake, was about the same age as Roy. A few months later, while playing football, Blake suddenly died from an undiagnosed congenital heart condition. While the family were dealing with the death of their son, Mrs Carter, middle-aged by then, discovered she was pregnant.

Towards the latter stages of her pregnancy, things were not going well. To be able to better manage their own situation, the Carters handed Roy back to the orphanage. Soon after that, Roy had his first brush with the law. According to more than one source, the young Roy was a wrong'un, but clever with it – streetwise and cunning."

"That's just about the picture I'm getting of my client's husband. I suspect he's almost succeeded in pulling off his master plan to give himself a real leg-up in life. But why was his passport issued in the name of Blake Carter? Are we confusing him with some other Blake Carter living in Tasmania at that time?"

"Nah, it was Roy who applied for the passport. I have a 'friend' who has the authority necessary to access application files. I miraculously have acquired copies of the documentation submitted with the application.

It goes without saying, I followed up on all of it. There's no doubt. Roy assumed the identity of the then long-dead Blake Carter by using a copy of Blake's birth certificate. He forgot to mention that the real Blake Carter had been dead for about nine or ten years by then."

"What about the Carters – Blake's parents – were they aware of this?"

"They were gone. Roy couldn't have chosen a better persona to assume. Mrs Carter died of complications right at the end of her pregnancy. Life became all too much for her husband. Let himself go, became an alcoholic, and died a couple of years later in a homeless shelter away from the town where the family had lived. It's possible Roy knew what happened to the family and capitalised on it when he needed a new identity.

Anyway, that's about as much as I've discovered. I won't be dropping the investigation. I won't sleep at night if I don't know the whole story. So, anything you dig up at your end would be greatly appreciated."

I let out a low whistle after the call ended. It was almost better than winning Lotto. I had recorded the entire conversation and was keen to produce a hard copy of all James told me, but there was something else to do. I sent James the two images of the motorbike rider Nick identified as Blake Carter. Then it was time to transcribe the recording of James's call.

My grumbling stomach alerted me that lunchtime had passed by without my noticing. After a quick trip downstairs, I returned to my office with a fish and salad sandwich and a newspaper. I made another coffee. How many have I had today? Who knows? But I need caffeine, and I felt it critical to heed my survival instinct before studying the transcript.

While I munched my lunch, my mind roamed free. It began reviewing and assessing everything from James's call. "I think James nailed it when he called Blake Carter a wrong'un," I told my empty office, "but something doesn't quite fit with my end of the story." James had him pegged as clever, crafty, and cunning. Someone with those attributes wouldn't do his own dirty work, like trying to kill people … and, so far, three times unsuccessfully. I had almost convinced myself that my attacker, while I was on surveillance of the Thomlinson Estate, was Blake Carter.

Now I had given myself a new problem. Do I continue to think of this bloke as Blake Carter, or train myself to call him Roy Gilham? Nah, reverting to his real name would only lead to confusion, mostly for me. "Blake Carter it shall remain then," I confirmed for the universe.

Before returning to the transcription of James's call, I tried calling Ben but reached his voicemail. I left a message asking him to call me when he was free. Then it was back to transcribing. About twenty minutes later, as the printer spat out another copy of the transcript, Ben called.

He was busy and couldn't talk now unless it was urgent. If it wasn't, could it wait until tonight? And, what did I want for dinner? My side of the conversation was brief and simple: no, it wasn't urgent … yes, tonight would be soon enough … Chinese would be good.

All pressing matters now dealt with, I put my feet up to read the newspaper. And that's what I tried to do, if only my mind would switch off from Blake Carter. I ran up the white flag and admitted defeat. With my hands behind my head and the paper abandoned, I stretched back in my chair. Something about Janine's case was begging for attention, but I couldn't figure out what. I created a mental timeline of the case from its outset.

Somehow, Janine's initial concerns about her husband's possible infidelity that brought her to my office now seemed almost ludicrous in the light of everything that had happened since. Almost like a blow from Thor's hammer, that elusive 'something' finally slammed through to the forefront of my thinking… Griff Davidson, Janine's missing forensic auditor. Where the hell was he?

Had the police turned up anything on his apparent disappearance? Normally, I would immediately put that question to Ben. But I knew he was busy, so it would have to wait until tonight. In the meantime, I would pray whatever was making him busy would be settled before this evening, and he wouldn't have a reason to opt out of dinner.

Despite trying to prevent it, my mind insisted on revisiting the crime scene in Davidson's apartment. Perhaps because it was so confronting, my mind didn't linger there, instead dredging up another thought to throw at me. Janine's unit in the city was no safer than Griff Davidson's, probably less so since Blake Carter had his own key. I toyed with the idea of calling Janine to discuss the matter before remembering my early morning call already had unsettled her today. I gambled she would be safe enough for a while and decided not to call her until I spoke to Ben this evening. I could call her then, but if not, it would be first thing tomorrow morning.

Such thoughts made me consider my office here on the first floor of this city heart building. This upper floor is divided into two distinct areas. One-third is occupied by the headquarters of the business venture that owns this building and several other properties in and around Millhaven. It has its own private access. The remaining two-thirds of the floor is divided into three separate office areas. The second one is about the same size as my office space, while the third office is about twice the size.

For the last few months, the largest space has been unoccupied after the previous occupants had complained long and hard about the rental. While it is a prime city heart location, it's hard to justify the rent they were asking for that double space. Using the ancient lift is akin to taking your life in your own hands, and the stairs are steep and not 'client friendly'.

"Is any of that important?" I asked the universe before answering my own question. Of course, it's important – if I aim to be safe and secure up here. The only other occupant of this part of the first floor rarely visits his office. When he does, he spends no more than a day there. That line of thinking had me out from behind my desk and on my way to lock my door. Perhaps a security camera of some sort to monitor traffic to my door would be useful. I called the security firm I use. They would come to work out the best option for me to install.

About fifteen minutes after they arrived, they were sitting in my office outlining their proposal. It all sounded straightforward. A discreet camera would be mounted across the hallway and along a bit from my door to provide continuous feed to a monitor in my office of everything happening in the hallway. It would allow occupants of other offices to hook into the system at any time in the future if they wished. The equipment will be installed tomorrow.

When I left my office, I intended to go home. Somewhere between locking my office and unlocking my car, the plan changed. Something suggested a cruise past Janine's block of units might be worthwhile. It didn't come as a complete surprise when no one appeared home. It was too early for her to be home anyway. But, seeing as I was taking the scenic route home, perhaps a drive past Griff Davidson's unit wouldn't go amiss.

No surprises at Griff's place either. I didn't really expect there would be any evidence of activity there, but something suggested I should drive past anyway. And it wasn't a complete waste of time. It brought to mind something I needed to follow up. The resultant mental note was a reminder to ask Ben about footage from the CCTV cameras at Griff's block of units. It would be nice if he brought a copy of it with him tonight, but I was almost certain he wouldn't.

My scenic tour meant I wasn't home long before Ben arrived. He bounded in, carrying a bag of Chinese food in one hand and a bottle of white wine in the other. Our preferred practice, when Chinese food was on the menu, was to eat as soon as it arrived rather than to let it go cold while we had a pre-dinner drink. We followed that practice this evening, with only occasional small talk interrupting the eating process. Then, with bowls of fruit salad and ice cream, and mugs of coffee, we retired to my lounge room. It was time for a serious conversation.

To avoid forgetting it later, I asked about camera footage from Griff Davidson's unit block. Ben scratched around in his pockets. The look that spread across his face told me his search was unsuccessful, and it mystified him.

"I'm sure I put it in my pocket," he mumbled as he checked again. "Damn; what else would I have done with it? Oh, I know." He bounced out of his chair and disappeared out to his car, returning a few moments later.

With a sheepish grin, he admitted, "I slipped it into my jacket pocket, which I left in the car. Anyway, here's a copy of the footage I received late this afternoon. I haven't looked at it yet, so I've no idea if it's captured anything useful."

"We could adjourn to my office to look at it now if you're up for it."

Of course, he was up for it, but we did delay relocating to my office until we finished our desserts. A couple of minutes later, images from the memory stick Ben gave me were filling my big screen. In the mistaken belief that this would be the same as all camera footage-watching sessions, we sat back and sipped our coffee as the first images scrolled across the screen.

About a minute later, coffees abandoned, we were both sitting upright and on the edge of our chairs. This would not be a long boring session. Already, the screen commanded our undivided attention. And Ben's earlier murmurings about an early night were forgotten.

Chapter 23

A dark-coloured van drove up to the building housing Griff Davidson's unit. It reversed into the entrance of the residents' basement carpark. Two people alighted and disappeared into the carpark.

When the vehicle arrived, I slowed the feed to the big screen. It made waiting for the next activity to appear on the screen seem interminably long. Later, watching it in real-time, it was no more than about half an hour after the car first appeared until the two blokes reappeared at their vehicle.

"This was when it happened," I yelped as the two figures loaded something into the rear of the car. "That bundle they lugged out to the vehicle; I'll bet that's Griff Davidson."

"We can't be sure on that image alone. We need a clearer image to identify the two doing the heavy lifting."

Ben was right. From a police perspective, clearer images were required for them to take action. But I was only half listening to him. Something about the image frozen on the screen rang an alarm bell for me – a distant alarm bell.

"Are you listening to me?" Ben demanded.

"Yes, but let's watch more of the footage to see if anything else interesting happens." He gave me a sceptical look but gestured for me to play the recording.

Nothing much of note was recorded until the next day when Janine's car parked out front of the building. We watched her disappear into the building and come back out not long after.

"A quick visit to find out why he was absent and not answering his phone," I murmured. "No wonder she was concerned about him." Ben nodded and motioned for me to move on with the recording.

Various vehicles accessed the building and the basement carpark, but not many. They provided little to see. The next image of interest was our arrival, followed by the arrival of the forensic team and Ben's various officers. No news there, so we watched another five minutes of the footage before calling it quits.

"We've seen all we need," Ben announced, "but I'll ask the Tech boys to see if they can enhance any of it."

Again, I only half listened but nodded anyway. That little bell I heard earlier kept ringing in my head. It had become louder when the two figures carrying the large bundle appeared on the screen. I didn't argue when Ben announced he would go home for an early night. I wanted to be alone, to try to figure out why that bell kept ringing.

I took a long shower to help me relax before embarking on a long session in my office. I restarted the recording and watched the entire footage, but found nothing else of interest. That box ticked. I was ready to run those few images of interest through another program to try enhancing them.

My limited ability meant the process took longer than expected, but I enhanced the first of the images. Enlarged, cleaned and sharpened, the shot of the two men alighting from the car before disappearing into the building held my attention. Finally, the little voice in my head reminded me something was familiar about that vehicle — that I knew something about it.

The mental gymnastics were slow, but eventually, a memory emerged from the murky mess of my recent recollections. I knew the car was familiar, but why continued to elude me. To think about something else, I noted the vehicle's registration number. No lightbulb moments there. After spending time on the other enhanced images, I was drawn back to that first one again.

"Okay. I accept this one holds the secret," I barked at the screen, "but that's not helpful."

At midnight, I gave up and went to bed. I would have trouble sleeping, but the alternative was to spend the rest of the night in my office and still be none the wiser in the morning.

Sweet oblivion refused to arrive. But, as I lay there dozing, the recollection that had tried to come through earlier finally arrived. I recalled seeing where that same vehicle was parked during my visits to Janine's workplace. Springing out of bed, I raced to my office and booted up my computer. I waited for the enhanced images from the CCTV footage I'd studied earlier to fill the screen again.

"Yes. Gotcha!" I yelped as I stared at the image on the screen. "I remember you."

As I was leaving Janine's complex after my first visit, I was forced to wait for local traffic to pass before exiting the property. The car now occupying my big screen was parked across the road from the entrance to the Thomlinson complex. The other interesting fact I recalled related to the sole occupant of that vehicle. The bloke sat scowling at me. Although, at the time, I thought his dark look was meant for the traffic that prevented him from leaving. Now I wasn't so sure. That same face now featured large on my screen.

Was he scowling at me on that earlier occasion? I cast my mind back to recall what happened when I finally drove away from Janine's complex. My memory of the incident swam back into focus. I thought the bloke would make a U-turn at the first opportunity. As I was a vehicle entering onto the roadway, he had right-of-way. I had to wait for him to turn and move off along the road before I could drive out. As I replayed my memory of that event, the next image I recalled jolted me.

He didn't make a U-turn and drive off. I saw him start his vehicle, but instead of making a move, he just sat there with the engine idling while continuing to scowl at me. I remembered thinking he was waiting for me to move off before he made his turn, and he glared at me because I just sat there, further delaying his departure. So I drove out and headed back towards the city. I don't recall anything significant after that ... until now. As I replayed my memory of my drive into town, an image slammed to the fore.

A clear image of that same car emerged from the mass of nothingness that was my recall of the drive into the city. I recalled being stopped at a set of lights. A squeal of brakes somewhere behind made me check the rearview mirror for the likelihood of a rear-ending. There was no threat, but I did notice the car now gracing my big screen was only two cars further back in the queue at the lights. It followed me into the city until I turned off to park behind my office building.

Was it a coincidence, or was there more to it? Given the CCTV footage I'm looking at, I'm now inclined to the latter assessment. But, as my mind searched its recesses for more information, my gut suggested there'd been another sighting of that car. It came to me just as I was about to give up and go back to bed.

The first night I drove to the park for surveillance on the Thomlinson Estate, that vehicle passed me going the other way. Not a big believer in coincidence; I knew these memories weren't that. My big question now was, what was Scowl-Face's role in what's going on in Janine's life? One thing was clear. I need a long and in-depth conversation with Millhaven's top cop, Ben Richards, tomorrow … argh, now that's today.

After only a couple of hours of sleep, I wasn't at my sparkling best at breakfast. As I lingered zombie-like over my coffee, I tried to plan my day. The only thing I achieved was the realisation that there wasn't anything definite I could do, and there was nothing else on my agenda. Before leaving for the office, I called Janine. I heard her go into instant alarm mode.

"I'm just checking that you are okay and there have been no further unforeseen incidents since we last spoke." She assured me all was well, so I pressed on with what I really wanted to discuss with her. "Janine, I know this will sound strange, but does Blake have keys to your city apartment?"

"Blake…? Yes, of course, he does. He lives here. Well, he lives here when he's not staying at the estate. What's this about, Sonny."

"No need for concern but, until we know more about Blake's current situation, there is something I'd like you to consider. Please think about having a locksmith change all the locks at your unit." I heard a sharp intake of breath and rushed on. "Maybe I'm being over cautious, but we'll both sleep better knowing you won't have any unwelcome visitors in the middle of the night. The reality is, we don't know where your husband is or what his condition might be. And we don't know where his keys are." After further discussion, she agreed to call a locksmith this morning.

"That's one matter dealt with. Now to try my luck with the other," I muttered as I called Ben.

"Do I want to know what has you calling me at this hour of the morning?" His opening line was not encouraging and stirred my dark side.

"And good morning to you too! Before we proceed, I should warn you that I have had precious little sleep. Now…."

"Christ, what happened after I left last night?"

"Eh? Oh, no, nothing worth mentioning. I worked most of the night, that's all. Anyway, the reason for this call is to ask a favour," I heard him groan and ignored it. "If you have a moment today, please look up a registration number for me. I'll tell you why I need it when I see you tonight."

"Okay, hang on a minute." I heard the soft click of a keyboard in the background. "Right, what's this number I'm to look up?"

After giving him the number, his keyboard was given a workout. A few moments later, he gave me the details. As he read out the information, I scribbled it down and then ended the call. For a moment, I sat staring at my scrawl. The vehicle's details were correct for the car in question. Good. At least it is not driving around wearing 'funny' plates. And that speaks volumes about the driver's confidence that he wouldn't be pulled over for anything.

The most exciting morsel of information Ben provided was the registered owner's address. Now, that's worth a look, but it could wait until later today. On the way into the city, I decided the best use of my time was to compile a list of things to do or follow up. Sitting around doing nothing did not sit well with me. Some of my investigations were slow-paced and difficult, but this one has me spending all day, every day, just spinning my wheels and going nowhere.

Having dealt with all the usual routine admin tasks, I made a start on compiling my to-do list. I had managed to head up a new page on my pad before a phone call interrupted. It was my ten o'clock appointment apologising for having to cancel her meeting and promising to reschedule as soon as possible. When she made the appointment, she didn't say why she needed to see me, but I had a fair idea why. My caller's hurried, whispered conversation told me someone she didn't want to hear was there. I figured she wanted to talk to me about a problem with a spouse who was unexpectedly close by.

Returning to my to-do list for Janine's case, a few minutes later, every line on the page was filled with a task or question requiring attention. There were bound to be other issues to add to it, but they escaped me for the moment. It was coffee time, and along with caffeine, a sugar fix might better stimulate my grey cells. After a quick trip to the baker downstairs, I was soon settled in one of my ancient lounge chairs with coffee and cake to aid the contemplative processes.

As I sat munching and sipping, I ran my recent to-do list through my mind. Something stood out immediately. Most of the items on the list were matters I needed to discuss with Ben. They were questions to which only Ben might provide answers. Normally, I would take them up with him when he came to dinner in the evening. But, this time, the list was long and involved, and many of the issues to be discussed would require Ben's access to information unavailable to me. One thing was clear. On this occasion, I needed a proper work session with him. The problem was that, as Millhaven's top cop, Ben has a heavy workload and doesn't have time for lunch some days. He is unlikely to have spare time to sit down with me to discuss my case.

Having dispatched coffee and cake and thoroughly depressed myself about my case, I remained slumped in my lounge chair until my phone demanded my attention. It was Ben ... *did I have any spare time today, preferably sooner rather than later?* After an appropriate delay – while I supposedly consulted my calendar – I was free for the next few hours.

"Good; I'll come over now ... but I will be needing coffee and cake. And this might be a long session. So we might need lunch later too."

"No problems," I assured him, and thought he might be surprised at just how long our session might develop into. In the meantime, I needed to fetch more cake and refill the coffee machine.

It takes a few minutes to walk from his office to mine, but today, he opted to drive and parked in the tenants' carpark behind my building. Armed with coffee and cake, we installed ourselves at my desk. Ben opened his laptop, and the long slog began. Before Ben outlined what he wanted to do, I jumped in with a question I'd been dying to ask since I noticed he had brought his computer.

"Before we begin whatever you want us to look at, please do one quick thing for me." He gave me one of his looks but agreed. "Thanks. Can you check for any vehicle registrations under the name of Roy Gilham?"

"Yeah... Okay, what do you want to know?"

"Everything...." I received another hard look and ignored it. With pad and pencil at the ready, I asked him to tell me what he found.

It appears Mr Gilham has two vehicles registered in his name: a car and a motorbike. Ben read out the details of the car and then paused. I looked up to see why. He looked as though he thought he had completed the task.

"Well, don't stop there," I snapped. "What about the motorbike?"

"Oh, I didn't think you would be interested in the bike." He read out the details. "What's so interesting about this bloke

Gilham? Does his wife think he is up to no good?" I was still chuckling as I tried to answer.

"In a manner of speaking, yes. But Gilham is interesting because my Tasmanian colleague has confirmed Roy Gilham is one and the same as Blake Carter." I explained the process behind the name change."

"Christ, the missing man...." Ben murmured. "How long ago did Gilham become Carter?"

"It's not recent. When he was about twenty."

"What else do you know that I might find useful?" His tone told me he was not a happy chap.

"I don't KNOW anything... not much anyway. But, between us, we might be surprised at how much we do know" God, this is becoming exasperating. "Have you anything back from forensics on the blood samples taken from both of my shooting sites?"

"They weren't from the same person, and we don't have an identification for either of them."

"Both of them looked as though they had lost quite a bit of blood. I thought they might have sought medical attention and, as they were gunshot wounds, the doctors might have notified the police."

"We found the first victim early this morning. He is currently in a serious condition in hospital in Ralston. We haven't had a chance to check his identity.

We don't have anything on the other victim yet, and have services outside Millhaven on alert for any gunshot wounds."

"I thought the first victim was in hospital here in Millhaven. Didn't the doctor alert your guys about his gunshot wound?"

"Yes, but after the guard on duty was fed some 'funny coffee' that knocked him out, our patient was spirited away and ended up in Ralston hospital, where he now is in isolation with a *staph* infection."

"That's interesting. From the blood at the scene and the severity of his wound, I wouldn't have thought the victim was in a fit state to drive to Ralston. In fact, I'm surprised he survived the four-hour drive, even though someone else drove him there.

Now, the second victim…," I continued, "I can tell you something about him, although it has nothing to do with his injury. From the security image of the bloke on my deck the other morning, he has been positively identified as Blake Carter. I also sent a copy to my Tasmanian colleague, who compared it to a photo in a police file of a young Blake Carter/Roy Gilham. He is reasonably confident of a match."

"So the missing man is not really missing. He just hasn't gone home. Is that a fair assessment of the situation?"

"Yep, but there are a couple of things that don't add up. My investigation failed to find any evidence Carter went to Tasmania as his wife believed because we now know he has been in Millhaven the whole time.

That gives rise to a number of questions. Where is he living? Does he have one or more accomplices helping him stay under the radar? And, was he responsible for drugging Brett while he was on duty at the Thomlinson Estate the other night?"

"Interesting questions, and for none of which we have answers."

"I'm not sure that's true. The camera footage from Griff Davidson's block of units shows a bundle, surprisingly like a body being loaded into that van. You gave me the registration details of that van this morning. Is it a coincidence that Griff Davidson just happens to have disappeared, or is his disappearance involved with whatever Carter is up to? I believe it's the latter, and Carter is not working alone."

"Right. So we know the identity of one of those two blokes and his supposed address. I'm not sure what we do with that. Any thought of Davidson's disappearance? Has Janine given you any clues?"

"Possibly. Davidson was her forensic auditor. There were some funny goings-on in the accounts. I don't know who alerted whom about the possible discrepancies. Although

Janine didn't want to believe it, I think she suspected Carter was somehow siphoning money out of the company. It could be that Davidson's digging about in the accounts might be responsible for his sudden disappearance.

Ben, I don't want to suggest this, but I don't like Davidson's chances of still being upright and breathing. Why keep him alive? At some point, they'd either have to let him go and run the risk of what might follow, or get rid of him permanently. I believe this mob are more inclined towards the latter option."

"It seems the two most urgent tasks for my teams are: to search hospitals and doctors outside Millhaven where Carter might have sought medical attention after you wounded him, and to impound that van for forensic investigation."

"Agreed … but, as I recall, your visit was to discuss something bothering you. All we've done so far is discuss stuff from my investigation. So, what prompted your visit?"

"Argh, hell, I'd forgotten about that. We managed to obtain some CCTV footage from the time of your unwelcome visitor the other morning. It's from a building across from the entrance to your street. The Tech staff worked on the recording last night. If we go through it together, you are more likely to spot something out of place than I am. Should we run the footage now to see if it tells us anything?"

Silly question…. I held out my hand for the memory stick containing the recording. Scrutinising CCTV footage required my bigger monitor. I wheeled over to my desk a 36 inch monitor on a trolley and connected the monitor to my computer. Then we both shuffled forward on our chairs to wait for the file to load.

"There it is!" I squawked. "There's the motorbike turning onto my street. What's the time stamp on that frame?" It was about the correct time for my unwelcome visitor's arrival.

"The image doesn't tell us much. It's just a black blob on something black that's the shape of a bike," Ben said with a shrug. "No help there. Either the light is bad in that area, or he smeared something over the number plate."

"Sssh, keep watching," I hissed. "There might be a clearer image when he leaves. If the time stamp on that first image is right, we have a lot of footage to watch before he leaves. He would have been here for over an hour."

"That's if it is the right bike. It could be anyone on a bike going home after a night out."

Ben had a point, but my gut told me something about that bike and its rider was familiar. We had to sit patiently, watching the images roll across the screen as little happened in my part of the world on the night in question. A car, one truck, and a security firm's vehicle were the only other traffic recorded. I increased the playback speed slightly, but not enough to risk missing something pertinent. The minutes ticked by. Frustration levels increased. Ben became irritable.

"For God's sake, speed it up until the next time there's some action," he demanded.

"We might miss something important. If you can't handle it, make another coffee. I'll have one too, thanks." He didn't. Instead, he continued sitting there watching images rolling across the screen. It was some time before the situation suddenly changed.

"Whoa! Rewind…," I yelped as I clicked on the left arrow below the images. "Did you see it? Yeah… Look, see this frame.

That's the bike coming back towards the camera across from the intersection." Ben shuffled forward on his seat and craned his neck towards the screen.

"Well, that's more helpful. This time he has his lights on – if it is the same bike."

"Of course, it's the same bike. Who else would be riding along my street at that hour of the night? This neighbourhood isn't overstocked with motorbikes. In fact, I don't know of any other riders around here apart from me." He chose to ignore me.

But Ben was right. The bike's lights were off when the rider entered the street earlier. Now, desperate to get away, the rider didn't bother with such precautions. This time, the bike headed towards the camera with its headlight on. I rewound the footage to the first image of the bike departing my street before slowing the play speed until it moved forward frame by frame.

"Look. The rider is slumped over the petrol tank." I did a fast rewind back and forward through the recording. "See the difference. The rider was upright when he arrived earlier, but slumped over when he left. I'd say that's the bloke who was on my deck. I wounded him, and that's why he is slumped over." Ben grudgingly agreed and also agreed the rider probably was Blake Carter.

Carter was seriously wounded. How could he have his wound treated at a health facility without the police being notified of a gunshot wound? I was about to ask Ben that when my phone chirped. I didn't recognise the caller ID, but it could be a potential new client, so I answered the call. It was a male voice I didn't recognise but felt I should know it.

"Miss Whittington, apologies for bothering you, but do you have a minute to talk to me?" I assured the caller I could spare a couple of minutes. "Thanks. It's Brett, Brett Galbraith, the security guard from Thomlinson Estate. I know calling you is a bit of a cheek, but it was the only way. You seem to be close to Superintendent Richards, and I'm wondering if you could get a message to him for me."

"Why not ring him directly?"

"In case something happens, I don't want my phone to show I called him. But there are a couple of things I need him to know, and I hoped you might pass on a message for me."

"I could pass on a message, but I can do better than that. You can tell him yourself. He is here with me. I'll just put him on." As I handed the phone to Ben, I mouthed 'Brett Galbraith'.

Ben wandered away from the desk to take the call. I gathered up the coffee mugs and took them to my kitchenette. As I returned to my desk, Ben ended the call and strode across my office. We arrived at my desk together. Ben's face suggested he was troubled by whatever Brett's message had been. I didn't speak.

Waiting is not my strong point. After a minute of sitting silently staring at my desk, I reached my limit.

"On the assumption Brett's message has troubled you, I need to ask whether it will likely trouble me as well, or at least involve me?"

"Oh, sorry… Yeah, it does involve you. I told Brett we would meet him at the estate at two o'clock. It has to look like an impromptu visit, not prearranged."

"Okay, that's fine. It would be handy to know why we are going to meet him. Has something else happened? What was his call about?"

"Two things: I should look into Stan, the other security guard currently doing twelve-hour shifts with Brett, and he thinks something funny is happening in that house on Thomlinson Estate."

"What sort of 'funny'?"

"Things that go bump in the night and make funny sounds when there shouldn't be sounds."

"Ah hah, I see. This case becomes more interesting and complicated by the day while seeming not to progress at all."

"I need to make a couple of phone calls. I need officers to start looking into Stan, the security guard. But it is lunchtime. So, while I make phone calls, perhaps you could do the hunter-gatherer thing and find lunch – and something sweet for afters."

While it was tempting to point out that this was my office and I wasn't just the office girl, I thought better of it. Something occurred to me as I was about to go.

"Might be worth looking into the other security guard too."

Then I headed downstairs to find food. When I returned, the hot beef and gravy rolls and a box of assorted pastries met with his approval. Everything was on hold while we dispatched lunch. To fill in time until we went to meet Brett, Ben asked if there was anything else I wanted him to look into today. What a silly question. I always have something only he can help me with, and this case has loads of questions needing answers.

"Ben, where do you think Carter has been living since his 'disappearance'? We don't think he left Millhaven. I've drawn a blank on his possible whereabouts because I know nothing about his friends or close acquaintances. But now, the information on the van involved in Davidson's disappearance has me wondering if he is holed up with the van's registered owner. In that rural area, few nosey neighbours keep tabs on who comes and goes." Deep in thought, I continued, "Davidson's disappearance would have to be a helluva coincidence if it wasn't part of the Thomlinson case."

"My instinct says it is part of it. It doesn't take much imagination to see how the Davidson disappearance fits in with the rest of what's been happening. I know you are going to ask when I'm going to pull in Joe Costanzo, the owner of that van. The short answer is, I'm not going to do anything other than watch the bloke until we have sorted out the rest of the case. Well, unless he does something to grab my attention.

Anyway, we need to see what happens this afternoon, and it is time we left for the Thomlinson Estate to hear what Brett has to tell us. Hopefully, Stan has gone by the time we arrive."

Stan wasn't a problem. Brett told us when he arrived early for the midday changeover of shifts, Stan, claiming he had urgent business to attend to in town, left the Estate at 11.30.

Ben called Brett as we approached. The gates swung open. Brett met us at the front door. Brett acted unmoved when Ben announced he had only come to have another look inside the house. This wasn't a surprise visit, but one carefully choreographed during that phone call in my office. I kept my mouth shut and fell in line as, in silence, Brett led us up to Janine's apartment. We didn't enter. Instead, we talked outside her door.

"Tell me about these sounds you've heard," Ben asked to open the conversation.

"This week, because my shift is midday to midnight, I don't hear them during the day, but I do sometimes at night. They're occasional and quite soft. It would be easy to miss them if you dozed off, were reading a book, or something. With that TV set in the control centre switched on, you wouldn't hear them at all."

"So what do these noises sound like?" Ben asked as he glanced around us. "And you think this is where those sounds come from?"

"Hard to describe the sounds because they are so muted. From the control centre, they sound like something being dropped onto the carpet. It's a bit muffled. At other times, it sounds like a chair being moved. A chair pulled out from a table or put back under the table."

A moment of silence ensued as Ben and I considered Brett's information. Brett was becoming nervous about something and shifted his weight from foot to foot. Both Ben and I noticed, but it was Ben's show, and I shouldn't be asking questions – yet. I was relieved when Ben finally asked the question.

"Is everything all right, Brett? You seem anxious to be elsewhere."

"It's time for me to patrol all the external doors and windows. We have to key each one on a special device as we check them. It would be best if, when you arrived unannounced, you came straight up here on your own while I went about my duties as normal."

"Good point; Go and do whatever you're supposed to and we will see you on our way out," Ben instructed him before turning his attention to me.

"We'll check Janine's apartment, but our main target is Carter's rooms. Did you bring those photos you took when you inspected these apartments with Janine?"

"Of course, but why didn't we discuss all this with Brett before we came up here."

"He suspects conversations in other parts of the house are recorded, but the recordings don't feed into the control centre. Only these apartments appear free of such intrusion into the occupants' private lives." I nodded and suggested we should make a start on Carter's apartment.

After wrestling the folder containing the photos out of my bag and dumping the bag outside Carter's door, I followed Ben into the apartment. I was ready to make an announcement after only a few steps into the living area.

"Someone has been here since Janine and me." I led Ben into the bedroom and strolled around, pointing out changes since the photos I had taken. As we wandered back into the living area, I told him of my previous visit.

"When we came up here, this apartment looked as though someone had left in a hurry. Some cupboard doors were ajar. Drawers weren't closed properly, and some had bits of clothing hanging out of them. Janine confirmed the state of the apartment was out of keeping with her husband, who she described as a bit OCD about tidiness.

The way this place looks now is more in line with Janine's comments about her husband."

The entire living area was visible from the kitchen and allowed for easy comparison with my earlier photographs.

"Right… we probably should have a quick look at Janine's apartment while we are here. But before we leave this one, I want to check a couple of things," Ben said. I was of much the same mind. As he spoke, I was about to open the fridge.

"I thought I would check for food or scraps in the place before we left," I said as I yanked open the fridge door. "Oh, yes. This is much better stocked than the last time I saw it."

The photo I took on my last visit showed the fridge almost devoid of anything edible. Now there was milk (still in date), juice, cheese, three takeaway containers of food, and a couple of apples, and the freezer compartment contained more foodstuff that required just reheating or some basic cooking.

"It seems we agree somebody has been here since Brett was drugged. Let's have a quick look at Janine's apartment and then have a brief word with Brett on our way out."

Ben was peering in the fridge as he spoke to me. Then, as he started towards the door, he flipped the lid of a rubbish bin in the corner of the kitchen on his way past. His face lit up.

"Aah, well now, that is interesting. Three guesses who might have been here and how recently," he chirped as he gestured for me to take a look.

I rushed over and then hesitated as a wave of apprehension flowed through me. What was in the bin? Something funny, something useful to our investigation, or something quite unpleasant? It proved to be the latter.

A discarded surgical dressing lay on top of everything in the half-full bin. It was not your average bit of gauze-and-sticking plaster type homemade dressing. It was a professional looking surgical dressing, and it still looked damp.

"His wound is still weeping," I murmured. Then, closing the bin, I said, "So, our Blake Carter has been in his apartment at some time since I wounded him yesterday. It looks as though he has been staying here, maybe not the whole time, but on and off since our last visit here. How can that be, and what do we do now?"

"We do as we planned to do: leave after having a quick look at Janine's apartment." The set of Ben's jaw told me I should fall in behind and not ask questions.

"Thanks for that, Brett," Ben announced on our return to the control centre. "We've had a bit of a look around and are ready to leave now. Perhaps you might let us out."

Brett sprung off his chair and led us to the front door before following us down to the bottom of the stairs.

It wasn't until I reached Ben's vehicle that I realised Ben wasn't with me. He had further quiet words with Brett after I left them. Intrigued, I had a whole raft of questions ready to ask as we drove off the estate. He pre-empted my move and stopped me before I could ask my first question.

"Yes, I know you have a myriad of questions for me, but please give me a few moments to sort something out in my head before you begin." I slumped in my seat and waited for my cue to speak.

We were almost in the city heart before Ben spoke again. "Do you suppose we could finish off those cakes you bought this morning over a coffee?"

He parked behind my office building, and we soon were sitting in the ancient lounge chairs in my interview corner.

"You really could do with some decent chairs, you know. Something a touch more modern and comfortable than these would be good," he suggested.

"What, and frighten off any potential clients who come to see me? The state of this place makes them think I don't charge very much if I can't afford something better than what I have."

He chuckled and agreed I had a valid point but seemed reluctant to launch the conversation we had to have. I stepped in to kick it off.

"What happens now?"

"Dunno ... not exactly anyway. I'll need to see what the boys found about the other security guard, Stan. It's a fair bet he's been aiding and abetting our friend, Mr Carter. It's the only way Carter could be staying in his apartment. I only have my gut feeling, but I don't think Carter has been staying there the whole time, and it's probably been no more than the last few days. Now I know about his other identity, I'll have a dig around to see what that might produce. What's your next move?"

"Not sure yet. I'm still trying to process everything that's happened in the last couple of days. My gut tells me Carter is either desperate or something is making him less cautious than he was up until now. The Griff Davidson matter is causing me indigestion. It's part of whatever is going on, but I can't quite get a handle on it. Perhaps what's causing the problem is our mutual belief that Davidson has already gone to meet his maker. And that tends to suggest that whatever we're dealing with here needs to be stopped and quickly. One last thing, maybe you should take my advice and look into that security guard who is off on sick leave."

"Agreed. I'll go back to my office now to talk to the security firm, then rattle a few cages to see what jumps out. I need to know how much of this you intend to share with Janine now. She is your client, and all this is part of the case she asked you to investigate. Remember, whatever you do could have wider implications. I don't want my chances of nabbing these bastards fouled up because we're both not reading from the same page at the same time."

I assured him his message was received and understood. In truth, I didn't have a clue what to do next, but I was sure I wouldn't be sharing any of the latest developments with Janine at this time. A few minutes later, Ben was on his way back to his office, and I was trying to coax the mass of stuff floating around in my mind into a positive train of thought.

"This case is getting the better of me," I confessed to the universe.

There was no way I would share that thought with anyone else, but this case has become akin to an 'onion'. It's slow progress having to peel it back layer by layer, like peeling an onion… And every layer peeled back uncovers a further deception. As with the real vegetable, peeling back each layer will likely result in tears – for my client. I need to strip back the layers of Janine's case more quickly to expose the heart of it and uncover the full extent of the deception. I suspect Janine will not be safe until I've done that.

Perhaps if I go for a drive somewhere and commune with nature for a bit, maybe I'll come up with something I can do. As it was already late, I packed everything I might need to work on tonight into my tote bag, locked my office and galloped down to my car. With no clear direction in mind, I drove out of the city and soon found myself in a semi-rural location on the edge of the city limits.

"What the hell am I doing out here?" I asked the universe. With no reply forthcoming, I simply continued driving along the road. A little further along, a track led off to the coast. I told myself that sitting and watching the ocean for a while might be just the thing to stimulate my grey cells. I turned off onto a rough track.

The track didn't look as though it had seen much traffic in recent times. Little chance of being interrupted here, I told myself as I eased into a clearing at the end of the track. Beyond the rocky cliff at the edge of the clearing, a deep blue ocean dotted with white caps stretched out before me. A flock of gulls searching for dinner squealed as they circled overhead. A sea eagle or kite of some sort, riding the thermals, described lazy circles high above the water. After admiring the view from my car for a few moments, I undid the seatbelt, slid out of the seat, and crunched my way across gravel that sprouted occasional tufts of spinifex-like grass.

Paper barks and eucalyptus surrounded the area and whispered gently in the afternoon sea breeze. The briny smell of the ocean filled the air. A couple of parrots chatted to one another, and in the distance, a kookaburra had an early practice session for tonight's choir recital. I relaxed as I took in the beauty and solitude of my surroundings. Now to find somewhere comfortable to sit and think.

In past times, this clearing had seen many more visitors than recently. The relic of a makeshift brazier that perhaps had kept young couples warm on winter nights now lay abandoned and rusting at one end of the clearing.

A large boulder caught my eye, and almost beside it, a grassy patch right at the edge of the cliff lured me to it. The perfect spot to sit and think while dangling my legs over the edge. I realised this spot was the clifftop of a small alcove in a much wider arc of cliffs. The colours of the rocks and the patterns they formed on the cliff face were breathtaking.

For a few moments, I stood looking out to sea, mesmerised by the beauty of the constantly moving blue seascape before me. My eyes were drawn to a line of driftwood slowly being herded into the alcove by a combination of wind, waves and tide.

The place offered the solitude and tranquillity I needed to make sense of my case. But I needed to sit and be comfortable. I could be here for a while. The clump of grass right on the edge near the boulder beckoned me.

I stepped right to the edge and peered down the cliff face below me … and caught my breath. Stunned, I dragged my phone out of my pocket, almost dropping it in my haste.

Bugger! No reception here. I sprinted to my car, sending the smaller loose gravel flying from under my feet as I ran.

Chapter 25

Restricted by the shape and size of the clearing meant executing a multi-point turn before heading back out to the road. With the pedal kept hard to the floor, my SUV bucked and swayed as it rocketed over the rough ground. Tree branches whipped it every time it strayed from the centre of the track.

With all four wheels on bitumen again and blatant disregard for the legal speed limit, I roared towards town. Although it was only a couple of minutes, it felt much longer before my phone found reception again. I told Siri to call Ben, and then, with my panic level rising, I waited for him to answer. I expected it to ask me to leave a message but Ben finally answered. He was not happy about my call.

"What?" he demanded.

I didn't have time for the reply I wanted to deliver. Instead, I barked. "I've just found something I think is important to our investigation. I think it's Griff Davidson, and he is at the bottom of a very steep cliff."

"Where are you, and what makes you think it's Davidson."

I gave him a brief description of my location and where I saw the body.

"What are you doing out there? Argh, don't tell me. I know why you're there. The address of that van owner is somewhere out that way. Whatever possessed you to go poking around out there without a backup?"

"I didn't deliberately come here. I just went for a drive … and hadn't thought about the van owner's address until you mentioned it. Anyway, I'm heading…. Shit!"

"What? Sonny, speak to me."

"I think I've picked up a tail."

"Tell me about it."

"There's a dark blue van following me and… yep, it's a tail and closing in fast."

"Which one of your vehicles are you driving?"

I told him it was the SUV.

"Christ… cumbersome and about as agile as a river barge. I'm in the traffic control centre now. Give me your exact location."

"I don't know where I am other than east of the city and heading back into town along a bitumen road through a rural area with few houses. There are no side streets or intersections anywhere in sight."

"Are you armed? Do you have your weapon?"

"Uhmm… yes, it is somewhere in the bottom of my bag."

"Take it out and have it ready – just in case."

"No can do. I need both hands on the wheel right now, and I'm praying I don't encounter any other traffic."

"What can you give me to help pinpoint your location?"

"Nothing … Oh, hang on, there's a side road coming up. Yeah, it's Millers Road. I've now entered a more populated area. I just passed a school, Sandcliff Primary School. A more populated area probably means more traffic. At the speed I'm going, that's not good."

"Okay, I think we have you on the map. Is there a road up ahead that goes off to your right?"

"I'm passing it now. It's Jansens Road."

"Right, we've got you. A patrol car in the area will pick you up soon, and a second car is on its way too. Up ahead is a major intersection with Neaton Road. Turn left onto Neaton Road and stay on that road towards the city."

"Yeah, the intersection is just up ahead. Jesus, I'll have to slow down, or I'll never make the corner in this wagon."

But I didn't want to slow down. The only thing keeping me safe was that my gutsy turbocharged SUV was faster than the van. What can I do to avoid a rollover at the intersection? I swung right, heading for the extreme right edge of the wrong lane.

The manoeuvre gave a wider, gentler arc to my turn. It was hairy, but I remained upright on four wheels and was tearing along Neaton Road. I heard the squeal of brakes behind me. That van is no more manoeuvrable than my great tank, but it hadn't prepared for the corner and had to jump hard on the brakes to prevent a rollover. By the time it was safely on Neaton Road and picked-up speed again, I had put a significant distance between us.

Familiar landmarks began flashing by. I alerted Ben to the fact that I was safely on Neaton Road and feeling a bit more comfortable.

"Ben, I know where I am now, but I don't see any patrol cars yet."

"The first one is close by. Keep coming along Neaton Road towards the city."

Not only did I know where I was, but I also knew that up ahead, Glendenning Trucking's headquarters was off to my right and along a side street. I checked my rearview mirror and judged the gap sufficient to accommodate what I was about to do. Up ahead, Argyle Street led off to the right. I employed a similar approach as at the last intersection, moving as far left as possible before hanging a hard right into Argyle Street. But I had to wash off some speed to turn safely onto the narrower street. It allowed the van to catch up a little.

Argyle Street only ran for two blocks before making a right-angled turn to run towards the city parallel to Neaton Road. The trucking company occupied the corner block between Neaton Road and Argyle Street.

Glendenning Trucking occupied an area two blocks wide and two blocks deep between the two thoroughfares. In the course of a couple of investigations in the past, I had occasion to visit here and became familiar with its layout. Apart from a couple of small shed-like buildings along one side, the only other building housed a combined repair shop and admin facility. The unattractive structure was huge, high, and devoid of aesthetic embellishment.

At a slightly reduced speed, I flew along Argyle Street, around its corner, and, a little further along, to the rear entrance to Glendenning Trucking's yard. Dashing in through the gates, I turned left and wove my way through various trucks and trailers along the side of the workshop building. Directly opposite the Argyle Street entrance to the property is the exit to Neaton Road. This arrangement provides a neat, clear corridor through the property for an easy flow of trucks in and out of the yard. It also means the main building is offset to one side of the corridor.

As I navigated through the big rigs and other trucking gear strewn around everywhere, I could hear Ben bellowing at me over the phone. I ignored him until I was nestled alongside the repair workshop and hidden from view by a number of prime movers. But as I was about to respond to Ben, I heard the van slow down at the rear entrance to the property. It had followed me along Argyle Street and had either seen me turn in, or guessed I had, when it lost sight of me.

"Silence!" I hissed at Ben, before spending the next few moments listening to my pulse almost drowning out the sound of the van as it sped through the yard a touch too fast for some of the truck drivers waiting to exit the property. They indicated their displeasure by loud blasts of their horns and bellowed expletives. Then there was silence… well, silence apart from the sound of truckers going about their business.

Safe to return my attention to my phone and Ben, who had maintained his silence as I had asked, I told him what happened and where I was and again asked about the patrol cars.

"Are you sure the van is back heading towards the city along Neaton Road?" he queried.

"As sure as I can be. I don't know what it might do when it can't see me anywhere up ahead. It might come back and cruise Argyle Street looking for me. Do you have any suggestions about my next move? I thought I might head back onto Neaton Road and hang well back as I follow it towards the city."

"Have you found your weapon?"

"Affirmative; it is now in my lap."

"Okay, then go ahead and ease back out onto Neaton Road … but check first that the van isn't on its way back to look for you. Then, keeping within the speed limit, if possible, continue along Neaton Road towards the city. It's likely the patrol cars will have apprehended the van by the time you next see it. Now, stay on the air and give me a running commentary as you go."

A couple of minutes later, and after holding my breath as I eased out onto it, I again travelled along Neaton Road. The van was nowhere in sight. This is not good. I need to know where it is. I don't want to be rammed by it racing out of a side street at me. My head constantly swivelled from side to side as I searched for the van. I became aware my hands were aching. I risked a glance at them. They gripped the wheel so tightly, the knuckles were white. I eased my grip a bit, but only enough to allow a little circulation to ease the pain. Having dealt with that problem, I became aware of Ben calling my name.

"What's happening, Ben?"

"No, that's my question. What the hell is happening? I haven't heard a word from you since you left Glendenning's."

"Because nothing has happened. I haven't laid eyes on the van since I rejoined Neaton Road. Not knowing where it is makes me nervous."

"Don't worry about it; just keep coming towards the city. I will pick you up at the city limits and shepherd you into town. Nothing to report from the patrol cars yet. Please keep talking to me, even if nothing is happening, keep telling me nothing is happening."

"Ben, it occurred to me that the van might have returned to Argyle Street when it realised it had lost me. Maybe I haven't seen it because it is now travelling along Argyle, and there's no opportunity to get off Argyle until it intersects with Neaton Road just before the city limits."

He didn't comment further, but I heard a murmured conversation between him and an officer in the traffic control centre. Had something happened with the patrol cars? I was tempted to ask, but the murmured conversation continued, and I didn't want to interrupt. They might be trying to devise a new strategy for apprehending the van. But, after a couple of minutes, I became impatient and was about to say so when Ben came back to me.

"You can stop worrying about the whereabouts of the van. The driver is now in custody. Your identification of the van was correct. It is the one we saw in the CCTV footage from Griff Davidson's apartment building. The driver will spend the next wee while *helping us with our enquiries* – as we say in our Press releases."

My breathing and pulse rate returned to normal as I entered the city and gained Ben as a 'rear guard'. He followed me back to the parking lot behind my office building, and then escorted me to my office. I unlocked my door, but he checked inside before allowing me to enter, and then he locked the door behind us.

"I don't know about you, but I could go a coffee right now – and some of those cakes if there are any left."

Although I laughed at his request, as I headed for my kitchenette, a thought occurred to me.

"Are you sure you want coffee? I feel as though I've had enough for one day. Are you still on duty, or are you inclined to join me in something a little stronger than coffee?"

"The answer to both those is 'yes'. Technically, I am still on duty, and yes, I would prefer something a little stronger. What are you offering?"

I waved a bottle of single malt scotch at him as I reached it down from a cupboard.

Then there was the usual faffing about organising glasses and ice cubes, and querying how many 'fingers' of scotch were required in each glass before we finally settled in my interview corner with our drinks, a plate of crackers and some old, somewhat dried-out, cheese.

After a couple of sips, reality returned with a vengeance. "What are we doing? Why are we sitting here when there is a body out there? You need to do something." I was almost shouting at Ben by the time I finished speaking.

"What…? Jesus, I forgot what started all this. You said you found a body you thought was Griff Davidson. How do you know it was him?"

"I don't know, but my gut, instinct, or whatever, told me that's who it was. It looks as though it was tipped over the edge of a cliff and landed on a rocky shelf some distance below. Because of where the body is, there's a danger of losing it with the next high tide. For the last few days, we've had neap tides. Their highest levels haven't been high enough to cover the ledge. But, if the tide is high enough tonight or tomorrow, the body will disappear out to sea. That probably was the intention when dumping it there."

"Is the site easily accessible for recovery of the body?"

"Not easily. I suppose you could abseil down the cliff face, but I don't know about appropriate anchor points for the ropes. It was low tide when I was there. The water was a bit below the level of the shelf where the body lies. Maybe, if the tide was a bit higher, you could bring a boat in there, but you would have to know the area and choose exactly the right time. The only other way I can think of is to drop a basket down from a chopper. With the chopper hovering a safe height above the cliff and the surrounding trees, it would mean a long drop and might require more than one person to deal with the body."

"You're convinced it isn't some unfortunate bushwalker who fell over the edge."

"The body is not dressed for bushwalking. It doesn't matter anyway. You still have a body to recover."

Ben was on his feet, had his phone in his hand, and was walking away from me. He made his call from my kitchenette. I don't know who Ben called or what was said, but he was in 'business mode' on his return. He didn't regain his seat but stood in front of me, flicking through something on his phone as he spoke.

"Sonny, I need to know exactly where you were when you found the body. Can you show me on this map?" He shoved his phone under my nose. I took one look at it and shook my head.

"Too small to see enough detail," I announced. "I'll try to bring up a better one on the computer."

With the help of Google Maps, a few moments later, I was using the cursor to trace the road in question.

"There… see that track going off to the right? That's where I turned off."

I moved the image across the screen to bring up more of the area east of the road. Then moved it more to bring the clearing at the end of the track and the large boulder onto the screen.

"See the grassy patch there just along from the boulder…," I hovered the cursor over the spot where I had intended to sit. "that's where I was standing when I looked down and saw the body." He moved in close and photographed the image on my screen.

On his way to the door, he sent someone the image he had taken. He barked at me as he walked.

"Don't stay here, and don't go home. Go to my place and stay there until I come home. Go now. Don't argue with me. Just go to my place and stay there."

"Yes, Sir." Although the temptation to argue was strong, his tone cautioned against it. "Where will you be, and what will you be doing? Will I be there for a while before you return?"

"Possibly…." But the door slammed shut, and he was gone.

His words managed to shake me to the core. Unsettled once more, I definitely needed to finish my scotch… but first, I locked my door. As I drained my glass, I thought about Janine. I had kept everything from her to avoid causing her further stress, but it was time to talk to her. Now I was even more concerned about her safety. She needed to know the whole story and why she needed to exercise extreme caution.

Janine answered her phone almost on the first ring. I intended to arrange a meeting for tomorrow, but when I explained my reason for calling, her response surprised me.

"If you are free, I'll come now."

I checked the time and didn't need to be a genius to work out that it would be quite late by the time she drove in from her office.

"That would make it a late day for you. I am free now, but I'm happy to leave it until tomorrow if you prefer."

"This is early for me. I can be in your office in about five minutes."

"Five minutes… are you already in the city?"

"Oh, sorry. Yes, I'll work from here in my finance department's office suite for a while. I've taken over Griff Davidson's former office and ruffled some feathers while I was about it. Actually, I have something to talk to you about, and I intended to call you today for an appointment. Then I was setting up my new office.... You know how it goes."

About five minutes later, Janine knocked on my door, and we were straight down to business.

"You said you had something to tell me. Should I prepare to be concerned?" I asked.

"To be honest, I don't know – yet. Anyway, here's the story. Please tell me what you make of it.

Late yesterday, I received a message from a phone number I didn't recognise. At first, I wasn't game to open the attachment. I gave it to my technical department to see if they could identify anything about it that might tell me who sent it. The concerning thing was that it claimed to be from Griff Davidson, my forensic auditor who disappeared."

"It only arrived late yesterday, although he has been missing a couple of days?"

"Yeah. At first, its timing made me inclined to dismiss it. Then I remembered that area where my company's complex is located was without reception for most of yesterday and part of the day before. We had no phones or internet. So this message came through with a whole swag of other stuff when communications were restored."

"What did your technical department find when they looked into it?"

"Nothing much; by talking to a friend of a friend who has access to the 'right' information, one of my team was able to establish that the message was sent from … what do they call them?... oh, yes, it was sent from a burner phone. That didn't make me feel any better about it. Griff had two phones: a work phone supplied by the company and a personal one. Mostly we communicated via the work phone, but sometimes his personal one. When he disappeared, I kept trying both of them without success, so you can appreciate how this burner phone made me nervous."

"Griff – if it was Griff – obviously had something important to tell you, something he didn't want others to know about."

"So it would seem. In his attachment, he said he suspected money was being siphoned off from the company via a sophisticated system of documentation that resulted in invoices for big dollars being paid to spurious companies… companies he didn't know anything about and suspected weren't genuine."

"Is that possible? I mean, is it possible for bogus documentation to make its way right through your system without detection?"

"Well, I wouldn't have thought so, but I had a suspicion some time ago, and that's why I brought in Griff Davidson. He immediately introduced a couple of new measures. It looked as though, if something fishy had been happening, his new measures had stopped it – until a few months ago when he thought he detected a whiff of the same thing happening again. I think he was close to uncovering the whole system and those involved."

"Good reason to remove Griff from the equation.

"Remove him! Sonny, What do you mean?"

"Do you have any ideas about who might have been involved or the amounts of money going 'missing'?"

"He did give me a figure but stressed it was still only an estimate until he finished his investigation. It was close to a million dollars, but most of it was during the last few months. He also intimated he was close to exposing an employee central to the operation at our end – a high-ranking but unnamed employee."

"Any other clues about the rogue employee?"

"No-o… but it's not too hard to draw conclusions. There are two managers, each responsible for a separate and discreet function in the finance department. One looks after investments, marketing, and infrastructure matters. The other manager looks after the traditional accounting function. They both used to report to me until I suspected something was amiss. I brought in Griff and made him the senior officer in the department. Both managers then came under Griff."

"While I don't know too much about your operation, and don't need to know, I don't have to think too hard to know which manager I would be having a hard look at. Have any changes or anything else of note happened regarding that staff member?"

"Not until today. When I arrived to set up in Griff's office, that manager – the accounting manager – had taken over the office, despite the fact he already had his own office. I'm afraid I turfed him out none too politely. He was extremely unhappy, especially about my becoming a permanent fixture in his domain."

"Cruelled his game no end, I should imagine, having you looking over his shoulder all the time and having to report directly to you now. Did Griff give you anything more to help you weed out your rogue operator?"

"Yes, but there is still more work required. I need to tread cautiously so I don't blow it. I hope I'm up to the task now Griff is gone. He is gone – I mean, gone permanently – isn't he? That's what you meant before, wasn't it?"

"I'm afraid that probably is the case, but it remains unconfirmed.

As for being up to the job, I'll need to talk to someone, but I think I might be able to organise something to help you with that.

The other thing I wanted to check was whether you had the locks on your unit changed."

"Yep. I did as you requested. Sonny, there is more going on than you're telling me about. Is there anything else I should know? I, too, don't need to be a genius to work out that, for you to tell me to change the locks, I am in danger. How serious is the risk?"

"Janine, I don't want to cause you undue concern, but the risk is significant. I want to show you something that you might find upsetting. Are you up for it?"

She took a deep breath, nodded, and held out her hand.

Chapter 26

"Before I show you, I'll tell you a story to explain what this is about. On a couple of occasions, an unwelcome visitor came calling at my home. He was frightened off by my neighbour's dog. The dog is in the kennels this week, so it wasn't around to scare off that visitor yesterday morning. I was awake at the time and decided to investigate. Things became interesting for a while."

I pulled up my sleeve to expose the large dressing strip. "I've gained a minor scar for my trouble, but my visitor came off second best. I shot and wounded him.

My security camera captured an excellent image of him, if you want to look at a copy of that image." Janine nodded and again held out her hand.

The photo went into her hand face down, and I watched her slowly turn it over. She gasped, and I saw the colour drain from her face. She tried to speak. Only a croak came out. After swallowing hard a couple of times, she tried again.

"This is Blake; Blake, my husband. This is your unwelcome visitor? It is Blake, isn't it?"

"Well, yes, it is Blake Carter … and no, it isn't. Let me clarify that. It is the man you and others here in Millhaven know as Blake Carter, but it's also a man named Roy Gilham. Blake is someone Roy has masqueraded as since he was in his early twenties."

"Did he do that?" she asked, pointing to my arm. I nodded. "Is he also responsible for Griff's disappearance?"

"He wasn't directly responsible. I don't know if he was involved… but somehow, I think he was."

"So, you're telling me my whole married life has been a sham?"

"Maybe not so much a sham as a long-range strategy."

"A strategy? What do you mean?"

"This is speculation on my part and may prove to be rubbish. I believe his initial plan was a get-rich-quick scheme. He intended to milk you of enough money to establish a comfortable future life for himself. Initially, your father's presence probably prevented his plan from gaining traction. After that, he saw himself free to get on with it.

Sometime during the last few months, his scheme underwent a major overhaul. The endgame changed. Why settle for milking a few dollars when he could take over the whole empire?"

With hardness in her eyes, Janine said, "All he had to do was remove the one major obstacle standing in his way… me!"

"As I said, perhaps I misjudge him, but I do believe you remain in danger while he is at large."

"That incident in the park, was that something Blake organised?"

How do I answer that? I shook my head while I searched for the right words and before deciding just to tell it as I saw it.

"No, Blake didn't organise someone else. It was Blake on that motorbike. We have an image of him from a security camera at the park. Only his eyes are visible, but I'll let you decide."

Again I slapped the photo from the park face down into her hand. She was even more cautious turning it over. This time, there was no shock, no dramatic response at all. She just studied the photo for a couple of moments before handing it back to me.

"Yeah, they're his eyes. It was Blake on that bike. It was Blake who tried to send me over the side of that bridge. And it was deliberate, wasn't it?"

"We believe it was. I'm sorry, Janine, but for your own safety, I felt you had to know despite it being painful for you."

"Thank you. But what about Griff? There's been an unsuccessful attempt on my life and one on yours. Was there a successful attempt on Griff's life? Come on, Sonny, level with me, please."

Her enormous blue eyes held mine. I saw no sign of hurt in them, just resignation. This lady is one helluva survivor, I thought before answering her.

"I believe so, but I have no evidence to back it up."

"How could I have been oblivious to what was happening? I would never have thought him capable of murder – even attempted murder. But you seem so sure that is the case.

"Janine, the information I've received from Tasmania suggests he honed his murderous skills at an early age."

"How can someone you know so well… someone who is so familiar in just about every way… be a complete stranger? Can there be such a thing as a familiar stranger?"

I had no enlightening answer for her.

My phone brought my meeting with Janine to an end. I checked the caller ID: Ben. This probably would not be pleasant. I asked Ben to hold before telling Janine I had to take the call. I offered to drive her back to her office or home as soon as it finished. She refused to be my offers, insisting she had thinking to do, and walking helped with that process.

Then, it was back to Ben and his opening greeting. "Where are you?"

"My office…."

"You are supposed to be at my place. Are you alone?"

"I am now. I had Janine here, but she just left. So, I am ready to leave now, but I don't think I need to spend tonight at your place. I'll talk to you over dinner."

"No. Stay there. I'm on my way to your office."

A strong argument followed but ended in a compromise. I went home to my place. About twenty minutes later, Ben arrived with an overnight bag in one hand and food in the other.

"My assumption is that your spare bed is made up as it usually is," he said as he dumped the bag of food on the kitchen bench before heading for the spare room.

"Am I to understand you intend spending the night?" I asked when he returned to the kitchen.

"Yes, and perhaps we should put that food in the oven to keep warm until we are ready to eat."

"Not the most romantic suggestion an overnight guest has ever made," I quipped before attending to the food.

In the bag were containers of various pasta dishes. Their aroma had me wishing we could eat straight away, but I did as I was told. After all, I already had stretched the friendship about as far as I dared. We took a pre-dinner drink out onto my back deck. A couple of sips later, I felt it safe to begin talking 'shop'.

"Ben, do you have anything more to report on the body I found?"

He checked his watch before speaking. "Before driving there myself, I organised our chopper to take a couple of officers up to look at the location. They checked the place while I was there and reported they thought the best approach was to have the water police bring in their big inflatable at high tide. If it hasn't already been lifted off, the body should soon be on its way to the morgue." He had barely finished speaking when his phone chirped. He took the call in the kitchen.

When he returned, he looked grim. "That was my Detective Sergeant who was with the boat crew. They recovered the body, and he confirmed the victim was dead before being thrown over the cliff. The victim was severely assaulted and strangled prior to being dumped."

"I suppose it is too early for an identification?"

He nodded, but I'm sure we both shared the same thought. The victim was the missing Griff Davidson.

"Janine shared some interesting information during her visit this afternoon. It might shed some light on the Davidson matter." I gave him an executive summary of Janine's story and explained how Janine was now installed in Davidson's former office in her finance department in the city. "Do you think she will be safe enough there?"

After a long pause, he simply replied, "I don't know." He shook his head and sat in silence for a few moments before continuing. "I cannot get a handle on this case. Nothing makes any sense. It appears we are dealing with a number of cases, but I know they are all part of one overarching situation that's becoming a big, well-orchestrated case. I'd welcome your thoughts on it."

In a repeat performance, I shared the same best-guess scenario with Ben as I had given Janine earlier. He sat deep in thought for a while before commenting.

"You're right about the outcome of his plan seeming to have changed over the last few months, but we don't know what might have motivated it. What triggered a perceived opportunity to go after the 'whole cake' rather than just a hefty 'slice' of it? Pure greed perhaps….?"

"No idea; only Janine might have clues to that. Now I've given her something to think about, she might come up with something. It might be useful for you also to have a word with Janine's secretary. She might have noticed something out of the ordinary a few months ago."

"We're a long way from wrapping this up, but I hope tomorrow will tell a different story. There are so many threads to this case, and I don't seem able to tie them together."

"I thought the same thing earlier today, but unlike you, I don't have any positive thoughts about tomorrow being any better than the last few days."

Until about ten o'clock, we continued discussing the case and sharing what each of us knew. It all came to a halt when Ben's phone demanded attention.

"Looks like you are wanted somewhere else tonight," I quipped as he took his phone out onto the back deck.

As I went for a shower, I hoped I was right about his being wanted somewhere else. I prefer to be on my own tonight. While they weren't definite plans, I did have a couple of ideas I might be tempted to explore. With Ben here, that would be impossible. When I emerged from the bathroom, he remained occupied with his phone call on the deck. To fill in time while he was engaged in what appeared to be an unusually lengthy call, I shut down my office for the night, tidied the kitchen, and started the dishwasher. As I wondered what I could do next, Ben wandered in from the deck.

"How do you feel about an early morning start tomorrow?" he asked.

"I'd need a damned good reason… but I'm not averse to the idea," I added after a second thought.

"Good; nothing definite yet, but it is likely to be about a three o'clock start."

"Yep, count me in," I chirped as I groaned internally. "Perhaps I might be allowed to know what is happening and why such an early start?"

"Nothing definite yet, but does it matter?"

"Probably not, but I do suffer from this perverse need-to-know syndrome."

"Right. Pour us a nightcap, and I'll tell you as much as there is to know.

My call was confirmation of the identity of the body they picked up earlier. It was Griff Davidson. The body matches the photo on Davidson's driver's licence, and a local dentist has confirmed its identity from his dental records."

"So, no real surprises then?"

"No, and now my detectives have dragged the van driver out of his cell and are applying considerable pressure about his role in Davidson's murder. The hope is he will feel inclined to share whatever information he has about the wider operation in which he was a player."

"Okay, but what's the early morning start supposed to achieve?"

"Ah, yes. I had a second call. There will be a two-pronged offensive. It will take place around three o'clock. The exact time will depend on when teams are in place and ready. One team will descend on the van driver's address out in that rural area where you found the body. The other team will visit Thomlinson Estate and, more precisely, Blake Carter's apartment there. We will accompany the second team."

"What do you hope to find at the van driver's place?"

"Uhmm… probably nothing much – and hopefully not Blake Carter – but maybe there'll be something we can use to nail others involved in this case. Are you right for an early morning jaunt to the Thomlinson Estate?" Ben does ask the silliest questions sometimes.

To ensure we were rested and ready to go when three o'clock rolled around, within minutes, we had said goodnight and headed for our separate bedrooms. I thought sleep would be elusive, but its oblivion arrived almost immediately. No dreams or anything else intruded until Ben's phone playing its tune in the spare room woke me soon after two o'clock. Perhaps it was someone telling Ben tonight's exercise had been called off, and getting out of bed would be a waste of sleep. No such luck….

A sharp staccato on my bedroom door told me the raids were going ahead.

"I'm already up," I lied in response to Ben's continued knocking – and promptly scrambled out of bed. "How are we going to play this?" I yelled through to the other room as I pulled on clothes. "One car or two?"

"Two… I'll be tied up for the rest of the night, but you can go home."

Ben pulled into the little park adjacent to the estate, and I followed him. Two other cars were there already, both of them multi-passenger vehicles. It looked as though a fair-sized team would descend on the estate.

After a few words to his officers, Ben strode over to me. "Leave your car here. Hop in with me. Once we go in, stay back out of the way and keep your head down. Stay with Brett in the control centre – but stay there even if he has to leave the centre at any time. Do you have your weapon with you?"

Another of his silly questions! I patted one of the pockets of my cargo pants to confirm I was armed. I'd never been on a raid with Ben, not officially anyway. Although, on several occasions, Ben had accused me of being an 'unwelcome distraction' by inserting myself uninvited into the action.

Tonight, everything seemed too calm, too easy.

As we approached the estate, Ben made a call. The gates swung open. I guessed Brett was forewarned of a possible raid. Our three vehicles roared through the gates. Two parked at the foot of the front steps, and the third parked in front of the garage. Again, the front door opened as if by magic the moment we pulled up. Ben led his ten officers into the house. I saw Brett say something to Ben, who dropped him a nod as he went by. I trailed along behind the team and stopped when I reached Brett.

"It's not your lucky night, I'm afraid, Brett. I am to remain with you in the control centre."

He grinned broadly and, with a flick of his head, motioned for me to follow him. While we stood around waiting for things to happen, I asked Brett about something that bothered me.

"Brett, the other security guard… not Stan….?"

"Mick? Do you mean Mick Delaney?

"Right, so that's his name. What sort of vehicle does Mick drive?"

"Uhmm… a small blue van." A niggling suspicion was about to be confirmed, but there was no time to think about it.

Although I was sure all of Ben's team were wearing rubber-soled shoes, it sounded as though a whole platoon of hobnail-booted combatants raced up the stairs. I heard shouting and looked across at Brett. He didn't appear phased by it. I tried to relax. The sound of a door being smashed in made that impossible. Then more shouting and sounds of a struggle.

"Stay here!" Brett barked at me as he raced out of the control room.

I've already been told that once tonight. I have no intention of obeying either of those orders. I peered out from the doorway of the control centre. Not a soul in sight. Sounds of a scuffle of major proportions raging upstairs continued. After venturing out of the control centre and a little way along the hallway, I stopped. Standing motionless, I kept my eyes on the staircase leading to the first floor. No sign of anyone coming down. I tiptoed a little closer to the stairs.

How could there be such a battle going on up there? The only person likely to be upstairs is Blake Carter, a wounded Blake Carter. I doubted he was much of a match for ten burly police officers. But my ears told me something different. As I pondered the situation above me, I suddenly noticed things had gone quiet up there.

Battle over perhaps… and I did not want to be found where I shouldn't be. I raced back along the hallway and stood just inside the control centre to keep watch. A shout rang out from amid a deafening commotion.

"A gun! He's got a gun." A youngish male voice, not Ben's.

Almost immediately, boots thundered down the stairs, just out of sight further along the hallway. Those boots were coming in my direction. I hauled my Glock out of my pocket and worked the slider. Two shots rang out. I heard a yelp from upstairs.

Someone was hit… please don't let it be Ben. More boots – lots of them –coming down the stairs in pursuit of the shooter.

The gunman was crab-walking backwards towards me, but his attention was focused on the stairs. As he came along the hallway, he continued firing shots at random intervals at those trying to descend the stairs. The officers were easy targets … and one of them would be Ben. Without a sound, I stepped halfway out into the hallway. The escapee directed another shot at the stairs. Another yelp was heard.

That's enough, I thought. I fired. My Glock sounded loud despite all the other racket at the time. The gunman dropped his weapon as he went down but scrabbled around on the floor and quickly regained it. Not the outcome I was hoping for.

Although struggling to lift his arm, he aimed at me. I fired again. It sounded like it hit something, but I didn't know what or where. I think I had my eyes closed. Then Ben was yelling.

"Cease fire! He's down. Sonny, hold your fire. You got him … twice by the look of it."

Three officers half dragged/half carried the wounded gunman out and dumped him on the doorstep. Two remained to stand guard over him while the third officer returned to help his wounded comrades. Everything was happening at once. Around me, the night's events had entered their final stages.

Brett was back in the control centre and feverishly making phone calls. Ben came and stood beside me. I braced for the blast I was about to receive but was saved when Ben's phone played its tune. He took the call in the control centre. As he did so, Brett passed him on his way out.

"Ambulances are on their way, and the paddy wagon," Brett told Ben as he left.

As the procession passed by on its way out to the vehicles, I counted two wounded officers, three unknown males in handcuffs and looking a bit the worse for their recent encounter … and Blake Carter. A Blake Carter who appeared in a deal of pain and barely able to walk.

It was as if someone had thrown a switch. It was so sudden. One minute there was so much commotion, and the next, an eery silence seemed to fill the place. I waited for at least a few moments before following Ben to the front door. He appeared to be okay, but I wanted to know what had gone down upstairs. And Ben knew I would be anxious to find out.

"Not now," he snarled as I followed him onto the doorstep. "Later; now, go home and have breakfast or something. Are you okay to walk to your car from here?"

There were so many things I wanted to say, but I just nodded and made my way down the steps. He called after me as I stepped onto the path, "Thanks for your help."

I started towards the gates. Brett rushed up to me. "Wait a minute. I just need to lock the door, and then I'll drive to your car."

"Thanks, Brett, but I don't want to land you in any trouble."

He laughed. "Trouble? After what's gone down here tonight…? Get in. Oh, and nice shooting by the way."

Chapter 27

Too early for breakfast, I told myself as I unlocked my front door. Instead, I went through to my office to compile a note of this morning's events to add to my case file. It was an incomplete account, and would remain so until I caught up with Ben for the rest of the story – hopefully sometime today.

After a quick shower and change of clothes, it was 7.30 and time for breakfast. I was filling the coffee machine when Ben called.

"What's on the menu for breakfast?"

"Anything you might like, from toast and vegemite to bacon and eggs. Put your order in now though, as I was just about to make a start."

"Bacon and eggs – with lashings of buttered toast – sounds about right. I'll see you in about ten minutes."

"If that's the breakfast you're having, I hope you're not scheduled for a medical any time soon, not until you've worked it off anyway."

Conversation was scant until we took our coffees through to my office after breakfast.

"Come on, Ben. Put me out of my misery. Did we wrap up Janine's case this morning, or are there still loose ends?"

"All wrapped up. As you are well aware, Blake Carter and three of his accomplices were rounded up at the Thomlinson Estate. Carter and one of his cronies are under guard in hospital, where, according to doctors, they will remain for two or three days. The one you drilled required some minor repair surgery. Two of my officers received medical treatment. Although their wounds are not life-threatening, they will likely be off work for a week or two.

Brett is no longer working as a security guard and will return to normal duties at the precinct tomorrow. Stan, the other security guard, has been taken into custody and is helping the police with their enquiries. For the next few days, recently graduated police constables will replace the security guards at the estate after Brett shows them how to operate the systems. That just about wraps up everything to report about the estate.

My second team also had a productive morning at the van driver's address. They took into custody one male and collected quite a bit of evidence relating to the deceased Griff Davidson. The bloke…"

"Mick Delaney…."

"Eh? Yeah. At least, he calls himself Delaney, but his name is Costanzo. He's the brother of the van owner.

Anyway, the bloke they picked up – Delaney – was the one who helped the van driver dump the body over the cliff.

It appears the other gang member, the one who visited Davidson's apartment and assisted the van driver, is the bloke you shot in the park. He is being detained in Ralston nick, and Ralston police sent us photos for identification purposes. Now, how and what do you know about Delaney?"

"Let me think…; Mick Delaney, as he calls himself, was the third security guard at Thomlinson Estate. The one who has been off on 'sick leave' for a while… and drives a blue van to work." Ben's demeanour told me more questions would be forthcoming, but I continued in the hope of fending them off. "Do you believe you have rounded up everyone associated with the case, or is there still more work to do?"

"No, we are confident we have them all. The process of extracting the finer details of Carter's plan is ongoing, although we know the basic story. His original plan was to secure enough of Thomlinson's cash to ensure a lavish lifestyle for the rest of his life, and we know he was assisted in this mission by Janine's accounting manager over whom Carter had some significant hold.

As is so often the case, although all was going according to plan, he became greedy and decided he wanted the 'golden goose' as well as some of the 'golden eggs'. He admits to never having any feelings for Janine but found her an easy mark. Then, when he got greedy, it was obvious she had to go. The contaminated toothpaste and other subtle devices were designed to reduce her to a psychological wreck, thereby opening the door for one of two scenarios to occur."

I felt so angry on Janine's behalf but bit my tongue as Ben continued.

"Carter planned for her state of mind to become so affected, she would lose touch with reality. Then he would have her committed and take over the company in her absence, or an even better alternative was for her to become so depressed, she would commit suicide. If the latter scenario eventuated, as her husband, he could lay claim to the entire Thomlinson empire."

"And his plan was well on its way to achieving his objective, except Janine is made of sterner stuff than he expected," I murmured. "Ben, what about the cash he has siphoned off from the company? Is there any chance Janine will recover any of it?"

"The forensic accounting team based in Ralston started tracing the money trail after they arrived here yesterday morning. As a replacement staff member for Griff Davidson, Janine will welcome a new 'forensic accountant' sometime today. I mean, she will, after you tell her she is being allocated one from our forensic accounting team."

"How is that going to work if the bent accounting manager is still in place in her finance department?"

"We have the information. Now we need to go after the evidence. We want the manager in place until we have the evidence to confirm our information – before charging him. Our problem now is that, as of today, he seems also to have disappeared. When he is caught, the charges are likely to be for more than embezzlement."

"Ben, a couple of things are puzzling me. Was Stan somehow helping Carter to stay in his apartment after Carter supposedly disappeared, or at least after I wounded him?"

"Yes. We've yet to establish the exact nature of the hold Carter had over Stan, but it was serious enough to have Stan become complicit in Carter's scheme."

"Hmm, so I thought. I was surprised Carter had his henchmen at the estate during Brett's roster tonight. Wasn't that a bit risky?"

"It wasn't as risky as you might expect. From the little we have extracted from Stan, we know their intention was for Brett's future to be similar to Griff Davidson's, and it was to happen within the next few hours. Luckily, Brett called about the suspicious noises when he did.

Last night was about preparations and a final briefing before Carter secured his prize. As far as we've been able to establish, tomorrow night, Janine was to be attacked. We don't know the details, but it would likely be in her unit and similar to what happened to Griff Davidson. That's why Carter had brought in the extra muscle. He needed to be sure it was a successful attack."

For a few moments, I couldn't speak and was barely able to comprehend what Ben had told me. Ben's glance at his watch helped me recover my voice.

"Right, Ben, I'm sure you need to be back at the precinct, and I have a difficult conversation to have with my client. Go now, and I'll talk to you again tonight, unless something comes up during the day. I need to call Janine before she becomes too embroiled in her day."

The minute Ben drove off, I called Janine. She had just arrived at her office in the finance department and had nothing urgent planned for today. About half an hour later, she was sitting opposite me in my city office, and I was trying to work out how to begin the conversation we had to have.

"Janine, there is nothing easy about the information I have to share with you this morning. I expect you will find it upsetting and probably difficult to accept, but you must hear it and must know about a strategy that will be put in place in your office sometime today."

Then I rolled it all out for her, every last skerrick of information. Details of everything that happened last night, what we learned of Carter's take-over plan, Griff Davidson's death, and Carter's planned similar fate for Janine.

When I was done, she asked her questions. The reality of it all began to sink in. I didn't offer her coffee.

"I know it's early in the day, but I have a fine bottle of single malt scotch in a cupboard. Will you join me in a dram or two?"

Ben called as I was about to pour our second drink.

"Have you had a chance yet to explain everything to Janine?"

"Oh aye, done and dusted and washed down with a scotch."

"Good to hear. Do you think it might be possible for her to be in her office in about half an hour to welcome her new forensic accountant?"

"I'm sure that can be arranged."

I didn't feel comfortable about allowing Janine to walk back to her office alone, so I insisted on driving her. Not surprising, I suppose, when she didn't put up much of an argument. On the way, I offered to stay with her until everything was in place at the office and then drive her to her unit. This time she refused my offer point blank. She had things to do, and she intended they would be done today. Besides, she didn't want to go home. She had to return to her office at the Thomlinson complex and settle in there again.

"Janine, are you sure you shouldn't allow yourself a little time to come to terms with everything instead of rushing around like this?"

"No. Sonny, I took my eye off the ball a long time ago, but I'm clear-sighted and focused now. It's time people realised I'm very much back in charge. The old me has returned. Oh, and I would be pleased to receive your invoice for services rendered as soon as you have it ready – and don't leave anything out."

My account was embarrassingly large but honest and accurate. Or so I thought until I realised I hadn't included James Rothwell's expenses because I hadn't received them yet. But I had already emailed my invoice to her. I would just have to wear it. About an hour later, when I was paying some bills, I discovered she had direct-deposited almost twice the invoiced amount into my account. Looks like I've been more than compensated for whatever James's expenses might be.

Later, an email arrived inviting me to dinner the following evening at the most expensive restaurant in Millhaven. She apologised for also inviting that incredible Police Superintendent to join us. She hoped I wouldn't mind, and assured me I would find him interesting and personable company.

I would love to have dinner with you and get to know Millhaven's top cop, was my swift reply.

The End

Other Books by the Author

Sonoma Whittington series:

An Ancient Solution

A Public Service

Missing!

Connections

A Different Obsession

Shattered Illusions

After The Ball

Unholy Secrets

Fateful Reunion

A Dark Place

Merivale Retirement Village series:

Close to Home

Growing Pains

About the Author

Neive Denis is the creator of the series featuring the Private Investigator, Sonoma (Sonny) Whittington. Neive Denis is the pen name of a writer who was lured from her usual genre to focus on the mystery and excitement that are a part of Sonoma Whittington's world. She came into being specifically for this series and, for the moment at least, intends focusing mainly on stories from Sonny's case files.

This series tells of the intrigue and scrapes – some on occasion life threatening – that are part of the life of Sonoma Whittington, an Australian Private Investigator, based in a Central Queensland coastal city. However, Sonny doesn't confine her escapades to Australia, and that provides Neive with an opportunity to weave some of her other areas of interest into Sonny's hair-raising adventures on occasion.

See more about Neive Denis and her work at

www.eaglemountbooks.com.au/neivedenis

or contact her at

admin@eaglemountbooks.com.au

www.ingramcontent.com/pod-product-compliance
Lightning Source LLC
Chambersburg PA
CBHW010259100726

47904CB00011B/2671